Today's Sacrifice

by

Richard Denning

Written by Richard Denning

© Copyright 2015

ISBN: 978-0-9568103-0-4

Published by Mercia Books

Book Jacket design and layout by Cathy Helms
www.avalongraphics.org

Copy-editing and proof reading by Jo Field.
jo.field3@btinternet.com

Author website:
www.richarddenning.co.uk

Publisher website:
www.merciabooks.co.uk

Richard Denning was born in Ilkeston in Derbyshire and lives in Sutton Coldfield in the West Midlands, where he works as a General Practitioner.

He is married and has two children. He has always been fascinated by historical settings as well as horror and fantasy. Other than writing, his main interests are games of all types. He is the designer of a board game based on the Great Fire of London and others. He is also the director of the UK's Largest Hobby Games Convention.

You can find out more about Richard and his work on his website: www.richarddenning.co.uk

Also by the Richard Denning

Northern Crown Series
(Historical fiction)
1.The Amber Treasure
2.Child of Loki
3.Princes in Exile

Hourglass Institute Series
(Young Adult Science Fiction)
1.Tomorrow's Guardian
2. Yesterday's Treasures
3. Today's Sacrifice

The Praesidium Series
(Historical Fantasy)
The Last Seal

The Nine World Series
(Historical Fantasy)
1.Shield Maiden
2. The Catacombs of Vanaheim

Here are the names of the important characters in The Hourglass Institute Series as well as some terms used in the books.

Tom Oakely – schoolboy whose discovery at the age of ten that he could travel through time began his adventures as a 'Walker' (*Tomorrow's Guardian*).

Septimus Mason – time-travelling adventurer who taught Tom how to Walk through time.

Professor Neoptolemas – Head of the Hourglass Institute and one of three brothers created during a fight between Knossos and Titus that led to 'the Event' (*Yesterday's Treasures*)

The Event – cataclysmic event that split reality into different versions of the world and Titus into three brothers: the Professor, the Custodian and the Colonel (*Yesterday's Treasures*).

Colonel Thielmann – one of the Professor's brothers, in charge of a special security force of time-travelling soldiers from the 'Twisted Reality'.

The Custodian – one of the Professor's brothers: cold, apparently emotionless, the Custodian is in charge of 'the Office' - a place between realities.

Edward Dyson – Victorian Officer rescued by Tom and Septimus from the Battlefield of Isandlwana (*Tomorrow's Guardian*).

Charlie Walker – World War Two sailor saved from drowning on a sinking submarine (*Tomorrow's Guardian*).

Mary Brown – 17th Century maid whom Septimus and Tom rescued from the flames of the Great Fire of London in 1666 (*Tomorrow's Guardian*).

Mr Phelps – assistant to the Professor and administrator of the Hourglass Institute.

Captain Redfeld – one of Thielmann's officers and a deadly enemy of Tom.

Rolf Lapace – thief, adventurer and former business partner of Septimus. Rival for the affections of Julia di Rivoli.

Julia di Rivoli – the woman Septimus loves but lost to Rolf.

Phil –Resistance fighter in the Twisted Reality.

Lieutenant Teuber – One of Thielmann's officers but secretly an ally of the Professor and working for the Resistance.

Persephone – Greek girl, former servant of Knossos and member of his Black Robes, a cult in Ancient Greece (*Yesterday's Treasures*).

Knossos – superhuman megalomaniac in Ancient Greece, once an ally of Titus in the fight against the Titans, he became a powerful enemy who almost destroyed world history during 'the Event'.

Titus – powerful superhuman in Ancient Greece, divided during the 'the Event'.

The Twisted Reality – alternate version of our world in which history took a darker path.

The Hourglass Institute – Based in London, an organisation dedicated to preserving the timelines.

The Office – a place between realities where history is monitored by the emotionless Custodian and his servants, the 'Men in Suits'.

Walkers – individuals who can Walk or travel through and manipulate time.

Wall – A barrier of frozen time that can shield and protect a Walker from bullets and other forms of attack.

The Titans - Coeus; Crius; Hyperion; Iapetus and Kronos.

Minor characters:

Andy –Tom's best friend at school.

Men in Suits - clone-like servants of the Custodian who occupy the Office.

Mr Fitzwilliams – Hourglass Institute's principal scientist and engineer.

Mrs Mackay – lady who manages the Hourglass costumes department.

Doctor Makepeace – Hourglass Institute's physician with special healing powers.

Mr Ryan – Hourglass Institute's expert in historical weaponry.

CHAPTER ONE
THE STUFF OF LEGENDS

"War? What war?" Tom asked, breaking the silence that had descended upon the Professor's study.

He gazed across the room at the old man who was sitting behind his antique desk in front of French windows, which were open to allow air to circulate. The noise of the London rush hour had subsided and the evening was cooling quickly after the hot September day. Feeling a draught, Tom shivered. The Professor felt it too and walked across to close the windows before returning to his seat.

"What war, Professor?" Tom repeated when the old man was seated again.

He did not reply at first. As was his habit when pondering how to broach a difficult subject, Professor Neoptolemas slipped off his glasses, retrieved a handkerchief from his breast pocket and vigorously polished the lenses. Finally he popped them back onto his nose and peered over the top of them at the five individuals who sat across the desk from him. It seemed to Tom that the Professor was weighing them up – perhaps seeing if they were ready for the answer to his question.

Tom glanced around the room at his companions – like him, all 'Walkers' or time travellers – with whom he had now shared two terrifying adventures. Next to him was the Welshman,

Septimus Mason, a mercenary who had first taught Tom how to travel through time. Together they had journeyed back through the years and rescued his other friends from certain death. These were Mary Brown, a baker's maid from Pudding Lane, just sixteen when she was plucked from the fires that destroyed London in 1666; Edward Dyson, the young Victorian lieutenant, whom Tom had saved from the sharp spears of the Zulu warriors in the battle of Isandlwana, and finally, Able Seaman Charlie Hawker, who had almost drowned during the Second World War having boarded a sinking U-boat in the Mediterranean sea.

The five of them had battled evil men from other worlds and hurtled through history on a treasure hunt that almost ended with the destruction of the universe. After all that, Tom was certain they were ready for anything else the Professor might care to throw at them. Not, of course, that he wanted any more adventures anytime soon. But if they came along, surely they could cope? If so ... why was the Prof so hesitant to answer?

Professor Neoptolemas was the head of the Hourglass Institute, whose role was to protect history. In the last few months his organisation had been busy doing just that and Tom had hoped that the troubles were now behind them. The Professor, however, seemed to be aware of yet another danger looming, and judging by his manner, one even more challenging than the last. Suddenly, Tom felt like a mouse caught in the open fields with an owl swooping down from the skies, its talons open and ready to seize him.

"Professor? What war?" asked Edward, his tone impatient and eager; a soldier wanting to know where his next battle lay and which enemy he must face.

At last the old man answered.

"I speak of a struggle from long ago: a conflict that was ancient

2

even when Titus and Knossos walked the Earth."

"So you were not involved in this war then?" Tom enquired.

The Professor's response was a loud snort. "Oh, I was involved in it, Thomas, as Titus of course. In fact we both were – Titus and Knossos I mean. Actually, you might say that we were up to our necks in it. But it is old ... so very old that now it is the stuff of legends, myths and – even – religion!"

"Legends?" Septimus put in, fingering his goatee beard. "Which legends?"

The Professor's reply was to walk across to one of the many oak bookshelves that lined the walls of the room. There were books on science, history, collections of maps and, Tom knew, old stories and legends: anything in fact that might help the Institute in its mission. The old man ran his fingers across the leather spines of several volumes before selecting one and tugging it off the shelf. Returning to his seat he blew the dust from the top of the book, opened it and flipped through a few pages until he found what he was looking for. Turning the book around, he pushed it across the desk towards them, then tapped his fingers on a picture that filled the double spread of pages.

There was a creak of chairs as all five of them craned forward and peered at the image. They studied it in silence for a moment before Septimus spoke.

"You are having a laugh aren't you, Prof?"

Neoptolemas' response was to treat the Welshman to an intense glare.

"You're serious then?" Septimus asked, his gaze flicking back to the picture and then up again to the old man.

A curt nod was the only answer.

Not understanding the unspoken conversation, Tom frowned and bent again to look at the picture. The image showed a battle raging. Some of the figures were humans – or at least they seemed to be. Others were far from human and he could see ferocious-looking creatures with wings, others with tentacles and still more made – or so it appeared – from water, fire or ice. It was hard to see who was fighting whom. He glanced at the writing at the bottom of the page. It read: '*The Titanomachy. Led by Zeus, the Olympians defeat the Titans and become the gods of Greece.*'

It did not mean much to Tom. Puzzled, he looked up at the Professor and saw that the old man was now studying him.

"I don't understand," Tom shrugged.

"Nor I," mumbled Mary. "What is this a picture of?"

It was Edward who answered. "Before Zeus and the other Greek gods came to power, the ancient world was ruled by a race of powerful beings of immense strength. They were the Titans. Let me see now ... there was Kronos, Hyperion, Oceanus... er... Iapetus, Rhea and some others whose names I have forgotten. They each had different abilities, such as control over minds, the elements, the oceans, life and death and so forth."

As he paused to gather his thoughts, the others, used to Edward's seemingly limitless knowledge of arcane subjects, grinned and rolled their eyes.

The Professor shook his head at them. "Please continue, Lieutenant."

"Well anyway," Edward said, unruffled, "as you might expect from legends, their rule was cruel and harsh and their own children, led by Zeus, overthrew them and became the Olympian gods. The picture depicts the final battle between the Titans and the Olympians."

"Impressive," Septimus muttered.

"Learn that in the army did you?" asked Charlie, "Cos they

never taught it to me in the navy."

Edward grinned. "I told you before – the benefits of a classical education in a Victorian grammar school." His grin faded as he turned back to the Professor. "But surely this is just myth. All religions have tales of a war in heaven, or a war of the gods – the Vikings, the Babylonians ... even the Christian Church. What are you saying, sir? Are you saying that it actually happened?"

The Professor drew in a deep breath. "Yes, Lieutenant, that is exactly what I am saying. Or rather, what I am saying is that a war did occur involving great and powerful beings that men called 'Titans'. The war raged for years and the Titans were defeated in the end."

Now Septimus spoke, his voice filled with incredulity. "Defeated by Zeus, Poseidon and Hades, if I recall correctly," he said and then winked at Charlie. "We did have schools in Wales too you know, boyo." He threw Neoptolemas a challenging look. "That is what you are saying, Professor, isn't it?"

"No."

"No? What do you mean, no?"

"I mean, Mr Mason, that the Titans were certainly defeated, but not by the Olympians."

"Then by whom?"

There was silence again.

A flash of memory came to Tom. One of his unique abilities as a Walker was to inhabit the minds of others in dreams and not long ago, when he and his friends had been battling the black-robed Cultists from Ancient Greece, he had dreamed he was Knossos, their master. Something had struck a chord. What was it? Narrowing his eyes Tom thought back, trying to recall Knossos' thoughts. Then it came to him: Knossos had been thinking of the time when he and Titus were friends and together had destroyed an ancient enemy of humanity. Another memory surfaced – this time from his dream of being Titus when he had been approaching the fateful confrontation with Knossos, who by then had become his enemy. As Titus he had been thinking about how they had once been the saviours of Greece and had defeated Hyperion, Coeus and their brothers.

Tom gasped as all the pieces came together: Edward had said that Hyperion was a Titan which meant that...

"It was you, wasn't it Professor? Before The Event changed you, you were Titus: so it was you; you and Knossos who fought the Titans and destroyed them."

Neoptolemas eyed Tom with a glint of approval. "That is right, Thomas. Or rather, we defeated and imprisoned them. You saw that in your dream of being Titus I take it?"

Tom nodded. "And also something that Knossos was thinking when I was him. But Knossos believed he had *destroyed* the Titans."

The Professor barked a harsh laugh. "Knossos sometimes believed what it suited him to believe. But yes, he and I battled the Titans and in the end got the better of them. But I fear they were never destroyed...."

Stunned by this news, no one spoke as they all gazed back at the images in the book. Looking more closely, Tom thought the picture of Zeus with a thunderbolt in his fist did look a little like a young Neoptolemas – a little like how Titus had looked, in fact. With a nasty feeling in his gut he stared up at the Professor. Was the old man implying that the forthcoming war was against the Titans? Tom dared not ask, in case the old man confirmed it – and there he was, only moments ago, thinking they could cope with anything!

Finally, Septimus coughed. "Wow, Prof, that's... er... quite a story."

"Oh it is, it is," the Professor replied, staring at the Welshman over his spectacles before adding, "so, would you like to hear the tale?"

CHAPTER TWO
A TEMPORARY SOLUTION

Septimus scratched his head whilst he pondered a reply.

"Professor, I respect you, I really do. You are a man of great wisdom and vast knowledge. Now, I wanted to say all that before we go on so there is no misunderstanding."

Neoptolemas smiled. "It is very kind of you to say so, Mr Mason."

"It is true. That said, what you just told us sounds completely insane! What do you think Tommy?"

Tom shrugged. "A year or two ago I would have thought you insane if you had spoken of travelling through time, rescuing people from the Great Fire of London or visiting alternate Earths. Yet we have done all that and a lot more besides. Is this any less likely when you think about it?"

Septimus grimaced. "I guess you are right, boyo. Very well then, Professor. Tell us how you defeated the Titans."

The old man was flicking through the mythology book again. He left it open at a page entitled 'The Titans'. On the double spread were images of powerful figures striding through the waves, marching through a whirlwind, or with hands ablaze with flames.

"Greek mythology describes the Titans as being the first deities. They were in turn offspring of the first ever beings: Gaia, the Earth and Uranus, the sky. There were twelve of them in fact – six male and six female. They were powerful creatures but not all of them were evil. Nevertheless, according to the legends several of them were tyrants. Their leader was Kronos. Kronos killed his own father, Uranus – supposedly by… ahem… cutting off his private parts."

"Ouch!" Tom exclaimed. "Are you saying his own son chopped off his—"

Before he could finish, Edward, his face flushing crimson, held up his hands. "Please Tom, there is a lady present!"

Far from being offended, Mary actually laughed and laid a hand gently on Edward's arm.

"Oh, Edward you are wonderful, but I heard far worse in the taverns and coffee shops, please believe me. London in my day was not as polite as it was in yours."

"Good heavens!" Edward exclaimed, still blushing slightly.

"Carry on, Professor. I think we get the idea," Charlie said with a wink at Tom.

Tom grinned back and glanced across at Septimus expecting that he would be sharing the joke. But in fact the Welshman's expression was distant. He was absent-mindedly staring out of the windows, apparently watching the birds hopping along the fence in the garden.

"So," the Professor continued, "having overthrown his father, Kronos took over and ruled the Earth in a most tyrannical manner. His brothers helped him."

"His brothers?" Tom asked, turning to look at the old man again.

"Indeed. These five Titans were Crius, Iapetus, Hyperion, Coeus and the most powerful, as I have said, was Kronos."

"Where does Zeus fit into all this?" Tom asked.

"Lieutenant, you are the classical scholar, you tell them," the Professor said, leaning his elbows on the desk and looking over the top of his spectacles at Edward.

Getting up from his chair, Edward stood up straight and clasped his hands behind his back as he might once have done when as a schoolboy he was instructed to recite his Latin and Greek.

"The Olympian gods were the sons of Kronos. Kronos had been told that his own children would defeat him and so in order to avoid that fate he was supposed to have eaten every one of them as they were born. In the end Kronos' wife, Rhea, distraught at the loss of her children, hid the youngest, Zeus, and gave Kronos a rock to eat in his place. When Zeus grew up he gave Kronos a drink that made him sick and all the Olympian gods where vomited back up."

"Yuck! I bet they were not happy," Tom said.

Edward shook his head. "Indeed not. The Olympians started a war against the Titans."

"The Titanomachy?" Tom said, beginning to feel like he was catching up at last.

"That is correct, Thomas," the Professor now took over the tale. "The Olympians won. Seven of the Titans had surrendered and submitted and in time became accepted by Zeus and his siblings. The five Titans who had been the most destructive fought on to the end and when finally defeated were banished to Tartarus. That is the deepest pit of the Underworld. There they remain, entombed for ever."

The Professor flipped the book over a couple of pages. It now showed an image of the defeated Titans in chains in a bleak-looking dungeon – presumably Tartarus.

"Over the centuries, the Greeks embellished and elaborated

10

the stories so that what really happened became lost in myth and legend. Yet sometimes you can see through the story that developed and perceive the essence of the original truth," Neoptolemas said quietly, his expression solemn as he studied the picture.

"What truth?" Charlie asked, craning his neck to look at the same picture.

The old man leant back in his chair and closed his eyes. It was so long before he said anything that Tom would not have been surprised to hear him snoring. Eventually, though, he opened his eyes and began speaking again.

"The Titans were in fact vastly powerful humans from a very ancient time. Ancient even when Knossos and Titus walked the Earth. They could manipulate the very elements and all the forces of the universe. In time they made themselves immortal and essentially invulnerable and they developed powers of a terrifying nature. Through these powers they enslaved and dominated humanity."

The Professor paused and looked at them each in turn, frowning a little when he saw that Septimus was still gazing out of the window. Then he cleared his throat and continued with his tale.

"Titus and Knossos travelled back in time and became involved in the wars, eventually defeating the Titans and so in time becoming the basis for the legends of the Olympian gods. As I said, the five Titans were Crius, Iapetus, Hyperion, Coeus and the most powerful of all, Kronos. We, Knossos and I, defeated and captured them, but we discovered that we could not destroy them. So what we did was to imprison them in the void between realities. In the legends this became known as Tartarus, but in fact this was a time cyst – a bubble of time pulled off and separated from the universe – a pocket universe if you like.

11

Or in fact a multitude of cysts, for each Titan was separately trapped in his own bubble. We knew at the time that this was only a temporary solution and Knossos, who thought that given enough time he could devise a permanent solution, immediately began to work on one."

"What solution?" Charlie asked.

The Professor suddenly slammed the book shut making everyone jump.

"That is the problem! Knossos never told me what the solution was. I know he was writing it down, but before he could tell me what he had come up with, he and I..." Neoptolemas shrugged, his voice trailing away.

"You had started your own private war," Tom said, looking around at his friends. That story each of them knew only too well; they had all been involved in it and only by the skin of their teeth had they come out of it alive.

"You said that trapping the Titans in these time cysts was only a temporary solution, Professor. What did you mean exactly?" Edward asked.

"We... that is, Knossos and Titus, knew that the time cysts would not last forever. You see, they did not so much imprison the Titans in a physical location as such, but more within a piece of borrowed time. Time that would one day run out and, well... this was all a very long time ago."

Tom's eyes widened as he took in the implications of what Neoptolemas was saying, but he kept his thoughts to himself, his attention riveted on the old man's worried face.

"After The Event, my brothers and I became aware that the cysts were decaying and would one day open back into actual time, thus releasing the horror of a Titan invasion. An odd feature of the cysts, however, is that they will empty backwards into time.

12

Thus, once it is detected that they are beginning to open, it will be at some point in the past. The problem being that until each cyst actually decays there is no record of the moment and by the time we know when and where it opened, it will be too late."

Septimus let out a strangled cry, finally returning his gaze to the room and apparently paying attention once more.

"What you are saying is that the Titans could pop up anywhere and in any time period!"

"That is indeed what I am saying, Mr Mason."

Tom had a sudden image of the fabled *Koh-i-nor* diamond on display in the Crystal Palace. Not the Crystal Palace that had stood in his own world nearly two hundred years ago, purpose-built to house the Great Exhibition, but the one they had tracked down in the Twisted Reality, a dark, sinister mirror world where the worst events of history had occurred. A world that was controlled by the Professor's brother, Colonel Thielmann.

"I assume it could be in any reality too?" Tom mused with foreboding.

The Professor nodded. "Yes, it could be in the Colonel's world."

Tom frowned, remembering the catastrophic moment when the Crown of Knossos had shattered. It was not just an ordinary crown, it was an ancient artefact imbued with unimaginable powers. With it Knossos had planned to destroy all worlds but his own, new world where, assisted by his black-robed Cultists – themselves imbued with special powers – he meant to enslave all other beings and rule supreme. But Titus had defied him and in their battle for supremacy the Crown had broken, destroying Knossos's power. That cataclysmic moment, referred to as 'The Event', had split Titus into three identical individuals: the Professor; the Colonel and the Custodian. And it had led to the

13

creation of three distinct realities: Tom's own, familiar world; the Twisted Reality inhabited by the Colonel, and the strange world in between, which Tom knew as 'The Office', from where the Custodian' monitored the three realities and tried to keep them in balance.

"Or indeed in The Office," the Professor said, as if reading Tom's thoughts. "So you understand the danger. The risk here is that this could alter time. Moreover, the cysts may decay at a varying rate, releasing the Titans at different points in time. They won't all pop up in the same place and date. The Custodian has been working on a means of trapping the Titans. He has already created miniature time cysts which are portable. They can each contain a Titan for a short period, but what is urgently needed is a permanent solution. We are working on this, my brothers and I. But we do not yet have one."

"Can you trust them, do you think? Both your brothers have taken great risks with the universe and even tried to invade our own world," Edward pointed out.

The Professor shrugged. "They have their own motivations, that is true, and yet long before The Event they and I were each a facet of Titus. They recall, as I do, the horrors of that war; the first war in history – or so the Greeks believe. They will want to make sure the Titans do not return every bit as much as I do."

"So what do we do now?" Tom asked.

"Now? Nothing for the present. Return to your family and your school, Thomas. When I know something, I will send for you. Meantime, I will continue to work on a permanent solution. It is regrettable that we have no record of the work Knossos did on this...." his voice trailed away.

A thought occurred to Tom. "Professor, I wonder if Persephone might know anything?"

Neoptolemas considered this. "Because she was once one of the Black Robes you mean?"

"Yes, she may have seen him working on something."

The old man shrugged. "It is possible, I will allow that, but she may not be aware of what she has seen. I take it that you mean to ask her some questions?"

Tom nodded.

"I am not sure that is such a good idea," Charlie said. "I mean, she was as you say a Black Robe. More than that, she seemed to have been central to Knossos' plans and undertook many tasks for him."

"Only whilst under his control, Charlie. Her mind is free now since we rescued her and Walked her to our time," Tom said.

Charlie looked doubtful. "Even so, how sure can we be that she is not under some hangover aspect?"

"I will just have to be careful what I say. But let me try."

Having considered the idea for a few moments the Professor nodded his head. "Very well, Thomas, but say nothing about the Titans."

"I won't, don't worry Professor." Tom turned to say something to Septimus, only to find he was once more staring outside at the garden.

"Earth calling Septimus, come in Septimus!" Tom whispered as he leant across.

"What?" the Welshman asked.

Tom grinned. "This saving the world stuff boring you?"

Septimus blinked and turned to look at him then laughed. "Sorry... it's just that what with all that *Koh-i-nor* business and having to spend time with Rolf Lapace again, I find that... well, let's just say it's revived old thoughts."

"Thoughts of Julia, you mean?" Tom asked.

15

Septimus gave him a sharp look. "Yes, how did you guess?"

"It's not exactly rocket science, mate. You and Rolf loved the same girl. She fell for him instead of you, but when he betrayed her, stole from her and blamed it on you, you ran away. And now you are thinking about her again. I may only be twelve, but I'm not stupid!"

Septimus patted him on the shoulder.

"You certainly aren't, boyo. Don't worry. I am back now. I am never going to see Julia again so I might as well just put her out of my mind. Come on, let's get you home. I will give you a call when the Professor needs you. Time you had a bit of ordinary life at that school of yours."

CHAPTER THREE
MODERN TIMES

"Tom mate, there you are. Where've you been? I need to ask you a question," Andy said.

Tom was sitting at his desk in his classroom waiting for the English teacher to arrive. There were moments when he found it hard to get his head round how strange his life had become since he discovered he was a Walker. In his own personal time line he had spent the last few days rescuing the universe from certain destruction and then, only yesterday, discussing Titans and the threat they posed to the world. Yet here he was, about to start a day in which the most challenging problem was probably going to be the quadratic equations they were studying in third period maths. Oddly, however, he felt quite relaxed. Maybe the normality offered by the school day helped. Or perhaps he was just getting used to it.

"A question? What about?" Tom replied.

Andy, Tom's best mate since the day he had clobbered him with a ruler, shuffled across to his desk, dropped a rucksack on the floor and then threw himself down in the chair.

"That girl – Persephone. Do you fancy her?" he asked.

Tom glanced around. The classroom was filling up with his classmates who sat around in small groups chatting about a hundred subjects: homework; the latest boy-band craze;

Mrs Jones the geography teacher's choice of lipstick; the new reality TV programme and the best new console games. A buzz of conversation filled the room and as a result no one seemed to have overheard or be paying any attention to Tom or Andy.

"What ...?" Tom hesitated, unsure how to reply.

The Greek girl was new at the school having turned up out of the blue at the start of term. Tom would have to admit he had quite liked the look of her and when she had paid him attention and wanted to go to his house after school to talk, he had thought she fancied him too. He had not been displeased by the thought, if he was being honest.

Yet it all turned out to be a complete lie. When she first arrived Persephone had told everyone that her family had moved from Greece to open a delicatessen in the city. That was all Tom knew about her. He'd had no idea then that she was lying, was in fact a Black Robe; a servant of Knossos and under his complete control. Far from being attracted to Tom, she was merely following orders, trying to get close to him because Knossos had told her to for reasons of his own.

Knossos had long held the Black Robes in a type of hypnotic trance. Persephone herself had been lost to her parents when she was just eight years old, taken into the Cult and trained as a Black Robe. When The Event had flung the Cultists forward in time from Ancient Greece to twenty-first century Britain, they had attempted to bring their master back and fulfil his plan to destroy the modern world. The plan had failed and thanks to Tom and his friends, Knossos had been blasted into oblivion. Persephone, released from the mental control she had lived under for so long, had come out of her trance-like state to find herself alone in the twenty-first century.

Concerned for her, Tom and his companions had gone back to rescue her parents and brought them to the modern day to be reunited with their daughter. The Professor had then instructed Doctor Midas, an archaeologist who had been caught up in their last adventure, to help the family recover from the shock and adjust to their new life. Because Persephone was already known at the school – albeit for only a brief time – the Professor had thought it best that she continue there where Tom could keep an eye on her. However, since the chaos of the conflict against Knossos, Tom had not seen much of her, nor even thought about her until yesterday when he had wondered if she might be of help in this Titan affair.

Lost in thought, Tom became aware that Andy was persisting with his question.

"Well? Do you fancy her or not?"

"Why do you ask?" Tom said.

"I was planning on asking her out. Maybe take her to a movie at the weekend."

"Oh, I see. Andy, you do know she is a couple of years older than us?"

Andy blinked. "Really? Why did she turn up in our lessons then?"

Tom shrugged. The real reason – that Persephone had lied about her age and infiltrated his class to get close to him – would be hard for Andy to believe.

"I guess… I guess she is having to catch up a bit. Being foreign and all. But she is fourteen."

Andy pursed his lips whilst he considered this fact and then shook his head. "Don't see as that matters. I am sure she would be happy with a mature chap like me," he said, puffing his chest out.

Tom's laughter at this display earned him a punch on the shoulder. "Ouch, that hurt, mate!" he protested.

Andy just shrugged. "Serves you right. So then – is it alright if I ask her out?"

"Well er…" Tom hesitated again. At that moment Persephone walked in the door. It was the first time he had really looked at her since rescuing her parents. Now he noticed again her beautiful olive-green eyes and the shining dark hair that fell gently onto her shoulders.

"I guess so, Andy," he replied absently, suddenly wondering if it was alright after all – for all sorts of reasons, not least the jolt of excitement he felt as she spotted him across the room and smiled at him.

The English teacher walked in behind her and rattled his knuckles on his desk. The class fell silent.

"Listen up – Persephone here is joining your class for English. Some of you will have seen her around the school over the last week or so. Her family has moved here from Greece. She has been placed in year nine, but as English is not her native language and she has some catching up to do, she will take some lessons with you for the time being. I am sure you will welcome her."

"You bet, sir!" Andy shouted.

Her face flushing, Persephone found an empty desk at the back of the room and taking her seat, got out a notepad then held up her hand.

"What is it Persephone," the teacher asked.

"Please sir, I have no pen."

Andy was on his feet in an instant. "Here you go," he said, passing her a ballpoint pen.

Persephone stared at it.

"Can I borrow some ink?" she whispered.

Andy now looked confused. "It's alright. It's a biro. Got ink in it."

"What is a biro?" Persephone asked.

This earned her an even more puzzled expression from Andy and a titter from Kyle Rogers, the class bully, who sat with his cronies a few seats away.

Andy scowled at Kyle and then turned to the girl, who by now had tried the pen on the paper in her notebook and was drawing something. Andy stared for a moment and then suddenly he beamed at her.

"You were having me on – nice one."

"Hurry up and sit down Andy, so we can begin," the teacher instructed.

"Yes sir, sorry sir," Andy said. Returning to his seat he leant across and whispered to Tom, "Strange girl. She was drawing something that looked like a Greek pillar."

Glancing back Tom saw that Persephone had drawn four pillars and a roof. From what he could make out it was a sketch of the Temple of Knossos.

"Very strange," he murmured. "Still want to ask her out do you?"

Andy nodded. "Way I see it she needs guidance."

"And you think you're the one to give it do you?" Tom snorted.

Before Andy could reply the English teacher's voice boomed out accross the room.

"SILENCE CLASS! Turn to page eighty-eight and complete the exercise on alliteration."

With a few groans and a shuffling of chairs the class settled to the task.

After English was the maths lesson. Persephone was not in their year for that subject – her skills in maths being more advanced than her English. Tom spotted her next at lunch. She was wandering around the dining room looking lost and carrying an empty tray. Andy spotted her too and leapt to his feet.

"Come and sit next to us, Perseph'," he shouted across the noisy room. He then elbowed Tom. "Budge over to that space, mate, you're cramping my style."

Tom glared at his friend but did as he was asked and made space for Persephone to sit down.

"Give me your tray and I will get you some food," Andy instructed the girl. He then pulled out a chair and gestured at it. "You sit down. There you go, nice and comfy."

The Greek girl sat next to Tom and handed Andy her tray. "Thank you," she said.

Once his friend was out of earshot, Tom took the opportunity to talk properly to Persephone for the first time since they had parted after the Knossos incident.

"How are you?" he asked tentatively.

She shrugged. "I am well," she answered.

"I meant how are you finding getting used to life here?"

"It is strange not having Knossos in my mind Thomas. Not having him there telling me all the time and having to decide what to do for myself is very strange indeed."

"What about your parents?"

"The Institute has found us a nice house and that Dr Midas is being kind and visits often. He speaks Greek and English so is helping them learn English."

"Good, but I meant how do they feel about what happened?"

Persephone checked to see that no one was listening. Andy was over by the counter that was serving the special of the day – lamb curry – or so the sign said. He gave them a wave. Persephone gave a weak wave back and then turned back to Tom.

"I think it is just as hard for them but also…" She hesitated and looked down at her hands.

"What is it?"

"They don't say anything and they are kind, but they are finding having a girl who is no longer small…"

"You mean a teenager?"

"Yes that is the word. Well they find that having a teenager around is difficult."

Tom laughed. "I think that many parents feel that way."

"Yes, but to my parents I was eight and now I am suddenly ten and four…"

"Fourteen," Tom prompted her.

She nodded. "Last night we had an argument, Thomas. I shouted at them. I never did that before. They were telling me…" she now blushed. "Well, it was about boys and not being too friendly."

"Oh, I see," Tom said.

"I suddenly got angry and ran to my room while they were still speaking. I even slammed the door!"

Tom grinned. "Is that all? That's what teenagers do. It just shows that you're a teenager now. They'll get used to it in time."

"Maybe you are right." She smiled at him and once again he felt a little thrill of excitement.

"Anyway Thomas, there is something I need to ask you before Andy—"

"Before Andy what?" Andy interrupted, slamming the tray down on the table. "Hope you like curry. Afraid they ran out of poppadums though. I think Rogers ate them all."

"What are poppadums?" Persephone asked.

Andy stared at her, then suddenly laughed. "You're teasing me again aint you?" he said. "Look, I was right." He pointed to where Kyle Rogers was sitting with a stack of six poppadums piled up beside his plate. "Greedy sod. Wait there and I'll get you one." He jumped up and ran over to Rogers' table.

Tom turned to Persephone. "What was it you were about to say?"

The girl opened her mouth to reply, but at that moment Tom felt the sudden sensation of motion that told him someone was Walking; travelling in time or through space. An instant later Persephone vanished leaving Tom staring at the spot where she had been sitting.

"Hey, where did she go?" Andy said as he returned clutching two poppadums.

Rogers was scowling at them both but when he caught Tom's eye he quickly looked away. Tom smiled. Not long ago he had used his Walker's abilities to best Rogers in a confrontation. It was not something he would normally do – it was against the Institute's rules except in a life or death situation – but on that day he had been goaded beyond endurance. Typical of all bullies, Kyle Rogers was a coward and now he was somewhat afraid of Tom.

"I don't know, Andy," Tom said. "She just shot off."

"Well, how did she get out the hall so quickly? She can't just evaporate into thin air can she? Where did she go?"

Tom just stared at him. "That's just what I was wondering," he replied.

CHAPTER FOUR
PERSEPHONE

A few minutes later Tom was in the boys' toilets. Andy had gone outside to look for Persephone in the playground. As soon as he was out of sight Tom had popped into the toilets and locked himself into a cubical.

'*Now what do I do?*' he asked himself. '*Where has she gone?*' From the sensation he had felt he knew she had definitely Walked, but where to? 'Anyway, why did she leave in the first place?' he wondered. He realised he was panicking and forced himself to take some deep breaths.

'*Think, Tom,*' he ordered himself. '*What should I do now?*'

Once his mind had stopped spinning it took him only a moment to work out what to do. Edward was the answer. He would go and find Edward. The Victorian soldier had one particular talent that had proven invaluable in the past: he could track any Walker wherever they were in time or space.

Visualising the Hourglass Institute, Tom closed his eyes. Walking was so familiar to him now that he was barely aware of the juddering, sinking feeling as he hurtled through space. Moments later he was in the Institute. He located Edward in the library, sitting next to Mary, a book open between them.

Edward looked up as Tom ran in. Something in the lieutenant's face suggested he was not that happy about being interrupted. "Can I help you Thomas?"

He had asked politely enough, Tom thought, but in the way you might say things when you would rather the other person went away and you did not really want to help them at all. Tom glanced across at Mary. She seemed more relaxed and smiled at him.

"Well, Thomas?" Edward asked.

"Sorry to interrupt, Edward, but…" pausing to catch his breath, Tom explained the problem.

With a sigh, Edward pushed his chair back from the table and stood for a moment with his eyes closed. Then he opened them and reached out a hand for Tom to take.

"Found her," he said, as they both vanished.

They materialised beside a swiftly flowing stream that was jumping and swirling around and over rocks and boulders. Mountains coloured with shades of green, purple and grey rose all around them, creating a bowl in which they stood. The stream passed under a bridge a short distance away before emptying into a long lake or maybe an inlet from the sea. It was a peaceful, beautiful spot with cool clean air and majestic surroundings.

"Where are we?" Tom asked.

"The Isle of Skye. It's the year 1900. Persephone is here… look, over there," Edward pointed.

Tom spotted Persephone nearby, the girl was sitting on a rock beside the stream and staring with an unfocused expression into the water. He scrambled down the bank and hopped across the rocks to reach the one she was sitting on.

"Persephone," he called as he neared her. "Are you alright?"

She looked up at him with a confused, almost lost expression on her face. "It's difficult to explain," she said.

26

He sat down next to her. "What is?"

She shook her head and looked away. A branch, which must have fallen from a tree higher up the mountain, bobbed down the stream, swirled in the foam near a rock and then plunged on towards the distant loch.

"Come on, you can tell me," Tom said.

The girl looked up at him, but did not speak.

The scrape of a boot on a nearby boulder heralded the arrival of Edward, who was crossing the rocks towards them. "Are you alright, Persephone?" he asked. "Do you have any injuries?"

She shook her head and then once more looked away, apparently reluctant to tell either of them what was on her mind.

"Thanks Edward, we'll be fine now," Tom said, suddenly keen to be alone with Persephone.

"You sure?" Edward sounded doubtful.

"We will be fine. I will take her back to school."

Edward nodded. "Very well. I will be at the Institute if you need me." He turned away, clambered back onto the bank, raised a hand to Tom and then was gone.

"So then, what is this all about?" Tom said, turning back to Persephone. "What's got you so upset?"

The girl pushed her hair back from her face, composed herself and then answered.

"Well, it's like this…" she began, but got no further because at that precise moment the air seemed to shiver and she vanished again.

"Damn it!" he swore. "Now where has she got to?" What was he to do? Did he go and get Edward again? By the look of things the Victorian lieutenant and Mary were getting more than just friendly. Tom had already interrupted them once today and was reluctant to do so again. But there was nothing else for it, was there? Or was there? Edward was the only Walker who seemed able to track others, yet, Tom thought, he might be able to do the same trick. After all, according to the Professor he was a Potentate – a remarkably powerful Walker, who in theory had access to more powers and talents than any other. During the encounters with Knossos, Tom had discovered this for himself and had started to develop his skills, but he had never tried tracking a Walker as Edward did. Now seemed the right moment to give it a go.

So, in his imagination he focused on the map in his mind that enabled him to navigate in time and space. He tried to spot Persephone on the map. He had travelled with her through time and knew what she looked like – not just physically, but in terms of the temporal energy she radiated. This was a type of energy unique to Walkers. It was by generating this energy from within themselves that they could travel through time and manipulate the world about them.

At first Tom could not see Persephone anywhere. Then, just as he was about to give up, he spotted her energy signature, faint but definitely present, much further to the south. It seemed she had gone back to the school. Whatever was she playing at?

Pleased to find that, like Edward, he was able to track another Walker, Tom cast a final appreciative glance around the peaceful Scottish island, then Walked back to the school toilets, returning to his locked cubicle. Persephone's signature was brighter now. She was near, apparently mere yards away in the corridor outside the toilets.

He left the cubicle, passed the wash basins and opened the outer door. Then he stopped and stared. In his mind the signature was right there in front of him, yet the corridor was empty – most of the school were still outside on lunch break.

"So she is here in this location – but I can't see her. Which means she is here but not in this time," Tom murmured to himself. "She is some when else then. But when?"

In the way Septimus had taught him when he had first been made aware of his powers as a Walker and was learning to control them, Tom imagined the clock in his mind and began to spin the hands backwards, all the while keeping a strong grip on his location. As the clock hands span faster and faster Persephone's signature grew brighter – so he knew he was closing in on her. Letting go of the present he Walked backwards through time into the void.

Checking the clock, Tom saw that he was approaching the tenth century and the signature was now fully bright. He was close. *'Almost there,'* he thought, preparing to step out of the void onto the hill where the school would one day be built. Persephone, it seemed, was standing on the hillside in the year 986 AD. Then, just before he could reach her she was on the move again. The glow of energy flashed past him. For a moment he caught a glimpse of her face and saw that she was screaming. Then she was gone, hurtling forward through the years. Tom was immediately after her, pursuing her energy across the centuries. As she Walked forward she started to drift away from their location by just a few dozen feet. Tom followed.

'Where is she going? It's almost as if she has lost control!' Tom thought, pushing himself on after her. Just as they reached the present day at the moment in time when they had left, Tom saw the energy slow down, turn around and start moving back down the time line. An instant later he saw Persephone hurtling towards him through the void. Instinctively he reached out and seized her, wrapped his arms around her and Walked them both out of the void back into the real world.

They materialised in the chemistry classroom, which fortunately was still empty. Persephone was screaming and tumbling out of control and Tom found himself tugged sideways over one of the lab benches. They crashed into apparatus that had been set up for an experiment, smashing glass test tubes and bottles and landing heavily on a stool, which under their combined weight collapsed with an ominous splintering sound.

Finally they were still. Tom could hear shouting and laughter drifting through the open window from the playground outside. Persephone had stopped screaming, but was still breathing heavily and was staring at Tom. After a moment she pulled away from his arms, picked herself up, dusted glass fragments and splinters of wood off her school uniform skirt and then spoke.

"That is what I was about to tell you. I am struggling to control the... er... how do you call it?"

"Walking? Tom asked.

Persephone nodded. "Yes, Walking."

Getting to his feet, Tom frowned. "I don't understand. When you were a Black Robe you were all over the place. Why are you having problems now?"

"Knossos was in my head then. He directed us and guided us. I did not learn to Walk on my own. I was never taught. Suddenly he is gone and yet these powers remain. Sometimes they just take me. I fight them and try to get back to where I started, but it's so hard. I don't suppose you can understand it."

"Actually, I can." Tom smiled at her.

They sat down on a pair of stools and he told her about the confusion and ridicule that had been his lot when he had first discovered he could Walk – how he would find himself randomly vanishing and appearing at different locations in space and time.

30

"So can you help me, Thomas? Can you help control it?"

"I can try. But first I think we should get out of this room before—" Tom broke off, "Oops! too late," he hissed.

"Before what, Oakley, hummm? Before what?" Mr Yardley, the round-faced chemistry teacher asked from the doorway.

Taking in the smashed apparatus he moved into the room and shut the door. "I think you had better explain yourselves," he said.

In the end there was nothing to be done but accept the blame. Tom made up some story about playing football and kicking the ball through the open window. He had come into the classroom to find the ball, he said, and thrown it back outside just before the teacher came in. Persephone had heard all the glass smashing and come into the lab to see what was going on. She had nothing to do with it, Tom insisted. He did not think Mr Yardley fully believed him, but since Tom was clearly willing to accept full responsibility, his punishment was less severe than might otherwise have been the case.

Mr Yardley decreed first that they must tidy up the lab before anyone got hurt on the broken glass, then that Tom would have to serve detention every night for two weeks. Finally, a letter would be sent to his parents asking them to pay for the replacement equipment and stool. That decided, the chemistry teacher stood and watched Tom and Persephone clear up the debris before evicting them from the lab and sending them back to the playground.

"Sorry Tom… for getting you into trouble I mean," said Persephone as they strolled disconsolately outside.

"It was not your fault, was it," Tom replied, "but we need to do something about controlling your Walking."

31

She nodded. "That is what I wanted to ask you. Will you teach me?"

Tom thought about this. He had never taught anyone to Walk and was not sure how good a teacher he would be. However, if he did this then at least he could keep an eye on her and given the excuse to spend time with her, he would also have the opportunity to ask her more about Knossos.

"OK, why not?" he said.

At first it was not easy to find time when Andy was not hanging about trying to talk to Persephone. If ever Tom found an empty classroom and he and Persephone met there, you could guarantee that Andy would turn up, poke his nose in and ask something like, "What are you two up to then?"

He became more and more suspicious as time went on and when he and Tom were walking home after school one day, Andy stopped abruptly and said, "Look, about you and Persephone... you two are going out aren't you? Only I can't help noticing you're always together these days."

"What?" Tom shook his head. "No, we are not, honest. She's just a friend."

"You promise?"

"I promise," Tom replied, holding his hand up like someone swearing an oath.

"You sure?"

"Aaaaghh!! Yes I am sure!"

"So you don't mind if I do ask her out?"

"Well I..." Tom hesitated then forcing a grin, said, "No of course not."

Andy slapped him on the back. "Cheers mate."

After that Tom had to work harder to find time to teach Persephone without Andy finding out. It would be possible, Tom knew, to take Persephone away to another time or location, just as Septimus had once done with him and indeed, he did occasionally do this. However, Persephone wanted to be the one who did the Walking. She wanted to feel in control of where they went and when. He found that if he transported her she grew frustrated and as a result seemed to gain less and less from each trip. She responded much better if instead they snuck away to a quiet corner of the school or he invited her to his home. The only problem with either of these options was avoiding Andy, who would grow suspicious again if he saw them together.

Over the next couple of weeks Tom tried to pass on what he knew about Walking, as well as helping Persephone to develop a strategy designed to control the spontaneous, unintentional time travel that plagued novice Walkers. Thinking back a couple of years to when he himself was randomly travelling forwards and backwards in time and getting into all sorts of bother as a result, Tom tried to get across to Persephone the technique of pinning oneself to both time and place. She was eager to learn but easily disheartened by early failures.

The worst of these happened one Sunday afternoon when she and Tom were at his house. His father had asked him to wash the car and Persephone had volunteered her help.

"I don't understand how you pin yourself, Thomas. I am Walking without warning and at times I could not predict. How do you focus on maintaining that link?"

Tom frowned. "You don't. It's like… um, let me think… Yes, I know! It's like a ship's captain who does not consciously have to do anything to stop his ship, he simply has to drop the anchor and it works; the ship stays where the anchor falls. The captain forgets about it until he wants to move his ship again then he

33

pulls in the anchor and off he goes. It's the same with Walking. You just have to learn how to anchor yourself in time and place. Then, when you want to Walk, you simply let go of the link, that is to say, you pull in the anchor! Do you see what I mean?"

"I think so." Persephone stared at him. She had just picked up a bucket of water in preparation for throwing it over the car to rinse off all the suds and foam. "It sounds easy enough," she said, swinging the bucket towards the car, "but—"

Persephone got no further because at that moment she vanished.

"Blast!" Tom cursed and set off in pursuit.

He was focusing so hard on keeping track of the girl and materialising at the same point that he did not give any thought to where and when she had appeared. So it was with horror that he realised they had both materialised in the Head's office on a school day and that Persephone had just managed to throw the entire contents of her bucket right over the Headmaster's head!

As the spluttering Headteacher glared at them, quick as a flash Tom pushed Persephone towards the door and out into corridor then Walked them away from the building. As soon as they had materialised behind a stand of trees on the far side of the school, he checked the date and time.

"Oops!" he exclaimed.

"What?" Persephone asked.

"It's tomorrow!" he said.

It transpired that they had arrived in the Headmaster's office during the lunch hour on Monday, one day after they had been washing the car. Still stunned by the experience, Tom Walked them back to Sunday afternoon, hoping nobody was around to see them materialise in his driveway. He wished there was a way he could change what had happened, but he had found out early on in his time-travelling experience that he could not simply revisit a point in time where he was present and prevent or alter an event, at least, not without great difficulty and if he did so there was always the risk of causing a chain of other, unforeseen consequences. So he just had to live through it all again.

There then followed a very unpleasant twenty-four hours waiting for time to tick round to lunchtime the following day. At the appointed time, he and Persephone shuffled gloomily back along the corridor outside the Headmaster's office, timing their arrival to a few moments after their earlier selves had just run out of it and vanished.

The Head's door flung open and there he stood in the frame, dripping and steaming at the same time. He glared at them, looked down at their school uniforms and back at their faces. A confused expression crept across his features. Then he shook his head and a steely glint was fixed upon them both.

"You two hooligans, come here! You think that by quickly changing your clothes you can fool me? What is the meaning of this… this outrage?"

Unable to come up with a plausible excuse, Tom remained silent. A tirade, letters to their parents and another two weeks of detention ensued. Tom was relieved; he had feared expulsion or at least suspension. The Headmaster had let them off lightly in the circumstances.

So, that same evening, for the first session of their punishment Persephone and Tom sat in one of the classrooms used for detention. The end of the school day bell had just rung and out of the window they could see their classmates streaming home, laughing and joking, listening to music or running for buses. The story of the bucket incident had already somehow passed like wildfire around the entire school and no doubt some of the laughter was from children retelling a story that would pass into legend.

Sighing, Tom opened his exercise book and began writing out an essay on appropriate behaviour in a school and why drenching a headmaster was not a suitable example.

Up at the front of the classroom Mr Franklin, the teacher assigned to the detention class, cast a glance full of distrust and contempt at Tom before returning to marking some homework. After a few minutes he stood up and looked at them then coughed to summon their attention.

"I'm just going to get something I need from my form room," he said. "I will be back in a few minutes. Get on with your work and no talking!"

When he had gone, Persephone leant towards Tom and tried to attract his attention.

"Psst! Thomas…"

He frowned. "What?" He was feeling decidedly grumpy.

"I am sorry about this," she said in a low voice, looking as if she was about to burst into tears.

Tom looked across at her thinking that the expression puppy-dog eyes might have been invented for just such a moment. Once again he sighed. It was impossible to be annoyed with her.

"It's not your fault, Persephone. You are trying hard to control Walking. Don't worry… we will get there."

She smiled. "Do you think so?"

"Yes indeed."

"Well I hope so."

Remembering that he had not yet asked her the questions about Knossos for which the Professor was awaiting answers, Tom bit his lip. This was probably as good a moment as any.

"Um… Persephone?" he began.

"Mm, what?" She was chewing on her pencil as she studied

what she had so far written in her essay.

"Can I ask you something?"

She nodded.

"It's about…" he hesitated, "Knossos."

Persephone gave a little shudder at the name and looked across at Tom. "What…what about him?"

"Apart from the Crown did he build anything else?"

She looked confused. "What do you mean?"

"I mean, did he talk about any other similar objects or artefacts or did you see him making anything? Something a bit like… oh, I don't know, something a bit unusual maybe?"

Persephone screwed up her face as she thought back. Slowly she shook her head. "My time with him is shrouded in a deep mist, Thomas, I do not recall anything like you describe. Sorry."

"You sure?" Tom asked, but got no reply. Mr Franklin had returned and stood glowering in the doorway.

"What is this?" he roared. Coming fully into the room he glared at Tom. "What did I say about being quiet, Oakley? That is thirty more minutes of detention you just earned yourself boy!"

An hour later Tom staggered out of the detention room on his own, everyone else having left earlier, including Persephone, who cast him an apologetic glance as she passed his desk. The school was deserted and he had missed the school bus. He could, of course, Walk the long route home, but having sat for over an hour in the stuffy classroom he felt in need of fresh air and exercise, so he set off at a brisk pace, his thoughts occupied with Persephone. He was half way home, just passing the park, when his mobile rang.

It was Andy. "So, you were lying to me, Tom!"

37

"What?"

"You said you weren't going out with Persephone!"

"I'm not."

"Liar! I have not been able to get her alone to ask her out these last few weeks. Now I find out that you have been seeing lots of her. Sneaking into the gym or classrooms, thinking no one had seen you. Inviting her home weekends. Turns out you've been seeing lots of her."

"Andy, it's not what you think. It's just—"

"Oh come on. The pair of you are practically joined at the hip – even pulling pranks on the Headmaster I hear."

"Andy..." Tom hesitated.

"Oh shove off, Tom, just shove off!" Andy said and the phone went dead.

Sitting down on a nearby park bench Tom tried to call him back, but all he got was a message saying Andy had switched off his phone.

"Damn!" he swore.

It started raining. Soon Tom was drenched through. Cold and wet and in a very bad mood, he stomped on home, all the while imagining what would happen when he got there. In his pocket was a letter from the Headmaster and another from Mr Franklin about his 'behaviour'. He had some ideas about how difficult the conversation he was inevitably about to have with his parents was going to be.

"Damn and blast!" he cursed.

CHAPTER FIVE
THE FIRST TITAN

*"*Thomas, wake up please."

The words came seemingly from far away. Tom was dreaming. It was a bizarre dream: he was a great big grizzly bear that had just scooped a sparkling trout from a fast flowing river and tossed it, still flapping about and dripping, onto the river bank. Yet, as he climbed out of the river and turned to pick up the fish, it jumped about five feet away from him. The bear, who was Tom, growled and pounced upon the trout, but again it leapt high and evaded his grasp. Two and three times more he grasped and lunged with his great hairy paws, and two and three times more the slippery fish evaded his grip. Finally, roaring in triumph he seized the fish, but as it turned and struggled in his paws he caught sight of its head. It looked exactly like Persephone. "I am sorry you got detention on my account, Thomas," the fish said...

"Thomas! Wake up!"

Tom woke with a start and stared around his bedroom. His radio alarm clock read 8:15 20 Dec. Sitting on the end of his bed was Lieutenant Dyson.

"Do you know that you growl in your sleep, Thomas?" Edward asked.

Tom yawned, sat up and stared down at his hands, half expecting to see hairy paws and extended claws. Coming fully awake he looked up at Edward and grimaced. "There was a time

39

when I was a normal boy you know. Before I met you all."

Edward smiled. "Speaking as one who was about to die in battle when you turned up, I am glad we did meet. Septimus, mind you, would no doubt point out how boring your life could have been had you never met him."

Tom shrugged. "I guess we will never know. You do know it's not a school day and you have woken me at 8:15 – and on the first day of the Christmas holidays too!" Tom moaned, pulling the bed sheets up over his shoulders. It was two weeks after the incident with the Headmaster. Two weeks of days full of Andy sulking at him or ignoring him completely; two weeks of detention every evening and then, to top it all, two weeks of interrogation by his parents wanting to know what had gone on at school every time he arrived home. Now, at last, the holidays were here and Tom had planned a long lie-in this morning, but it seemed this was not going to happen. 'What is the use of being a so-called Potentate!' he thought bitterly, glaring at his Victorian tormentor.

Edward tugged Tom out of bed and thrust some clothes at him. "Come on lazy bones. When I was in the army I would have been awake almost two hours by now. There will be time for holiday later. For now get dressed, the Professor needs us all. You go ahead and get to the Institute. I will join you there."

"Why? Where are you going?"

"I am going to find Septimus. No one has seen him since the last time we all met. I am going back to locate him."

"Back? Back where?" Tom asked, tugging on a pullover.

"1516 A.D. in Bologna, Italy."

"What's he doing there?"

"I have no idea. Maybe he likes pasta?" Edward replied. "Anyway, I won't be long."

Then he vanished, leaving Tom reflecting on how stiff and formal Edward had been once upon a time and how he seemed lately to have developed a sense of humour. Dry humour perhaps, but the guy had certainly lightened up a bit. Tom wondered if this was Mary's influence. It seemed likely.

He had just left the bathroom after brushing his teeth and tugging a comb through his mop of jet black hair, when his dad emerged on the landing.

"Tom, what on earth are you doing up? It's not even half-eight on a Saturday!"

Tom thought quickly. "Yeh, I know Dad, but er… I still need to get Mum's present for Christmas. I was going to pop up to town before the crowds arrive. It's the last Saturday before Christmas after all and it's bound to be busy."

His father stared at him. "You're not meeting that Greek girl are you? What's her name again?"

"Persephone."

"Ah yes, Persephone. Well I'm not sure she is a good influence on you. You've had nothing but trouble since she arrived on the scene."

Tom shook his head. "Honestly, I am not seeing her, Dad."

"What about Andy?"

"No."

"You two fallen out? He's not been round lately."

Tom shrugged. "It's nothing."

His father still looked doubtful. "You sure you are OK going on your own?"

Tom sighed. "Dad… I'm almost thirteen! I have my bus pass to get there and back and I've got my mobile. I'll be fine."

"Very well, if you're sure?"

"I'm sure."

His father yawned. "Well I am going back to bed." He grimaced, "Your mum and I are doing the supermarket shopping a bit later so we might miss you. Be back for tea, lad."

Tom nodded, "Yes, Dad."

Going back into his room, Tom shut the door behind him then picked up his coat and mobile and Walked to the Institute. He arrived in Mr Phelps' office. The Professor's assistant dropped his pen in surprise and then, picking it up again, scowled at Tom and pointed at a new sign that had appeared on the wall of the desk behind him.

'No appearing or disappearing in this office!' it read.

"I have had enough shocks and surprises with you lot popping up like jack-in-the-boxes every five minutes nearly giving me a heart attack. Right then; I had better check you in. Name please?"

"Mr Phelps, you ask everyone their name every time they come. It is Tom Oakley as you very well know."

The administrator leant over and using an old fountain pen ticked off Tom's name in his appointment book.

"That is better. Now all is correct. The Professor is expecting you."

"I know! I wouldn't be here if he wasn't," Tom said.

Phelps nodded toward the door. "In you go then."

Rolling his eyes Tom entered the room to find that Charlie and Mary were already present. The Professor had a map out on his desk, as well as an open book, which was face down on the map. Tom peered at the title. It was 'The Storm' by someone called Daniel Defoe. Tom had heard of neither author nor title. He turned his attention to the map. It took a while to realise that from this side of the desk he was looking at it upside down, but after some moments of squinting at it he recognised the South of England from the Thames Estuary around to the Bristol Channel.

Actually, there was something else odd about the map. Apart from the coastline and the names of towns along it there was no detail of the land at all. No roads, railway lines, forests or hills. However, the area of the map that covered the sea was full of detail. The English Channel was crisscrossed by lines. Every island, substantial rock and sandbank was outlined and many areas showed the sea's depth at that particular point.

"A sailor's map?" Tom asked as he pulled up a chair and sat down next to Charlie.

"In fact it's a nautical map of the English Channel drawn up around 1700," Charlie said.

The Professor finished polishing his glasses and popping them back on his nose nodded a welcome to Tom.

"It is the closest cartographical representation we possess or can obtain to the target date."

Tom tilted his head. "Target date? Do you mean..." he hesitated.

"Yes, Thomas. We have detected that the first Time Cyst is emptying its content – one of the five Titans will emerge over the Channel."

The door opened at that moment and Edward, followed by Septimus, entered. The Welshman was wearing what appeared to be tights and an elaborate jacket.

Charlie tittered, "Didn't know you had the legs to pull off that kind of costume, mate," he said.

"What's with the tights, Septimus?" Tom asked with a wink at Charlie. "Been doing a spot of ballet have we?"

"They are called 'hose', ignorant youth, and they are the height of fashion in Italy," the Welshman replied curtly. "Five hundred years ago anyway," he added.

"Now we are all here," the Professor interrupted, "perhaps we can begin. Thank you Lieutenant for finding our waif and stray. What were you doing in sixteenth century Bologna anyway, Mr Mason, if you don't mind me asking?"

Septimus glared at the Professor and it was a long few seconds before he answered.

"As it happens I do mind you asking, as it's nobody's business save my own," he said with a sniff. He turned his head to look out of the window where rain was pattering against the glass. For a moment it was the only sound that could be heard, but then a log burning in the fireplace collapsed into the ash and there was a loud crack accompanied by a shower of sparks.

If the Professor was offended or surprised by the Welshman's surly response he gave no indication. "Oh, I see. Well, my apologies if I am intruding. Do you mind if I continue with my briefing?"

Septimus shook his head but said nothing, returning his attention to the window.

Tom stared at his friend. Septimus was usually so cheerful and happy. What was wrong with him?

The Professor patted the map. "As I was saying, the first Time Cyst is emptying. We have discovered the location, date and time. It is here, in the English Channel on November 26th 1703. Our trackers are having difficulty giving an exact fix. It seems to be travelling from west to east through the Channel from around 2 a.m. that morning onwards. What form or appearance it will take is hard to tell. I think we need to get you back there and you will have to use your intelligence and skills to locate it. There is a complication, however…"

"There usually is!" Charlie muttered to Edward.

The Professor glared at him for a moment then opened his

mouth to continue, but it was Edward, learning forward to stare at the map, who spoke next.

"November 26th 1703 was the day of the Great Storm."

"That is well remembered, Lieutenant," the Professor nodded.

"Did you read about it?" Tom asked Edward.

"Yes, Defoe was one of the authors I read at school. That book," he pointed at The Storm, "tells of the great gale that devastated southern England on that day. It came from the Atlantic and swept across the nation. Hundreds of people drowned in the floods that ensued in the West Country. Thousands of houses lost their chimneys in London. The forests in the South were flattened. Yet the worst of the storm was out there at sea," he gestured at the map and paused before continuing.

"A convoy of about one hundred merchant ships and escorts was scattered and some thirty were sunk that day. The Royal Navy was particularly hard hit with its Channel Squadron devastated, fifteen ships lost and over one thousand sailors drowned, many of the ships running aground on Goodwin Sands near Deal."

"Nasty," Charlie said sombrely.

"So, we must find this Titan amongst the storm?" Mary asked.

The Professor nodded. "I know this will not be easy, but if the Titan is allowed to roam free the effect could be catastrophic. He must be captured."

Mary frowned. "Yes, but how exactly are we to do this? How can we hope to contain one of these creatures?"

"I believe I can be of assistance in that regard," a voice spoke from the fireplace. They all swung round to see the Custodian standing there. He was dressed as ever in a formal grey suit and flanked by two of his featureless men, who were similarly dressed in smart suits. Tom had no idea how the Custodian

45

had managed to appear without anyone feeling him Walking, but that did not bother him as much as the actual presence of the man. He had held a grudge against the Professor's brother ever since the terrifying battle with Knossos for which, in Tom's view, the Custodian was largely responsible.

"What are you doing here?" Tom demanded.

"I bring a means to contain the Titans," the old man said, moving to the desk and placing a small cotton bag upon it. There was a tinkle of glass as he did so.

"I suppose you expect us to just trust you?" Tom said with a scowl. "For all we know you might be up to new tricks. Last time it was you who risked the universe by allowing the tablet to be found that brought Knossos back and almost destroyed everything."

"I don't have any interest in what you think about me, Thomas Oakley. What I did then was necessary for the prevailing crisis and I will say no more to defend my actions for they require no defending."

Tom was not convinced, but it was clear they needed some means of dealing with these Titans when they met them. If the Custodian brought that means then it would be necessary to listen, much as he did not want to.

"Oh, very well," he said at length. "So what have you got in the bag?"

The Custodian opened the bag and looked inside it. "A temporary solution only," he said, reaching inside and pulling out an object. It was a blue glass bottle with a cork stopper. In many ways it looked like a perfume bottle, similar to the dozens Tom's mother kept on her dressing table at home.

"Have you heard of the legend of the genie in the bottle, Master Oakley?" the Custodian asked.

"What, Sinbad, the desert and so on?"

"Just so."

Septimus snorted and turned his attention from the window back to the meeting, but he did not speak.

"You must be joking!" Tom exclaimed. "You don't mean this bottle is like the genie's lamp, do you? What are you saying? Do I get three wishes like Ali Baba?" he smirked.

The Professor reached over and took the bottle from the Custodian. "You should not be so fast to ridicule myths and legends, Thomas. Many of them have some origins in truth. In ancient times there were many so called gods, demigods, spirits and fairies. What were these creatures – men with powers like ours or something more? In truth we still don't know, but what we can say is that ways were developed to contain them. What the Custodian has brought us here is a miniature pocket universe. Or rather, the portal or opening to one. Point this bottle at a Titan, open the stopper and you will draw the creature into the pocket universe and trap it there for a while."

"So it is just like a genie in a bottle!" Edward said.

The Professor nodded.

"How long for? How long will it hold?" Charlie asked.

The Custodian shook his head. "Months perhaps; weeks maybe. I cannot be sure. I located five of these glass vials just after The Event because I knew this current time would come and was prepared for it."

There flashed into Tom's mind a brief image of the Custodian and the blank-faced men of the Directorate poring over the table in The Office boardroom, where a large open box, full of constantly swirling silver and copper sand, enabled them to monitor patterns of harmony or disturbance in the different realities and, more importantly, predict what might happen if they did not intervene.

"What then? What happens when the vials cannot contain the Titans any longer?" Tom asked, taking the bottle from the Professor and examining it. It felt cold and was significantly heavier than it looked.

There was no answer.

Tom looked up. Neither of the brothers had said anything.

"You still don't know do you?" Septimus asked.

The Professor shook his head. "No, Mr Mason, we do not yet have a permanent solution. Let us tackle the first Titan and then think further on that."

Tom shrugged. "Very well. But if there is going to be a storm I suggest Septimus changes out of his tights!"

Half an hour later they had visited Mrs Mackay's costume rooms upstairs and returned to the Professor's study to find that the Custodian had gone. Tom and the men each wore short trousers that went down to just below their knees, long socks and black shoes with brass buckles on them. Completing this apparel was a shirt, which had rather too many frills for Tom's liking, a fitted coat and a triangular tricorne hat. Edward was loading a pair of flintlock pistols and Charlie and Septimus were examining their long, thin swords, which looked rather like those Tom had seen in a film about the Three Musketeers.

The door opened and Edward gasped as Mary sidled in. She was dressed in a long, deep green dress with a lot of lace around the collar and sleeves.

"You look beautiful," Edward said, his eyes out on stalks.

"Thank you, Edward," Mary said, her face flushing slightly.

Septimus grinned at them, "Come on you love birds, it is time to go."

Edward looked shocked, but Mary just giggled as she slid her hand around the lieutenant's arm. "Yes, but where? The south coast is a big place, where do we start," she asked.

"One of the first reported incidents early in the storm was the total destruction of Eddystone Lighthouse." The Professor pointed at the map, "That was here on Eddystone rocks, a few miles off the coast near Plymouth. Given the ferocity of the storm, actually visiting the rocks would be too dangerous. The nearest land point is here at Rame Head, which is about nine miles from the lighthouse." He moved his finger to indicate a headland just outside Plymouth. "Go there at around 1 a.m. on that day and be careful – the storm will be approaching its full fury."

Edward frowned. "At one o'clock in the morning in the middle of a storm I cannot see how we will be able to spot the lighthouse from nine miles away, Professor."

The old man nodded and picked up his phone. "Mr Phelps, you can send in Mr Fitzwilliams now."

A moment later there was a knock on the door and a gentlemen entered carrying a leather case. He was a thin gangly fellow with long white hair, whom Tom did not recognize.

"Mr Fitzwilliams here is behind some of the gadgets we use in the Institute, such as those trackers you might recall using to follow the course of that merchant ship out of Malta Harbour during the Second World War. Remember?"

"Too right!" Charlie grinned.

Tom nodded, thinking back to when he and Septimus had rescued Charlie. He recalled the tracking device a little like a mobile phone and the tiny bead-like objects, one of which they had dropped in a packing case on the deck of that ship.

"So he is a bit like 'Q' in James Bond you mean?" Tom said,

looking at Fitzwilliams. In fact he looked less like Q and more like some sort of mad scientist.

"Absolutely not!" Fitzwilliams said in a hurt tone, but just as Tom started to apologize, he added, "Actually, Q is my brother, but I can't talk about him. Official secrets you know!"

It took Tom a moment to realize the man was pulling his leg. He smiled at the scientist and received a kindly smile back. Fitzwilliams then placed the case on the desk and popped the catches. Reaching into it he withdrew five metal tubes. He held them out and the Walkers each took one. Tom examined his. It was a small telescope of copper and glass.

Edward smiled and shook his head. "I used to have a spyglass when I was a boy. This is a nice instrument, Mr Fitzwilliams. But in the dark I don't think—"

Fitzwilliams held up his hand to silence Edward. "No, not exactly a spyglass, Lieutenant, nor is it merely a telescope. These instruments are specially adapted spotting scopes. They have powerful magnification yet will contract to a size that fits in your pocket. More to the point, they have infra-red technology built into them."

Edward and Mary both looked confused.

"You mean they can see in the dark?" Tom asked.

"Exactly," Fitzwilliams nodded. "Many miles, in fact. They have the same technology the army uses in night vision goggles, but we've enhanced it."

"Cool, how does it work?"

"Like this," Fitzwilliams said, and proceeded to show them how to zoom in an out and also how to activate the night vision feature. "Just don't leave them in 1703," he warned, "or you could change history with the technology that's inside them!"

Tom shook his head and turned to ask Septimus what he

thought. The Welshman was leaning back in his chair peering through his telescope, which was angled up towards Neoptolemas. The old man was currently sitting at his desk, eyes closed in thought.

"Professor..." Septimus said.

"What?" Neoptolemas answered vaguely as he opened his eyes.

"I can see right up your nose!"

Charlie snorted.

"Well," Tom said hurriedly, "no point in wasting any time. Come on, let's get on with it."

Pocketing his scope, he held out his hands and the others clustered around him. In his mind he then reached out for the map and the clock... and Walked.

CHAPTER SIX
THE GREAT STORM

They went from the warmth of the Professor's brightly lit study with its inviting fire crackling in the hearth, to the depths of night and a spot perched high on the top of a barren cliff, the sea crashing in fury and foaming white at its base. Instantly they were assailed by the shrieking gale and drenched by the rain.

Almost swept off his feet, Tom peered out to sea, blinking his eyes to clear the moisture and trying to make something out. At first he could see nothing, so heavy was the rain. Then there was a flash of light far out over the water. He tried to focus upon it. After a moment he could make out a shape there: something dark and tall. Then the rain grew even heavier filling his eyes with water and it was gone.

"This is impossible we can't see anything!" he shouted as he rubbed his eyes again. Similar activity on the part of his companions suggested that he was not the only one struggling.

"Mary, can you do something about this?" Septimus shouted.

"What did you say?" Mary shouted back.

Septimus cupped his hands and bellowed, battling the whistling wind. "I said can't you do something about the storm?"

Mary's face twisted into a frown as she pondered the question. Then she raised her hands skyward, closed her eyes and shouted, "WALL!"

In an instant the air around them seemed to shimmer and sparkle and a transparent dome of frozen time materialised around and over them to form an impenetrable barrier. Outside it the storm still raged: the winds blew, the sea surged and the rain fell. Yet inside the dome it was quiet and calm and – Tom was very glad about this – dry. This particular skill of Mary's to manipulate a piece of time in this way was unique among the Walkers. It had saved them from disaster many times in the past, but it drained her of energy and Tom knew that in these conditions she would not be able to hold the dome for long.

"Well done Mary," he said as she opened her eyes and smiled at him. "I wish Mrs Mackay had thought to give us oiled cloaks, I'm soaked through already."

His voice seemed to echo in the silence that now surrounded them. Drying his eyes with the large, lace-edged handkerchief he found in his trouser pocket, Tom then retrieved the telescope Fitzwilliams had given him. Raising it to his eye and activating the Infra-Red night vision function, he stared out at the storm again. After a moment he relocated the light far out at sea. Fiddling with the zoom on the scope he was able to bring the light into focus. He studied it and realised that it was a light at the top of a tall tower: a tower that stood on rocks some miles away. It could only be the Eddystone Lighthouse the Professor had referred to. The waves were surging around it, pounding against its walls. Yet, for now, the twelve-sided stone tower stood firm.

"Over there!" he announced. "Use your scopes." Around him he heard the sound of movement as the others fiddled with their telescopes and looked through them.

"It's amazing anyone could build such a thing in such a place!" Mary said in awe, her dress clinging to her like a sopping wet rag.

"It was the first of its kind," Edward said, knowledgeable as ever. "In earlier times, the Greeks and Romans built lighthouses in the more tranquil Mediterranean, but—"

"More tranquil?" Charlie interrupted, quirking his eyebrow. "You mean not counting the earthquakes – or have you forgotten the one we were caught up in when we were trying to find Alexander the Great's tomb in Alexandria?"

"Of course not, but earthquakes are a lot less common than storms, fortunately," Edward said. "Anyway, as I was saying, before Henry Winstanley built this one in 1698, just five years ago, no one had built one for hundreds of years and certainly not in Britain's wild seas. This was a model for ones that would follow. Yet, it did not survive this night – unlike the Pharos lighthouse, Charlie, which did survive the earthquake we witnessed in 365 AD!"

Turning to Mary he added, "Mary, can you let us hear what is happening? Keep us out of the storm but let the sound in?"

Her face white with effort, Mary nodded her head and Tom felt a slight shift in the energies around them. The Wall of frozen time was still solid, yet somehow holes appeared in it – enough to let the sound in. With a great crash of thunder the din of the storm came rushing in again.

Below them and nine miles away the waves pounded Winstanley's tower. Above it the clouds swirled and raced, dark against the moonlight. Out of the clouds forked lightning stabbed, thrust and darted. Then it seemed to Tom as if a darker shadow had appeared within the clouds. The shadow surged towards the lighthouse and the clouds seemed to change direction and go after it, like a wolf pack following its leader. In moments a hurricane was spinning round the tower. Zigzag light, shaped like the teeth of a buzz saw, flicked out of the swirling cloud.

The force of the wind drove the waves on so that they were rising up and smashing down upon the lighthouse – waves twenty feet tall, some fifty feet, even seventy feet now.

"Can't we do something?" Mary said. "There are people in that tower."

"Are they Walkers?" Septimus asked.

Tom reached out with his mind but felt nothing there. He looked at Edward.

The soldier shook his head. His expression was grim because he knew, as they all did, that only Walkers could travel through time and space the way they all could. "Alas not," he said.

"No Septimus. Not Walkers," Tom said.

"Then there is nothing we can do for them," the Welshman said sadly.

As he spoke, a wave more than one hundred feet tall surged up and crashed down upon the tower. There was an almighty crack and, like a sandcastle demolished by the incoming tide when it races up a holiday beach, the tower crumbled, tottered and finally fell into the sea. Abruptly the light went out, extinguished by the rage of the elements. Not wishing to watch any further, the Walkers lowered their telescopes.

No one spoke.

Then, out of the shadow that still spun around the space where the tower had been, they heard a new sound – a sound that sent a chill through their bodies. Tom did not believe what he was hearing at first. Booming out over the din of the storm came the unmistakeable sound of laughter: a deep rolling laugh, as if some monstrous creature was revelling in the destruction of the lighthouse and the people within it. For a few moments the shadow lingered then raced away eastwards along the English Channel, the laughter lost on the shrieking wind.

"It is worse than we thought," Septimus said after a moment.

"Why?" Charlie asked.

"The Professor was concerned that the storm would get in our way and be an obstacle to us."

"Well he has got that right," the sailor said, pointing at the huge seas.

"No, it's more than that. It's no coincidence that the storm happens to be here this very same night the first Time Cyst has deteriorated. Doesn't this whole scene strike you as something out of a Greek myth – raging tempest; surging seas? Don't you see? The storm isn't here by chance; the storm IS the Titan. Crius has escaped!"

"Oh my God!" Tom gasped. "Then what you are saying is that the heart of the storm is where the Titan will be. Which means that is where we have to go!"

Septimus nodded, "Afraid so."

"Out there?" Mary pointed, a horrified expression on her face.

"What are you suggesting… that we walk on water?" Edward said. "That's impossible; we can't simply Walk out there. We will all be drowned."

As moonlight shone through a gap in the scudding clouds Tom studied the waves for a while and caught a glimpse of a small, one-masted fishing boat a mile or so out to sea. It was obviously in trouble. With every wave it seemed to submerge, yet it bobbed up again, each time lower in the water.

"Look, over there!" he cried, struggling to focus his telescope on the boat.

They all looked through their scopes to where he pointed. The boat was being tossed about like a cork on the water. The crew had taken in the sail and were clinging on to whatever they could get hold of. Tom hoped they might make it back to land, but it was a faint hope. As he watched, the boat plunged deep into another furrow, the sea rose over its deck and this time it did not emerge again.

"Those poor fishermen," Mary said quietly.

Once again they fell silent, but after a moment, Charlie spoke. "We may not be able to walk on water, Edward, but we can sail. That's what we need: a boat. I will sail it close to the eye of the storm while you sort out capturing the Titan."

Tom shook his head, "In this weather? You saw what just happened."

"It can be done though," Edward said. "I once sailed a skiff in bad weather around the Orkney's when I was a student – that was before the army of course."

"Besides," Charlie pointed out, "you are forgetting we have some talents and abilities ordinary sailors do not possess. Mary can shield us and I am sure you can do your bit, Tom."

Tom sighed. "I guess it is the only way to get close. But where will we get a boat?"

"Plymouth is over there," Septimus pointed, "just behind us. You'll be spoilt for choice there, boyo."

Charlie shook his head. "That's no good. This storm is moving fast. We have to get ahead of it. Take us to Weymouth, Tom. On the south side there is an old fort on the headland there. The modern one, still there today, is from the 1860's, but in 1703 where we are now, there is an earlier one. I think it was built during the Civil War."

"I'm impressed, Charlie," Edward said.

Charlie smirked, "Yes, well if there's something I know more about than you, Edward, it's the coast. Anyway, below the fort we should find some boats right at the harbour entrance." He grinned, "Probably easiest to... ahem... 'borrow' one of those than half-inch one from the main harbour."

Tom nodded. "OK, Weymouth it is. Mary, you can let down the Wall now. Grab hold, everyone."

A moment later they materialised in Weymouth just outside the small fortress that had once guarded the entrance to the harbour. The main harbour was off to the west – a forest of masts just visible in the moonlight. The chief part of the town was opposite them across a narrow neck of water that led into the harbour. They could see a few lights glimmering, but the majority of houses were dormant, their inhabitants having closed up the shutters and retired for the night or else taken shelter from the storm as best as they could. Out at sea the waves were already tall, but the full anger of the gale had not yet hit the area. Nevertheless, the trees above and around them creaked and groaned in the wind. Somewhere there was a crack and a crash as one of the trees came tumbling to earth. The rain had started here and was getting heavier by the minute.

"Come on, we don't have long," Charlie said, and led them down the track. He had been right: there were several small fishing boats, dinghies and skiffs tied up along both sides of the entrance to the harbour. The sailor examined a few and then waved Edward over to a solid-looking vessel with a single mast. The other three Walkers watched and waited. Edward must have agreed that it was suitable because he and Charlie climbed aboard then indicated that the others should join them. There was a small cabin at the rear of the vessel and Septimus and Mary took shelter in there. Lingering on the shore, Tom took a final glance around then untied the hawser that secured the boat to an iron ring on the harbour wall. Coiling up the rope he threw it aboard and clambered after it. Edward pushed them off with a pole before unfurling the sail while Charlie took charge of the tiller.

The sail caught the wind and they were away.

"Now I feel like one of those Barbary pirates," Mary commented as Tom joined her and Septimus in the cabin. "Stealing a boat I mean."

"All in a good cause though, Mary," the Welshman said.

As it sped away from the calmer water of the harbour, the little vessel began rising and falling with the swell and lurching alarmingly from side to side. Mary looked a bit green.

"Maybe piracy is not the life for you?" Septimus commented. "I always found it rather fun."

"Just when were you a pirate?" Tom asked, trying to keep his balance by swaying with the boat.

"I'll tell you the story one day," Septimus replied with a cheeky wink.

Charlie steered the boat out of the harbour and turned south. They passed the large bulk of Portland rising tall and black to the west and then they were out into open seas. A mass of dark clouds was coming alarmingly quickly towards them from the direction of Weymouth and beneath it the seas rose and fell like water boiling in a pot, the waves growing higher and higher until each one seemed like a moving cliff. At the same time the winds were howling around them and the rain was now so heavy that the pounding on the cabin roof sounded like someone was up there with a hammer. They could see that Edward was having a hard job controlling the sail, so Septimus went to help him. Meanwhile, Mary and Tom left the cabin and struggled to the small deck where Charlie was standing, clenching his teeth as he fought with the tiller. "Best take in the sail before it shreds and brings the mast down with it," he shouted to Edward.

"Grab a rope and hang on tight, Mary," Tom yelled, moving to lend Charlie a hand with the tiller. "The last thing we need is you falling overboard!"

"If Crius is in that mass of cloud we have to get up above this monster wave," Charlie said. "I don't think the boat can survive that. Any ideas?"

Tom could see what Charlie meant. They had come out of the harbour in front of the storm. That storm had now created a giant wave that was thundering like a tsunami down the channel. It would drive everything before it or, more likely, would simply roll over them, bury them in tons of water and leave a wreckage of timber, sail cloth, rope and their broken bodies in its wake. Tom wondered if he could Walk them and the boat up onto its crest and ride it, much as a surfer would ride the waves, but the effort to do that would probably be too much even for him.

"Mary, how wide an area can you affect with your talents? Can you freeze time over a cube of say fifty feet each side?" he asked.

Mary blanched at the thought. Then she slowly nodded her head. "I daresay I can, Thomas, but not for long."

"Then do so – all around the boat. Let the wind in if you can, but keep the water out as much as possible. Charlie, steer a course across the wave. I will try and Walk us upwards in small jumps. Come on everyone, let's go surfing!"

A translucent globe – more a sphere than a cube and around ten feet in diameter – extended around them and outwards. Charlie turned the tiller and the boat, which had been heading straight towards the monster wave, now turned and headed diagonally across it. Tom closed his eyes and concentrated on all five of them plus the boat. He reached out for the flow of time and gave the boat a little lift. As a surfer on a surfboard climbs a wave, so the little vessel rose up the towering wall of water.

All around them the mass of a million tons of seawater was thundering its apocalyptic way up the channel, flooding the

60

river valleys and ports, crushing ships into kindling and scattering fishing fleets as if they were so many matchsticks. Yet here, in the very heart of the storm, Tom's boat was climbing up the wave, cresting it and now riding it like a mighty sea god of old.

"Drop the Wall, Mary, so we can draw in the Titan," Tom yelled.

Mary nodded with relief and lowered her arms. As the shimmering sphere vanished Tom craned his neck and searched the skies. At first all they could hear was the roaring of the storm. Then a voice thundered out of the black clouds that were now right above them. The words were strange and Tom could not understand them.

"He is speaking Greek. Ancient Greek that is," Edward explained. "I will translate."

The words boomed again. Edward listened, head cocked over to one side, eyes closed in concentration. *"So, there are still some of your kind alive!"* he said after a moment. *"You are not mere mortals. Can it be that the distant children of those who fought us dare to challenge us today, all these eons later?"*

Tom pulled the vial out of his pocket and held it concealed in his hands. He winked at Edward. "We need to goad him into showing himself. Tell him this: 'That's right. Our kind kicked your butt last time around and we are not letting you back to cause havoc'."

Edward nodded, thought for a second and then shouted out in Ancient Greek an approximation of this reply.

To begin with there was no answer, but then, as the boat continued to bob along the crest of the giant wave, the blackness above it appeared to grow even darker and a piece of it seemed to break away. It shot down towards the little boat and for a moment a swirling mass of black cloud hovered over it.

61

Then from out of the clouds a tall man, clad in bronze armour and wearing a helmet, stepped onto the deck.

He studied them each in turn then uttered a stream of what to Tom sounded like gibberish.

Edward translated. *"Who is it that speaks now to Crius the Titan. You should be on your knees in front of my glory."*

"Get lost!" Mary spat at the Titan.

Crius might not speak English, but the venom in her voice made the meaning obvious. He clapped his hands and a blast of icy air slammed into Mary smashing her backwards. She tottered to the edge of the deck and then with a terrified scream fell over the rail that ran along the boat's sides.

Quick as a flash, Septimus leapt full length forwards and seized one flailing hand so that Mary was left dangling over the watery precipice. Face contorted with effort the Welshman struggled to pull her back to safety but could only manage to hang on to her single hand.

With a cry of alarm, Edward took a step towards them, but Crius forestalled him. This time a small whirlwind spun out of the Titan's palm. It sped towards Edward and seemed to pin him to the spot. Crius shouted out another command, "θα γονατίσει!"

Edward grimaced. "He is telling us to kneel, Tom."

Crius pointed towards Septimus, who was still clinging on to Mary's hand. He said something and then again those words, "θα γονατίσει."

"He says kneel or he will blast Septimus and Mary into the sea," Edward translated.

The boat suddenly pitched from side to side. Back at the tiller Charlie was clearly struggling just to keep it on the crest of the wave. It lurched again and was now tilting at a terrifying angle.

As Tom fought to keep his balance he found he was looking past the dangling Mary and straight down the front of the wave.

"Hurry, Tom! Do it now!" Charlie shouted.

Tom, clutching the blue vial behind his back, turned to Crius. "θα γονατίσει," the Titan repeated, fixing Tom with a dark stare and pointing down at the deck.

Tom nodded and stepping forward bent his knee and knelt in front of the arrogant Greek demigod, who smiled with satisfaction and spoke again.

Once again, Edward translated: "*Better. Now you others join your companion in worship.*"

Crius's gaze shifted from Tom and back across to Edward and Charlie. Finally it fixed on Septimus. "θα γονατίσει," he said again.

"I can't! I will drop Mary!" exclaimed Septimus, who had needed no translation.

"απελευθέρωση της," the Titan bellowed.

"He says release her," Edward said. "Well, we'll see about that!" Following Tom's example he made as if to kneel, but halfway through the movement he roared and launched himself at Crius. Before Edward could reach him, the Titan twisted around to face him and clapped his hands. Another blast of icy wind caught the soldier in the chest and flung him head over heels along the length of the boat towards the stern.

While this was going on Tom had made use of the distraction to pull the stopper from the neck of the vial. Now, raising his hands he pointed the open bottle at Crius. Immediately, the air between them seemed to distort and blur.

Crius cried out and swinging round to Tom he glared at him, shook his helmeted head from side to side as if dazed and spoke. Edward, scrabbling with his hands and feet to halt his slide

63

along the deck, shouted out the Titan's words. *"No! You cannot capture me again. Release me or I shall destroy you."*

"I don't think so!" Tom said and thrust the vial closer.

The blurring effect became even more pronounced. It was shimmering, rather like the heat haze above a road on a scorching summer's day or the mirage in a desert. Here, though, it was not heat distorting the light but the effect of powerful temporal forces reaching out from the vial and latching onto the Titan.

Crius gave another cry of panic and then he seemed distort, becoming long and thin, his cries growing weaker. Finally, his elongated body appeared to evaporate into a dark vapour that was now being drawn into the blue glass vial. When all of it was contained, Tom popped the stopper back in and pushed it tight, placing the vial in his pocket and thrusting it down as far as it would go.

At that moment the boat rocked violently from side to side before twisting to point bow first into the yawning chasm in front of the wave, which now seemed to be collapsing beneath them. Edward, unable to hold on any longer, disappeared over the stern and vanished into the waves far below.

"Edward!" Mary screamed, still dangling precariously over the sea.

Breathing heavily and stretched full length, Septimus strained to pull her back up towards the rail. "Mary, quickly, grab my other hand," he yelled.

"Here we go!" Charlie cried out as the boat plunged into the abyss.

CHAPTER SEVEN
THE GREAT STORM

As the boat went over the edge of the wave, Tom skidded down the steeply tilting deck, which was awash with seawater. Thrashing about wildly he managed to latch onto the rail. The bow end was below him now, the boat pointing directly down at the surface of the sea, the stern sticking up at a crazy angle above him. Septimus had managed to pull Mary back on deck and they too were clinging to the rail. Behind and above him Charlie was hanging onto the tiller, but now his fingers lost their grip and with a cry of alarm he plunged past Tom.

There was no sign of Edward. Tom could only hope the soldier had been able to Walk before he was drowned. As Charlie shot past him, Tom let go of the rail and he and the sailor fell side by side, tumbling towards Septimus and Mary. Tom just had time to register the look of alarm on the Welshman's face as he and Charlie ploughed straight into him, knocking both him and Mary away from the rail. In a tumbling mass of arms and legs the four of them slid helplessly towards the bows and the cruel sea that lashed and surged beneath them. And now the boat was falling too, plunging into the trough of the giant wave, the mast creaking and groaning as it began to crack. Five tons of wood and iron were about to hurtle down at them and behind it the wave was turning over, ready to rush down and dash them all to pieces.

"Walk! Tom! For God's sake *Walk!*" Charlie gasped as they clung together, mere seconds from certain death.

"I'm trying!" Tom managed to say. His mind was a whirl of fear and emotion as he battled to control it and focus on the flow of time.

Then… they were gone. The surging seas and terror of the Great Storm left far behind them as they landed in a soggy mass in front of the Professor's fire.

As they struggled to disentangle themselves a familiar voice rang out.

"Well? Did you get him?"

It was Edward. He was standing by the Professor's desk, a towel around his shoulders and water dripping from his clothes. It was the last thing he managed to say for a full three minutes because Mary gave a cry of joy and then jumped up from the floor, pushed him back against the wall and planted a kiss upon his lips, which went on, Tom thought, longer than was strictly necessary.

Untangling himself from Septimus and Charlie, Tom got to his feet and thrust his hand into his pocket, panicking slightly that the vial might have fallen out and into the sea, but it was still there.

When a blushing Edward had finally surfaced, he glanced at Tom. "Well?"

Clutching the vial, his hands held out in front of him, Tom puckered his lips at the soldier then grinned and backed away. "Look mate, I'm glad to see you too, but this is the best you're getting from me!"

"Very droll," Edward commented as Charlie and Septimus burst out laughing. He took the vial Tom held out to him and passed it to the Professor, who was looking on with the faintest hint of a smile on his lips.

"What happened to you?" Charlie said, patting Edward on the shoulder.

"Oh, nothing much. As I fell I managed to Walk myself here. The Professor and I were just... ahem… arguing about whether I should go back again, when you appeared."

"So then, that was easy. One down and four to go," the Professor said with a satisfied grunt, peering at the vial before placing it in one of his desk drawers.

Feeling battered and bruised, Tom glanced at his friends and rolled his eyes. "Well if they are all as 'easy' as that one was, Professor, this is going to be fun!"

A few weeks later, back at school, Tom was again teaching Persephone how to manage her Walking. Thanks to his tutelage she was now much better at controlling it and there had been no further embarrassing incidents. Even the situation with Andy had improved. At the end of the previous term Andy had avoided Tom and during the holidays they had not spent any time together. Tom had missed his friend and it seemed that Andy felt the same way because at the start of term he had come over to Tom and sat down munching crisps. He didn't say much, but then he smiled and offered Tom some crisps out of his packet, which as it happened, were 'Walkers'!

Tom took one and smiled back and everything was OK again. Even so, he wanted to clear things up regarding Persephone.

"Andy, mate, about Persephone…"

"Yes Tom," Andy replied, his tone slightly tense.

"Honestly, we really are just good friends. Nothing more. If you want to ask her out, go for it."

"Really?"

"Really."

Andy shrugged. "Well, I'm glad to hear that. Didn't think she was your type anyway."

Tom, thinking about Persephone's olive-green eyes, made no reply.

Matters having been apparently resolved with Andy, Tom focused on finishing the Greek girl's training. One lunchtime, when they had just appeared in an empty classroom and Tom was giving her some instructions, he decided to take the next step.

"I think this time I will let you try this again on your own. Why don't you walk back one hundred years and then return here. I'll stay around and wait for you. Don't forget to drop anchor first," he grinned.

Persephone nodded and vanished.

Waiting in the classroom Tom idly opened up a nearby textbook, which proved to be a physics text. He scanned through the pages not really focusing on them.

"What's this boyo? Studying for an exam?"

Tom looked up to see Septimus leaning against a desk. "No," Tom said, "I'm..."

"Never mind that, I've come to fetch you. The Prof believes he has located the second Titan. He sent me to find you."

"Oh, did he? Well you've found me. Right, best get to the Institute then."

"Let me come along too," said a familiar voice.

Tom spun round and gaped. For a second he had forgotten about Persephone. She now stood behind him looking slightly out of breath.

"You must be joking!" Septimus exclaimed.

"You're back," Tom said, stating the obvious. "That was quick."

Ignoring him, Persephone directed her gaze at Septimus and tapped her foot impatiently. "Why not? I can Walk now and I am getting quite good at it. Ask Tom if you do not believe me."

Tom nodded. "It's true. She is actually pretty good now, Septimus. She might be of use to the Institute."

Septimus looked doubtful. "Well... I don't know," he mumbled, studying the girl.

"At least let us ask the Prof," Tom suggested.

Septimus considered this for a moment.

"Very well. Come along both of you."

"I am not sure about this, Professor," Edward said.

The five Walkers and Persephone sat in the upright chairs that faced the old man's desk. Seated behind it he was examining the girl over the top of his spectacles. "I must confess to having doubts myself, Lieutenant," the Professor said.

"If you are worried that she can't Walk properly, you don't need to be," Tom said. "She can Walk well now. Took a bit of effort to teach her control but—"

"Quite the opposite, Thomas," the old man interrupted. "It's not that she cannot Walk, but that she can which concerns me. Or rather, that she can as well as you say she can."

Tom frowned. "Why?"

The Professor glanced at Tom before returning his stare to Persephone. The girl shifted in her seat, clearly discomfited by his gaze.

"Why are you worried, Professor?" Tom repeated. "I don't understand."

"Her powers, Thomas. How sure are we that they are indeed her own? Coming so soon after the episode with Knossos I mean."

Tom shrugged. "I don't get it. I don't see the link."

"Well," the Professor replied, "may I remind you that how-

69

ever she appears to us now, Persephone is at least as old as I am and has spent most of her life under the thrall of Knossos. On the one hand it might be that these powers she manifests are merely a lingering hangover from being under his influence."

Tom shook his head. "I don't see that, Prof. When she was actually born is meaningless. She hasn't lived for all those years like you have – we Walked her here as a teenager so she is still a teenager. And anyway, Persephone is getting better at Walking day by day: her powers are increasing not decreasing. If she had been under the influence of Knossos and the powers were just the residue of his and not her own, would they not be vanishing now he's dead and gone?"

The Professor shrugged, "Maybe so."

"You said on the one hand, Prof," Charlie piped up. "What's on the other hand?"

The old man stared at him as if unable to understand the question. After a moment he replied, "Ah yes. I meant that a more worrying possibility is that Persephone's powers are still obtained from Knossos; they are not diminishing because he is still channelling his powers via her."

Tom shook his head even more emphatically this time. "How can that be? Knossos is dead. I dispersed him throughout time. I felt it happen. I would know if he still existed."

Neoptolemas raised his eyebrows but said nothing.

"There is another possibility, Tom," Edward said in a low voice.

"What?"

"That she is in full control of her powers as you suggest and Knossos is indeed dead, but she is still loyal to him despite what you said and might be interested in revenge. She was a Black Robe after all."

Persephone was shaking her head. "No! You're wrong. I attacked Knossos, don't you all remember. I tried to kill him," she said vehemently.

"Yes Edward, she helped us, or have you forgotten that too?" Tom asked. "Why would she do that and now act for revenge? It makes no sense."

The Professor considered this for a moment. "That is a good point, Thomas but—"

Before he could finish, Edward butted in, "The thing is, Tom, we can't be absolutely sure and right now we haven't the time to find out. Her involvement with the Institute during this current crisis puts us at potential risk."

"And the risks are already quite bad enough," Septimus murmured.

"I am sorry, Persephone," Edward went on, "but I do not think we can fully trust you at this time. Please try to understand."

"What are you going to do with me then?" Persephone asked indignantly, her eyes glittering with tears.

Tom nodded. "Yes, we can't just send her back home and ignore her. She is a Walker now; one of us."

"You are right, Thomas," the Professor agreed. "Whilst we have concerns about her we will not simply abandon her." He reached out and pressed the intercom on his desk. A moment later, Mr Phelps walked into the office.

"You called me, sir?"

"Take this young woman down to the library if you please Mr Phelps. Make sure she is comfortable. I will call for her shortly."

Persephone scowled. "That's not fair, I want to be involved. I want to prove to you that I can be trusted. You saved me and my family from Knossos. Why would I serve him now he is dead?"

71

"Come on Miss," Mr Phelps said firmly and gestured towards the doorway.

"Oh… very well!" Shooting a look of appeal at Tom, Persephone gave in and climbed to her feet, stomping out unhappily after Mr Phelps and on down the corridor, not waiting while he closed the door behind them.

When they had gone Tom turned to Edward and the Professor. "I know you are just being careful, but I think you are wrong about her."

The old man took off his glasses and rubbed his eyes. "Maybe you are right, Thomas, but I just cannot afford to take any risks at present."

Thinking that the Professor looked unusually tired, Tom shrugged resignedly. "You're the boss," he mumbled. "So then, what did you call us about?"

In answer the Professor opened up a couple of the books that lay stacked up on his desk. "Edward, the map please," he said.

Edward picked up a map case from the floor, popped off its lid and tipped the contents out. A rolled up map unfurled across the desk. They all shuffled closer to take a look. The first thing that drew Tom's attention was the label on the map which read: 'Plan of the battle of Waterloo or Mont St. Jean, reduced from the large plan of the same battle, made up and published in 1816 by W.B. Craan, Engineer-Examiner of the Register of Lands of Brabant.'

It seemed that Tom's companions had read this at the same time because Septimus and Charlie burst out simultaneously: "Oh my God, Waterloo!"

"Waterloo?" Mary asked "What is that?"

"Waterloo, Miss Brown, was a little after your time," the Professor answered. "The Battle of Waterloo took place on June

72

18th 1815. It was the final and climactic battle of the Napoleonic and Revolutionary wars that raged almost without a gap from 1792 to 1815. It was fought between the super power of the day – France – and a series of alliances, which included at varying times Prussia, Russia, Austria and other states, but always Britain."

Tom noticed that Septimus was looking away from the map and towards the door, his head tilted to one side.

"What is it?" he asked.

Septimus frowned and then shook his head. "Oh nothing, I just thought I heard something," he said.

They all listened but could hear nothing.

"Maybe someone at the front door," the Professor said vaguely and they all turned back to the map, which depicted the contours of the land, streams, roads and buildings and several villages with strange names, among them Braine-Aleud, Plancenoit and Mont St. Jean.

"Why does it say 'The Battle of Waterloo or Mont St. Jean'?" Tom asked the Professor as they studied the map.

"The battle itself was fought, as you can see, between the crossroads of Mont St. Jean – in English you'd call it St. John's Mount – the village of Plancenoit and the inn of La Belle Alliance – meaning 'the Hotel of the Beautiful Alliance'. As a result it is often referred to in France as the Battle of La Belle Alliance. However, the Duke of Wellington, who was in command of the British and Dutch armies, had his headquarters in the village of Waterloo a few miles away. He rode back there to send his report of the victory, so the name Waterloo – which is easier to say for an Englishman than either of the other possibilities – is what stuck."

The map showed what appeared to be three armies. One,

whose battalions were outlined in red, stood in a line along a low ridge straddling the Mont St Jean crossroads. Another, lined up opposite it around La Belle Alliance, was coloured blue. The third, at right angles to the other two and outlined in black, was coming in long columns from the east towards Plancenoit.

The Professor explained what they were seeing. "The Anglo-Dutch under Wellington are in red. They are on the defensive, trying to repel an attack from Napoleon's French, who are in blue. Meanwhile, Wellington's Prussian allies under Marshall Blücher, who was, believe it or not, seventy-two years old at the time, are marching to Wellington's aid and hoping to catch the French in the Flank, but they were delayed and got there only just in time."

"What happened?" Mary asked.

"Napoleon's army attacked several times in an attempt to push Wellington off his ridge. The attacks were courageous, ferocious and bloody. At times thousands of cavalry were charging the allied lines, but Wellington kept his troops formed up into tight squares, which are difficult to attack on horseback. Thousands of French lost their lives galloping their mounts straight onto the allies' bayonets. At other times Napoleon's cannons were pounding away in an effort to break up the squares. Yet, under fierce bombardment, Wellington's British, Hanoverian and Dutch regiments showed outstanding bravery; they did not run, just stood and died. Their losses were eventually so high that by the middle of the day Napoleon's forces were in the ascendancy.

Meanwhile, the Prussians were force-marching to join the battle and during the afternoon and evening, when the outcome was hanging in the balance, they began to arrive in increasing numbers. With the threat of being cut off by the Prussians, Napoleon flung his best troops – the Imperial Guard – into a final

74

attack. It was repelled and the Guard fell back, French morale cracked and the army fled. It was the end for Napoleon. He was hunted down, captured and sent into exile from which he never returned."

Edward pointed at the map.

"Of course, I grew up knowing all about this battle and when I became an officer I learnt even more about it. Many of my colleagues had fathers or grandfathers who fought at Waterloo and every family knew someone who had died there. It was a bloody affair with one man in four or five a casualty."

"A bloody affair indeed, Lieutenant," the old man said sadly.

Septimus coughed. "So… are you saying this is where we must go?"

The Professor nodded. "All indications are that the second Time Cyst is emptying its content at around six in the evening on June 18th 1815, close to the farm of La Haye Sainte on the road between La Belle Alliance and Mont St. Jean." He tapped the map to show them the location and they all craned their necks to stare at where his finger was pointing.

Charlie whistled. "That seems to be pretty much bang in the middle of the battle as you've described it. Any other good news, Prof?"

The old man grimaced. "Actually yes, there is something else I must tell you…" He paused, apparently hesitant to proceed.

"Come on Prof, spit it out," Septimus said.

"Very well. The readings we are getting on the Cyst indicate that the content is the Titan, Iapetus."

"Good Lord!" Edward exclaimed. Seeing blank faces all around him, he explained, "Iapetus is the Titan god of war and battle."

With a creak of his chair, Septimus sat back. "Well now girl

75

and boys, what does that imply, bearing in mind what we learnt during the Great Storm?"

"If Crius could create a storm of that magnitude then Iapetus may be able to influence the soldiers at Waterloo," Edward said.

"And what's the betting he'll favour the French? Going to be fun, isn't it?" Septimus murmured to Charlie.

Charlie frowned. "You and I clearly have a very different understanding of the word 'fun', mate."

There was a clink of glass as the Professor opened his drawer. He brought out a small case and placing it on the desk opened the lid. Inside were the five blue glass vials, each standing upright in a separate compartment.

"So the plan is the same is it?" Tom asked. "We go back with one of those bottle, we locate Iapetus, point it at him, trap him and then bring him back here."

"Without getting shot," Mary commented.

"Without getting shot," Tom repeated.

The Professor shook his head. "No, it is far too dangerous. Two hundred thousand men fighting a ferocious battle in an area not much more than a mile across. I am very reluctant to send you there. I am trying to see if you might be able to engage Iapetus away from the battlefield. Maybe wait until he first appears and then seize him – somewhere safe."

Septimus raised his arms in exasperation. "Come off it, Prof, that will never happen. This guy thinks he is the God of War. He won't just walk away from one of the most dramatic battles of the last couple of centuries or so."

"Even so—" the Professor started to say, but got no further because at that moment the door burst open. Persephone stood in the frame, eyes bright with determination.

"I will do it!" she shouted.

Before any of them could act, stunned as they were by her sudden appearance, she jumped across to the desk, seized one of the glass vials and in an instant had vanished!

CHAPTER EIGHT
IN HARM'S WAY

Moments after Persephone's disappearance, Mr Phelps staggered into the Professor's study. He had lost his usual self control and stared angrily around the room, his face flushed, eyes narrowed.

"Where is she?"

"Who, Persephone? Gone – and with one of the vials too! What happened?" Edward asked.

"The little lady locked me in the library. I have been calling for help and banging on the door, but she closed the outer door to my office and that must have muffled the sound."

"I thought I heard something," Septimus said. "I should have trusted my instincts. She must have been listening to us outside the door."

"Very well, Mr Phelps, thank you. You may go now," the Professor said.

As a disgruntled Mr Phelps left the room, Edward turned to Tom. "Seems the 'little lady' is not to be trusted after all," he said.

Tom did not know what to say in reply. He was still thinking about it when he noticed the Professor was rooting through the vial casket.

"What is it Professor?"

The old man looked up, his face pale.

"Crius' vial... it's missing," he said in a quiet voice.

"Oh God, no!" Tom exclaimed. "Don't say she's taken the vial containing the Titan?"

The Professor nodded. "I'm afraid so, Thomas. Where has she gone, Lieutenant?" he asked, turning to Edward.

Edward closed his eyes and concentrated. Tom let his mind wander too and found that he was following Persephone's trail. He could not bring himself to believe that she was acting against them and hoped she had just walked randomly somewhere, perhaps back to school or even to Greece. Even now she could be safe on some idyllic island in the Adriatic. That would be nice. Yet with a sinking feeling in the pit of his stomach, Tom feared it would not be as easy as that. As he followed the little spark of energy that represented Persephone's trail from the present back through time, it became apparent just where she was heading. Tom realised exactly where she was just as Edward announced it.

"She's at Waterloo battlefield. Not far from the Mont St. Jean crossroads. June 18th 1815. She appeared there around six p.m."

"Professor... we have to go get her, don't we?" Septimus asked.

The old man nodded, his gaze drifting over the unrolled map, his fingers brushing the spot near a building. Tom read the name, 'La Haye Sainte' it said.

"I hate to have to send you there but yes, I fear you must. Iapetus is due to appear any moment after her arrival. If she releases Crius, or if Iapetus seizes the vial and frees him, the result would be catastrophic. Waterloo was a ferociously bloody battle. It will be incredibly dangerous. Perhaps you should not all go... maybe just Edward and Tom?"

"To hell with that idea," Charlie said.

"I will not be left behind!" Mary said, stamping her foot.

"We are a team, Professor. Let us act as a team," Septimus added.

The old man looked them over. Then he turned his head and looked at a picture on the wall near the fireplace. It showed a cavalry charge: men in green uniforms and bronze-coloured helmets riding huge black horses. Many of the horsemen clutched a broad-bladed sword or sabre, others further back wielded lances decked with black and red ribbon streaming in the wind. All around them cannon balls and shells laid waste to their companions, but still they rode on. The men's faces were twisted into screams and shouts, their eyes wide with the intensity of the moment, one which the artist had captured, full of glory, thunder, fear and death.

The Professor studied the scene before eventually nodding his head. "Very well. But be careful," he said quietly, "be very careful."

"So, what do we do?" Tom said, turning to his companions.

Septimus looked at Edward. "Could we get away with turning up in British uniforms do you think?"

Edward considered the suggestion. "It sounds the best idea. You, me and Charlie could go back as officers or sergeants."

"Make me a general then," Charlie said, winking at Tom, but the Professor was shaking his head.

"What's up Prof?" Charlie asked, but Edward answered the question.

"There were only fifteen or so generals on the British side at Waterloo – all pretty much household names and certainly recognisable by the men. Besides which, Charlie, you are too young to be a general. We will be junior officers. There are hundreds of them and so we can hopefully be less noticeable.

80

Anyway a general would be on a horse. Can you ride?"

The sailor shook his head.

"What about us two?" Mary asked, pointing at Tom and herself.

Edward studied them both for a moment and then smiled. "You two can be little drummer boys who have just joined the army."

"I can't play a drum!" Mary protested,

"Nor me," Tom put in, shaking his head.

"Don't worry you won't need to," Edward said. "If challenged, our company got separated from the rest of our formation – maybe from a light infantry regiment or the 95th Rifles. They often fought separately from the massed formations as skirmishing companies. It would explain us being on our own."

"What about me being a girl?" Mary asked.

"I doubt anyone would notice in the heat of battle, and anyway, it wasn't that unusual. You'd be surprised how many women joined the army in the guise of soldiers," Edward said. "Some of them got to be quite famous," he added.

The Professor opened a book that lay on the desk. He turned over several pages before stopping at one that contained a long list of all the regiments present at Waterloo. He ran his finger down the list and stopped at one. "I would make it the 52nd Light Regiment, Lieutenant. It's a big battalion so maybe some new recruits would not be recognised by all the officers. If you come across a captain from the 52nd you can pretend to be new troops from the regimental depot just arrived and looking for the battalion."

Edward nodded his agreement. "Right everyone, let's go get dressed," he said, leading them out the door and heading up to Mrs Mackay's costume department.

Half an hour later they were back downstairs. Edward, Septimus and Charlie were each wearing a smart uniform with black boots, grey trousers, white belts and a red jacket complete with collar and cuffs in bright yellow. They were pulling packs onto their backs, these held on by white straps that crossed their chests diagonally to form an X. On their heads were tall black hats that Edward said were called shakos. Each one had a regimental badge on it identifying them as belonging to the 52nd Regiment of Foot. Edward wore the slightly more elaborate uniform of an officer with gold-coloured braid on his shoulders, which he said were epaulettes, whilst the others had stripes denoting them as sergeants.

Tom's and Mary's uniforms were almost a reverse of the men's. They still had the shakos and trousers, but their jackets were almost all yellow with the collars and cuffs in the scarlet colour.

"I am always amazed how quickly Mrs Mackay can rustle up costumes for us. These details are very good," Septimus commented.

The old man tapped the side of his nose. "The good lady has her own talents, just like yourselves and Doctor Makepiece – whom I have alerted to your mission by the way. He commented that you had better not get yourselves shot. Even with his… ahem… skills, he would not be able to bring you back to life!"

"Dressed like this I can't see how we can avoid being shot. This is ridiculous. Not exactly camouflage is it?" Tom said.

"Nor is it meant to be, Thomas. It is intended to be prominent. Soldiers mostly fought in big blocks or formations of several hundred men. The idea was to make the units recognisable and even a bit intimidating. It was after Edward's time that khaki and other more subtle colours came in."

"Nothing wrong with a red jacket, Tom." Edward said in a slightly hurt tone. "I am... or was, at least, a British Officer in her Majesty's army. I was proud to wear it."

"You look very smart too, Edward," Mary said with a wink that made him blush slightly.

"Sorry Edward. No offence intended. So then, are we ready?" Tom asked.

"Not entirely," the Professor said and pressed a button on his intercom. "Send in Mr Ryan now," he spoke into the machine.

A moment later a red-headed man walked in carrying two polished wooden boxes, one considerably longer than the other. He laid the boxes on the Professor's table then turned to face him.

"Professor, with your permission?"

The old man nodded his head. "Mr Ryan here is our expert with historical firearms," he explained. "You are travelling back to a battle and we cannot be sure how long you will be there. Edward, Charlie and Septimus will take appropriate weapons for all of your protection in the event that you run into some French soldiers."

As Ryan clicked open the fastenings that held the first box shut, Tom half expected him to pull out some sophisticated electronic gadget, but in fact the larger box contained two long muskets and a smaller pistol, along with power and shot. Ryan picked up the musket, loaded it with power and shot and handed it to Charlie. After doing the same for Septimus he turned to them both.

"These are Brown Bess muskets: typical weapons of the British soldiers from the period. Point it at the enemy, pull back on

83

the flint to cock the weapon. Squeeze the trigger to discharge it. I will give you spare shot and powder should you need to reload."

"How accurate are they?" Charlie asked with a dubious glance at Septimus.

"Not very," Ryan answered. "Given a good aim you should hit a man at fifty yards. Hundred yards or so and the accuracy starts to wane. Over two hundred yards away and you could not hit a barn door with it. These soldiers fought in regiments to mass their firepower. However, they do have a bayonet which can be fitted to the end of the weapon. Makes it basically a spear."

Ryan turned to pick up the pistol but found that Edward had taken it and loaded it himself with smaller pistol shot.

"I am impressed sir. I understood you were from the 1870's and used revolvers and breech-loading rifles, not flintlock pistols like that Adams and Dutton."e

Edward shrugged. "My uncle was a soldier in India in the 1840's. Breech-loaders had not been introduced then. He had a collection of old guns and would let me practice with them. In point of fact he had a pistol just like this."

"What is in the other box?" Tom asked.

Ryan opened it. Inside was a gleaming sword; alongside it a scabbard.

"This is an infantry officer's sword," Ryan explained as Edward fastened the scabbard to his side and slotted in the sword, plunging it home. With his hand resting automatically on the hilt, he looked every inch the handsome soldier that he was and Mary gazed at him, her cheeks pink.

"Gentlemen, I have given you these for your own defence," the Professor said. "Please restrict them to that purpose and use them only when you have no choice. If you kill a man who according to history survived Waterloo, that would change history. The ramifications of that could be catastrophic. So avoid engaging the enemy where possible. Now, good luck!"

"Hang on, what about our drums?" Tom asked, glancing at Mary. "Shouldn't we be carrying them?"

The old man shook his head. "Remember, if asked, your story is that you have only just arrived and are looking for your battalion. The battalion's quartermaster would normally furnish you with a drum. Besides, if necessary you can always pick one up. I rather fear there will be plenty lying around, along with the bodies of their young owners."

Tom nodded grimly. "Where exactly shall we go and when?"

"Your first and most urgent objective is to find Persephone and retrieve the vial," the Professor said. "And pray to God she has not opened it!"

Edward concentrated for a moment. "I am finding it hard to get a precise location on her, but if we aim for 6.30 p.m. just here," he said, pointing at a road shown on the map. This appears to be sunk below the level of the surrounding fields, making it easier for us to hide. Persephone is somewhere near La Haye Sainte farmhouse, but I can't locate her exactly."

The Professor frowned. "I think it most likely that the emerging Titan is creating interference in the flow of time. Go quickly before it gets any worse." He delved into the vial casket and handed a blue glass bottle to Tom. "You'll need this." He paused and looked at each of the five Walkers in turn. "I say again, good luck. I am afraid you are going to need it."

About to pocket the vial, Tom changed his mind and handed it to Septimus. "Here, you take this one. I will get the other one off Persephone when we find her and they're identical. I don't want to get them muddled up."

"Good thinking, boyo."

Tom waited for his companions to gather around him and then they were off, back two hundred years to one of the most dramatic days in history: the Battle of Waterloo, June 18th, 1815, Belgium.

They materialised in the sunken road – a track leading down into a dip sufficiently deep that they could not see out of it. The first thing Tom noticed was the background noise: a cacophony of men screaming, muskets firing, horses' hooves pounding across the earth and, behind it all, the steady boom-boom of cannon fire. Then he spotted the body of a horse not five feet away and close to it, the rider. Both had been hit, it seemed, by the same blast of cannon fire. Tom swallowed hard. Seeing the dead man suddenly like that made it all seem very real.

Once he had checked that everyone had arrived they scrambled up the earth embankment and peeked over the top to check out the view. At once Tom regretted doing this for not twenty feet away to the south, a hundred or more horses were galloping directly towards them. The riders wore steel breast plates and amongst their ranks the tricolour flag of France flew below the bronze figure of a golden eagle – the symbol of Napoleon's troops. The riders' mouths opened to shout the French battle cry, "Vive L'Empereur!" – Long Live the Emperor! – as the cavalry charged onwards.

"Duck!" Septimus cried.

They slid back down the embankment and lay still pretending to be dead as the cavalry thundered towards them. A moment later the blue sky above their heads was blocked out as a hundred horses leapt over the gap, their hooves scattering clods of earth as they landed on the far embankment and charged on.

"Phew! A bit too close for comfort!" gasped Charlie.

"What's happening?" Mary shouted over the noise after the last horses had passed.

"Let's take another look." Septimus waved at them to cross to the far embankment.

They did so and, more tentatively than before, glanced over the top. Immediately in front of them was a battery of guns, the barrels pointing over their heads in the direction from which the French cavalry had come – so these were British guns then. But they had been abandoned, presumably when the cavalry had charged. Beyond the guns Tom could see a large open field of grass that gently sloped away from them towards a distant forest. Dotted all over the field were dozens of infantry battalions. Most were in red coats but there were also green jackets and blue ones too – the British and their allies, Tom reasoned. They had formed up into squares – each with four bristling walls of bayonets to keep the cavalry out. Tom now saw that the horsemen who had charged over their heads were only a small portion of the thousands of French cavalry who were swarming in and around the squares.

Close by them were French lancers, darting in to thrust with razor sharp lances at one of the British squares then retreating away from the reach of the bayonets. Even as he watched, one lancer was hit by a volley of musket fire from the vengeful redcoats. Each side of the square was four rows deep. The men in the front row knelt on one knee, muskets braced on the ground and angled forwards to present a viciously sharp fence of bayonets. Meanwhile the men in the second rank fired their muskets followed by the third. After each volley, they passed their muskets back for the rear rank to reload whilst they took loaded muskets and prepared to fire again. And so it went on with continuous rounds of musket fire operating like clockwork.

On the other side of the square, cavalry in green jackets, like those in the Professor's painting, were apparently trying to rally and preparing to charge again. A battery of British guns fired at them and a dozen of the green-coated men were shot to pieces, they and their horses screaming in agony as they fell. The rest scampered away to safety, jumping over the bodies of men and horses that lay piled up on the ground where they had fallen, not all dead but all dreadfully wounded.

Glancing at Mary, Tom saw that her eyes were full of tears. Not knowing what to say to comfort her, he put his arm round her and gave her a little squeeze.

"I am alright Thomas, don't worry," she said with a watery smile.

A little further away regiments of the riders with steel armour were circling a blue-jacketed battalion. This one had clearly suffered many losses and seemed to be wavering, on the verge of running away, yet their officer was bravely striding up and down the front rank shouting at them, cajoling them or so it seemed, to stand fast. Tom prayed that they did, for he could see that the foot soldiers' best chance lay in the security these squares gave them. And stand they did, bringing down horses with spasmodic sniper fire.

Gradually, as Tom watched, sickened by the carnage he was witnessing, the armoured men gathered their horses together and retreated. Tom was alarmed when a regiment passed close by the spot where they were hiding. However, although several of the French cavalrymen looked their way, none seemed interested in attacking them. Maybe they didn't realise he and the other four were alive, but actually, Tom thought they looked disheartened. He mentioned this to the others.

Edward nodded. "When I first joined the army we studied Waterloo along with other battles like Balaclava, Alma, Talavera and so on. What we are witnessing is the very end of the French cavalry charge. The British and allies had been holding on all day, but about two hours ago they pulled back a little to regroup. The French thought they were retreating and pursued with cavalry. It all got rather out of hand and what followed was a couple of hours of repeated cavalry attacks. At times up to ten thousand French cavalry charged in wave after wave at the allies. Wellington ordered the regiments into squares and repelled the attacks. The French have finally realized that cavalry alone won't break the British position and are having a rethink. What happens next is—"

Septimus interrupted with a grunt. "Whilst they do that, I suggest we do what we came here for. We find the Greek lass and get out of here as soon as possible. You can give us the history lesson later, boyo!"

Tom nodded and looked at Edward. "Well?"

"Yes, sorry," Edward said, "only it is extraordinary to see what I read in a text book actually happening for real. A bit like being on a film set. I just wish that's what it was!" He frowned in concentration, his eyes distant. After a moment he lifted one hand and pointed to the south and east. Easing back, they crossed the sunken road once more and climbed the south embankment in order to look that way again. The French cavalry was indeed retreating a mile or so, but even now was reforming into its regiments and divisions. In front of the mounted men were large blocks of French infantry, apparently waiting for the order to attack across the muddy fields, where crops of barley and wheat had already been trampled flat in earlier attacks. Slightly closer was a line of cannons pointing directly towards the sunken lane, their muzzles elevated to fire in the direction of the British battalions that were currently still hidden over the ridge.

Even as Tom and his companions watched, a battery of eight cannons opened fire in a cloud of smoke. There was a pause and then a whizzing noise and a tremendous eruption of earth only yards in front of them as a cannon ball bounced there. Automatically ducking, Tom felt a rush of hot air as the cannon ball passed close overhead and continued on towards the allied lines. He had not realised that the balls bounced like that, almost as if they were made of rubber instead of cast iron. Elsewhere the cannon balls were hitting the sodden ground and gouging great furrows through clinging mud. Trying not to imagine what a cannon ball would do to someone standing in its way, Tom saw that none of this was what Edward was pointing at.

They all scrambled into a better position to look east and a little south to where, a couple of hundred yards away, in a slight hollow and positioned beside the main north to south road that connected the British and French lines, they could see a stone farmhouse. It was painted white and had grey tiles on the roof. "That's La Haye Sainte," Edward said.

A solid-looking structure, La Haye Sainte was almost a fortress itself. Indeed, Wellington had clearly treated it as such and placed men there. A Union Flag was still flapping in the wind about the roof. Yet the farm was under attack. Smoke was rising from one barn and all around it like a swarm of ants were hundreds of blue- and white-jacketed French foot soldiers.

"Though the cavalry attacks failed to break the British squares, the French infantry were able to advance and take the farmhouse," Edward commented.

"*Take it?* You mean they are going to…" Charlie was saying, when there was a tremendous cheer from La Haye Sainte. The

Union Flag was pulled down and a soldier could be seen waving a French Tricolour from the roof. The rear door of the farmhouse opened and the surviving red-coated defenders streamed out through a garden and made off in the direction of the British lines, the French firing at them indiscriminately as soon as they realised their enemy was escaping.

"Edward, where is Persephone?" Tom asked, but in fact he had no need, for having focused his own mind he could feel the Greek girl's presence nearby, a short distance south and east. *"Oh God...!"* Tom thought, realising now where she must be.

"She is in the farmhouse. Somewhere high up – the loft spaces maybe," Edward said.

"Just where a thousand French soldiers are right now!" Septimus observed, pointing toward the flag-waving Frenchman.

"I am afraid so!" Edward's face was grim.

CHAPTER NINE
NOW'S YOUR TIME

"Regardless of the numbers, we have to go get her!" Edward said.

Septimus peered across the open field toward the distant farmhouse. The tricolour flag had now been secured to a chimney and flapped in the wind above the roof of the building. Below, French soldiers in their blue uniforms could be seen milling around it. There were an awful lot of them, thought Tom.

The Welshman looked as if he was thinking the same thing because he grimaced, but then he nodded. "Agreed, but how?"

"Tom, could you Walk us inside the loft area?" Charlie suggested.

Tom shook his head. "I did not get a look at a map of the farmhouse before we left and without knowing the layout we might arrive inside a wall or chimney."

Charlie sighed. "Then we will have to risk appearing on the roof and hope that with all the smoke and confusion no one spots us. We then break through the tiles and—"

Before he could finish what he was saying there was a loud eruption of noise close by on the French side of the farmhouse. It sounded like the detonation of explosives in a terrorist movie or maybe the charges used to demolish a derelict old tower block. They all turned to stare in this direction just as a flash of red light burst forth: bright, incandescent and almost blinding. As they squinted that way, trying to focus upon it, a blast of hot air shot outwards, like a wave radiating from where a stone has been dropped in a lake. The blast knocked Mary's and Charlie's shakos off and caused Tom to lose his grip and slide back down the embankment and out onto the sunken road.

By the time he had picked himself up and rejoined the others the red light was fading, revealing the silhouette of a man, well over six feet tall and with broad, muscular shoulders. The figure turned slowly to take in his surroundings and as he did so Tom could see that, rather like Crius, he wore old-fashioned armour. He looked like one of Alexander the Great's Greek warriors, complete with a helmet that bore bronze cheek pieces partially protecting his face. The helmet was crowned by a bright red horsehair crest that resembled a Mohican hairstyle.

The figure seemed to be taking in the battlefield around him where for the moment, with the French cavalry regrouping and La Haye Sainte in the hands of their infantry, there was a lull in the fighting. Then, clear and loud across the fields came a noise Tom would not associate with a battlefield. It was laughter: a deep, rolling laugh that built up and up and ended in a roar of triumph.

Three French light infantrymen, apparently braver than their compatriots who were cowering back in terror, were approaching the figure, muskets at the ready.

"They're probably *Voltiguers*," said Edward; Napoleon's special sharpshooters."

Before the Frenchmen could fire the figure saw them and raised his hands towards them, almost as if to show he was unarmed. Then out of his palms there burst forth a blast of fiery flame. It engulfed the *Voltigeurs* who fell screaming to the ground and then lay still, clearly dead, their bodies burnt and blackened.

The figure raised its head and laughed again. "*Polemos! Polemos! Polemos!* " he shouted.

"*War! War! War!*" Edward translated in an ominous tone.

Septimus grimaced. "Well, now, I think we can assume Iapetus has arrived!"

The Titan now pointed towards La Haye Sainte and slowly circled both his hands to sweep past Plancenoit, where Wellington's Prussian allies were assaulting the town, then take in La Belle Alliance, the small inn in the distance close to the spot where Napoleon was directing the battle. The Titan's hands continued to circle, moving to the Chateau of Huguemont lying to the west under the pall of smoke from its burning chapel, and passing Tom and his friends. Finally, circling back to the farmhouse, the Titan roared that word again.

"Polemos!"

Tom was suddenly overwhelmed by a feeling of extreme irritation and impatience. "Are we going for Persephone or are we just going to stand here gawping?" he demanded.

Edward turned to stare at him, his own face showing as much irritation as Tom's. "Yes, Thomas," he snapped. "We must go. What do you think we have been talking about all this time?"

"There was no need to snap, I only asked!" Tom snarled, reacting to Edward's sarcastic tone.

Mary jumped in at this point. "You shouted at Edward first, Tom!"

"That is true, boyo," Septimus said. Charlie nodded his head too.

"So, you are all picking on me now!" Tom yelled.

Now it was Septimus who was angry. "Oh, don't be so childish, petulant boy!"

Tom spun round to glare at the Welshman.

"We don't have time for this nonsense; we have to rescue the girl," Septimus said.

"Who died and put you in charge?" Charlie demanded.

"Yes, answer him," Tom said. He felt angry: really angry. In fact he could not recall having been so angry ever before. His fists curled and he brought them up, ready to strike the next one to make a foolish comment. There was the scrape of metal and he saw that Edward was drawing his sabre. Next to him, with a click, Charlie had cocked his musket. He levelled it at the Victorian officer.

"Put the sword away mate," the sailor ordered. His voice had a dangerous edge.

"Everyone, please calm down," Mary's voice cut through the tension. "What are we all arguing about?"

Tom turned to glare at her and then realised she was right. "Yes, what are we arguing about?"

"Well you started it," Edward said, but his voice was softer, a smile touching his lips.

Tom nodded. "Yes I did, but why? I felt… angry. No reason for it. Just irritated and boiling over with frustration."

To the south of them the sound of laughter rolled across the battlefield.

Septimus grunted. "It's Iapetus! When he circled his hands all around Waterloo, that included us. We know he is the Titan God of War. He must have the power to drive war and battle – to make men want to kill each other. What we are feeling all the men on the battlefield will also now be feeling.

"We must resist it and not fight amongst ourselves," Tom said. "Sorry everyone."

"Me too," Edward said.

"And me," Charlie chimed in.

Suddenly, from amongst the French lines beyond Iapetus there came a peal of trumpets. It was followed by a chorus of drums. From the edge of the sunken road the Walkers looked on as regiments of foot soldiers marched into a new formation. Battalion after battalion lined up in dense formation. A mighty French assault column was being created. Amongst them were hundreds of men in bearskin shakos. They looked a little like those worn by the red-coated soldiers who guarded Buckingham Palace, but these men wore blue uniforms and over their heads French tricolours flapped on flag poles topped with Imperial French Eagles.

"That is Napoleon's Imperial Guard. They are getting ready for the last attack," Edward said.

The drums were starting up again. *Rat-a-tat-tat Rat-a-tat-tat.* Then a pause and into the gap a powerful roar from five thousand French throats: *"Vive L'Empereur!"*

"They might be shouting for their Emperor but it's Iapetus that is calling the shots," Charlie observed.

"You say it is the last French attack. So it fails? The French lost Waterloo didn't they?" Tom asked Septimus.

"They did, but with a Titan urging them on and La Haye Sainte in French hands, this attack might well succeed."

"That can't happen!" Edward exclaimed. "Wellington's redcoats can beat the French bluecoats any day of the week," he added loyally.

"It's not patriotism that bothers me, mate," Septimus replied. "Waterloo was a pivotal moment in history. The aftermath defined the shape of Europe for a century and more. The British might well lose here unless we intervene. We can't let history change on that scale. Unless you've forgotten, that's why we're here. We have to stop Iapetus."

The drums grew more intense and now orders rang out from a hundred officers' throats: *"En avant!"*

"That's the order to advance," Edward said.

Half a mile away the dense column staggered forward and rolled towards them across the muddy field that was littered with the corpses of horses and men. At the same time the French artillery opened up again and the air was full of screeching cannon balls as they flew towards the sunken lane, throwing earth skywards as they bounced on by. Above them howitzer shells detonated scattering shards of metal all about.

"We have to act quickly, here they come!" Charlie shouted above the din.

Tom nodded. "Very well, spread out on either side," he instructed, reaching out with his arms. With Charlie and Septimus tucked in on his right and Edward and Mary on his left he Walked the short hop to the farmhouse roof.

"Mon Dieu!" cried a French sniper as they appeared. The Voltigeur was taking cover behind one of the chimney stacks further along the roof ridge. His face registered his shock, but he quickly recovered and swung his musket around to point at Charlie. He was already too late. Charlie, in that staccato-like stop-start motion that was so hard to follow, was on the move towards the Frenchman, who was trying desperately to keep the sailor in his musket sights. Reaching him Charlie gave the man a clout to his head. With a groan the *Voltigeur* tumbled off the roof and landed on a mound of hay on the ground below, stunned but still alive.

"Break through the roof!" Septimus shouted and slammed his musket butt against the tiles. Charlie was soon back with them and hammering away at the tiles with his own weapon. Then, attaching a gleaming bayonet on the other end of his musket he used it to prise the tiles away. Tom, Mary and Edward simply tugged at them with their fingers. Tom gave a cry of alarm as one tile broke away from the roof. Off balance, he stumbled a few steps down the slope, arms cartwheeling as he fought to regain his footing. Edward hastily reached out to him and Tom latched on to the soldier's outstretched hand, nodding his thanks as he scrambled back up the slope.

Shards of tiles broke away and gradually they revealed the wooden rafters beneath. At this point another French sniper had climbed up to the roof and fired a shot at them. Mercifully it drifted off target, but it grazed Edward's left shoulder and tore through his jacket. He let out a cry of pain and sat back on the roof, opening his jacket to reveal a bloodstained shirt. Grimacing, he pulled out a handkerchief from his pocket and stuffed it inside his shirt over the wound then, tugging his jacket back into place, he noticed the others had stopped working and were all anxiously staring at him. "Carry on. I will be fine, it's just a flesh wound. Nothing to worry about," he said between gritted teeth.

Hastily, Tom Walked to where the *Voltigeur* had almost finished reloading. Whilst the Frenchman stared at him, eyes wide, jaw-dropped, Tom shot out a hand and shoved the sniper off the roof.

"Get on with it!" he called over his shoulder. "There will be more coming to try their luck any moment."

Returning to their work they smashed away at the roof. The timbers started to split under the pounding of the musket butts and then, with a crunch and a splintering noise, they were through. Tom clambered down into the roof cavity. There, curled up in a ball on one of the beams, was Persephone. In one hand she clutched the small, blue glass bottle.

Tom, seeing the cork stopper was still firmly in place, breathed a sigh of relief. The Titan, Crius, was still contained.

"Persephone," he called softly. She did not respond. "Persephone, "he tried again. This time she lifted her head and peered at him, her face a tearstained mask of confusion and terror.

"It is Hades," she said. "The noise… the fire… the smoke. We truly must be in the realm of the dead! You should not have followed me here, Tom."

Overhead there was a sudden boom as a shell, fired from one of the British guns, detonated over the farmhouse. Pieces of shrapnel and musket balls showered the roof top. Mercifully, the bulk of the damage was on the far side of the roof, but Tom heard Mary give a squeal of pain. He glanced her way and saw that she had clasped one hand to her forearm. Blood was seeping through her fingers. Charlie went to her aid, tearing off a strip of his shirt to bind the wound.

"Tommy we can't stay up here long, we will get blown to bits!" Septimus shouted down and then ducked as a *Voltigeur* on the roof of a barn on the opposite side of the farmyard tried a shot at them. It went wide but not by far, as evidenced by the crack of the musket ball hitting a tile close by. "Or shot to pieces," Septimus added with an anxious glance at the tile.

On the far roof top, the Frenchman scowled at them and began reloading his musket.

Tom turned back to Persephone who was peering up at him, still with terror and shock etched on her face. "It might seem like Hell, but it's not," he said, hunkering down to her. "It's just a place…" Tom shrugged as he looked around him, "well, alright, a pretty horrible place. But we can't stay Persephone, we don't belong here. We need to get you out, trap the Titan and be gone.

Down on the battlefield there was a deep laugh echoing across the field and then again the cries of *'Vive L'Empereur'* ringing out.

Lifting himself up to see what was happening Tom watched as the Imperial Guard, their resolve strengthened by Iapetus, was closing on the thin line of redcoats clinging to the ridge. Tom knew that he had to act fast if history was not about to change on Waterloo field. He turned once more to Persephone, but was surprised to see that she was already scampering up and poking her head out of the roof to scan the battlefield. The powerful form of Iapetus striding along close to the French troops and egging them on was unmistakable. What did they think? Tom wondered, for they did not seem to fear him. Did they believe he was an avenging angel; proof that God was on their side? Could they actually see him? Maybe it was only Walkers who could. He was pondering this when beside him Persephone spoke.

"Yes, I remember now. That is what I was going to do here," she said, a sudden look of determination flashing on her face. "Indeed… that is what must be done." She raised the tiny bottle in her hand.

"Persephone no!" Tom cried out in warning, but it was too late, the girl had vanished.

'Oh God! I should have taken it from her. Why didn't I?' he thought, wracked with guilt. Everything was happening too quickly.

An instant later the Greek girl materialised next to Iapetus, very close to the French column as it climbed the slope towards the redcoats' position. Once again Tom heard the boom of maniacal laughter.

He took a look in the direction of the British lines. It seemed to him as if either the approach of the French guard or else some influence of Iapetus was indeed holding sway. Tom could see very few redcoats on the high ground. Here and there just behind the ridge there were flags, around which a few officers on horseback were just visible. Yet at the top of the slope and more or less in front of the advancing blue-coated mass, a single British Officer waited and seemingly with a lack of concern, studied the thousands coming straight at him. What was the matter with the man? Was he simply resigned to his fate or more likely, was Iapetus controlling him?

Tom turned his attention back to Persephone. She had raised both hands and even from this distance he could see she was fiddling with the vial's stopper. He gasped in alarm, glanced up at Septimus and saw that he was peering across at the girl.

"Don't tell me she's still got the vial, boyo!"

"Yes, sorry, she acted so quickly…" Tom faltered, seeing from the Welshman's horrified expression that they were both thinking the same thing: if Persephone opened the bottle she would not trap Iapetus, but rather would release his brother Crius. Then there would be not one but two Titans at the Battle of Waterloo!

"Mary, raise a Wall for you and Edward!" Tom shouted as he pulled himself out onto the unbroken tiles. Dodging musket fire that was coming from the barn roof opposite, he seized Charlie and Septimus. "No time to lose," he gasped and Walked the three of them down to a spot next to Persephone.

As they appeared, Iapetus turned his head to regard them. Then he smiled and strode toward them. He seemed almost eight feet tall and looked incredibly strong – a mighty warrior from ancient times striding across the battlefield. As he moved he drew a huge bronze sword and rotating his wrist swirled the blade around as if to demonstrate his prowess. Then he raised it and prepared to strike down at the girl.

"Persephone, wrong bottle!" Tom yelled as he lunged forward to wrest it from her grasp, but as he reached for it he tripped and fell flat on his face in the mud.

Standing over him, Iapetus swung the blade, but before the

edge reached Tom, Charlie was there, intercepting the blow with his musket. With a shower of sparks the sword glanced off the sailor's gleaming bayonet. Iapetus shouted out in frustration.

"Sorry mate, but you are not the only one with tricks. *Now* Septimus!" Charlie cried.

And the Welshman was there, un-stoppering the empty vial and thrusting it at the Titan. For the first time Iapetus looked uncertain, hesitant and then afraid. He tried to back away, shaking his head vigorously as the pocket universe within exerted its presence and tugged at the Titan.

Close by, the nearest French guards were peering at them, gawping like landed fish at what they were seeing. Then two skirmishers levelled their muskets and took aim at Tom and his friends. At such close range they could not miss.

There was a crack of musket fire.

Almost at the same time the air shimmered and the musket balls stopped in mid-flight. Struggling to his feet Tom glanced up at the farmhouse roof and saw that Mary was standing with her arms held wide. She had raised another Wall, catching the deadly bullets in a dome of frozen time.

The French soldiers gaped, frowned and then started to reload whilst a half dozen more moved out of formation and marched towards the Walkers.

"We have trouble, Septimus. Hurry up!" Tom shouted.

Septimus was keeping a firm grip on the vial as Iapetus resisted its draw. The Titan threw his sword at the Welshman, but as it cartwheeled towards the vial, it shrank, dissolved and popped into the neck of the bottle, drawn through the portal and away into the pocket universe. Now Iapetus fell to his knees and was clawing at the ground, growing thinner and longer as he shouted out in rage and terror.

Meanwhile, the blue-coated soldiers, their eyes out on stalks, were fanning out, preparing to fire at the Walkers and crying, "*Sorcellerie! Sorcellerie!*"

"I think they think we're sorcerers," Charlie snorted.

"Well I suppose we are in a way," said Tom, looking up at Mary. She was gesticulating and he could see her mouth working, but he was too far away to hear what she was saying over the din of the battle going on all around them. He didn't need to; he knew Mary would not be able to stop all of the Frenchmen who were advancing on them. She was already struggling to maintain two walls.

Then the solitary red-coated officer, still sitting on his horse above and behind them on the ridge, bellowed out an order, his parade-ground voice carrying down to them across the battlefield.

"Now, Maitland! Now's your time!" Then a pause and another order, "Up Guards and at 'em!"

Now Tom could see he had been very wrong before. The ridge was nowhere near as devoid of red-coated infantry as he had thought – it seemed Edward's patriotism was well founded. The redcoats had been kneeling down, just out of sight behind the brow of the hill. Now, as one, a thousand British guardsmen stood up. Muskets were levelled, there was a brief pause, and another officer, presumably this 'Maitland' shouted the command: "FIRE!"

The air was shattered by the sound of a thousand musket shots. The entire front row of the French column collapsed and a good many of the men in the rows behind. Half the skirmishers closing in on the Walkers were hit and knocked off their feet – dead or at least wounded, Tom was not sure. The frozen Wall held firm and was studded with British musket balls, but as he

103

watched it began to collapse. Tom looked up towards Mary and saw that she had dropped down onto her knees beside Edward. She was clearly exhausted and could not protect any of them any longer. Was it possible she had let go of the Wall around Edward at a crucial moment and the unfortunate man had now been wounded twice? Filled with dread that the Victorian officer might in fact be dead, Tom was more than relieved to see him lift his arm and wave. Then, as he watched, Edward put his arm around Mary and the two of them vanished.

"RELOAD!" The command came from the hill top. With the precision clearly learnt from many hours of practice, the British soldiers began reloading their muskets. It was obvious to Tom that this would not take long and that soon another deadly volley would be sent down the hill, aimed at the French column which was floundering around in the mud, officers barking commands, sergeants pulling the ranks into line and encouraging them to carry on the march up the slope. Aimed at these men the volley might be, but Edward's injury showed how easily stray musket balls could hit Tom and his friends.

"Septimus!" Tom warned but he could now see that the vial was pulling Iapetus in, the strong spatial and temporal forces within distorting and shrinking his form until, finally, the Titan, with one last scream of rage, dissolved into vapour and passed into the bottle.

Septimus jammed in the cork stopper and grinned. "Two down and three to go. Now get us out of here pronto, Tom!" he called, huddling around Tom with Charlie on his other side. "And don't forget to bring the Greek girl!"

Standing a few feet away Persephone was motionless, staring in horror at the vial clutched in her hand.

"As if!" said Tom, grabbing hold of her.

"FIRE!" bellowed the order from atop the ridge, but Tom was already dragging them all forward through the centuries, leaving that terrifyingly bloody battlefield behind and returning them to the present day.

CHAPTER TEN
INNOCENT UNTIL PROVEN GUILTY

"Just what do you think you were playing at young lady?" Edward rounded on Persephone just as soon as they materialised in the Professor's study. He was clutching his right arm, which was bleeding, and more blood from the wound to his left shoulder was staining his collar. Edward was clearly in some considerable pain, yet Tom, who was used to the Victorian Officer being the very definition of the phrase 'stiff upper lip', had never seen him so agitated, except perhaps on the day Tom had rescued him from the Zulus at the Battle of Isandlwana in 1879.

Tom, becoming aware that both his hands were cupped tightly around Persephone's, which still held the vial containing Crius, released her. Before she could move, Edward took two strides towards her and snatched the bottle from her grasp.

"I… I was going to give you that."

"How do we know? How do we know you were not about to release Crius?"

"I was not!" the girl insisted, stamping her foot.

"Ahem!" interrupted the Professor with a cough, "Can you please explain to me what is going on?"

"We found her at Waterloo, sir. She tried to open the vial containing Crius," Edward explained, lifting up the offending bottle by way of evidence.

Persephone shook her head. "No… it's not true! I didn't know—"

"You're lying. You did try to open it!" Edward interrupted.

Staring defiantly at Edward, Persephone was still shaking her head. "You've got it all wrong. Yes, I tried to open it, but I thought it was an empty vial."

"Why did you make off with it in the first place?" Tom asked. "What did you hope to achieve on your own? It was a stupid thing to do and I never had you down as stupid, Persephone."

The Greek girl flushed and looked down at her feet. "When I heard you talking about the Titan appearing at this Waterloo place I thought if I went there and captured him myself it would prove to you all that I am to be trusted." She looked up and gazed beseechingly at Tom then looked around at them all, her hands trembling now.

Edward seemed unconvinced. "Professor, I am concerned that Persephone may still be under the influence of Knossos."

The old man shook his head. "No Edward, Tom is right. I thought about this whilst you were away and Knossos is truly dead. He can never return and even if he could, Knossos and I fought against the Titans." He paused then added, "I don't see what she would hope to gain by releasing Crius."

"Her master may be gone but there is always revenge," Mary observed, looking down at her bloody forearm and wincing. "Releasing a Titan would cause the chaos and disruption that Knossos would have wanted."

Now Tom shook his head. "She was under his control before, Mary, but we released her from all of that."

"What if we did not, or not fully? She may be acting under some subconscious direction that even she is not aware of," Edward pointed out.

Tom stared at Persephone. It was true that she had been deeply under the sway of Knossos once. Moreover, Knossos had been the master of influence and persuasion. Was it possible that he was using his former Black Robe and striking out at them from beyond the grave?

Persephone seemed to sense his hesitation and her eyes narrowed. "I don't care what any of you say, I did *not* attempt to release this Titan. It was just mischance that I took that particular vial. Please believe me. I wanted to show that I belonged with you. I need to belong... to control these powers." She turned back to Tom, her eyes doleful and penetrating. "You know this more than anyone, Tom."

"I... guess so," he replied hesitantly.

"She might just be tricking you Thomas," Mary said.

Persephone stepped forward and thumped her fist on the Professor's desk in frustration. "Zeus and Apollo! What is wrong with you people," she shouted. "What must I do to prove it to you?"

"That is the point though, isn't it?" Septimus now commented. "None of us can be certain and you cannot prove it."

The Professor studied the girl for a moment and then spoke. "We have no convincing evidence either way. However, I believe that someone is innocent until proven guilty. For the time being I am prepared to give Persephone the benefit of the doubt. Tom, take her home."

Persephone seemed about to argue, but then her shoulders drooped and she turned away. As she did so, the Professor beckoned Tom forward.

"What, Prof?" Tom asked, leaning over the desk.

"Make sure she is safe," the old man whispered, "but keep a close eye on her, Thomas."

Tom nodded then stepping back said, "Come on Persephone. Let's get you home."

Moments later they were standing outside the Greek girl's house. "Here we are, you're home," Tom said.

She did not reply but merely turned those dark green eyes upon him. This time though, rather than being attracted by them Tom took a step back from her. At that moment, Persephone's expression was not exactly friendly. Hostile and threatening would be a better description. Those eyes were wide now, her face flushed red, lips drawn back over gritted teeth.

"I… er… said you were home," he said with a faint smile that she did not return.

"I can see where I am, I am not stupid," she said at last.

Tom was at a loss, "I only meant…"

Persephone took two strides towards him so that she was now staring right into his eyes from mere inches away. She thrust a finger at his chest. Startled, Tom wondered for a moment if she was under the influence not of Knossos but Iapetus – but no. This anger was no Titan-induced rage, this was all her own.

"You only what?" she snapped. "You only allowed your companions to accuse me of trying to release a Titan. Just think about that for a moment, Thomas. I am from a land and a time where everyone knew how dangerous the Titans were. To us they were not almost forgotten figures in the old stories. They were very real and very frightening. We worshipped the gods for defeating them and giving us peace from the chaos of their reign. How could you believe I would willingly release that terror on the world again? I thought you were my friend."

Tom reached out and put one placating hand on her shoulder. "Persephone, I am sorry, but look at it from our point of view. Only a few months ago you tried to kill us all. You were deeply

109

under the influence of Knossos. Maybe…"

The girls eyebrows rose dangerously and she swept his hand off her shoulder. "Maybe what?" she asked, her voice icy.

"Maybe you still are under his influence. Even if he is gone maybe something of that hold still lingers even if, as Edward said, you are not aware of it."

Persephone gasped and raised a fist. Tom tensed, waiting for the blow, but it never came. After a moment the girl dropped her hand and when she spoke she seemed calmer.

"For eight years I lived with his voice inside my head. Everything I thought and did was at his command. Believe me, Thomas, I would know if he was still in here." As she spoke, she repeatedly tapped a finger against her forehead.

Tom nodded. "OK. Let's say I believe you… and I do believe you, Persephone. However, I am not so sure about the others. Taking the vial had the opposite effect to what you intended. You can surely see that?"

"I guess so," she agreed reluctantly.

"So you might have some work to do to bring them around. That is all I am saying."

Persephone tilted her head. "So I'll find a way to convince them," she said, and then turned away from him and walked towards her front door, fumbling for her keys.

"See you in school tomorrow then, Thomas," she said without looking back at him, "after all, I am sure the Professor wants you to keep an eye on me!"

The following day began a wintry February morning. The snow was sufficiently deep to delay the bus, which Tom usually caught to get him to school. Eventually the vehicle heaved into view but was full and simply sailed on by. Tom glared up at the bus windows as if it was the fault of the lucky passengers on board that he was not one of them.

In the last but one window he caught sight of two familiar faces. One was Persephone's and beside her, clearly talking animatedly to her, was Andy. He glanced out of the window and caught Tom's gaze. Out of view of Persephone, Andy gave a thumbs up sign. Then the bus was gone.

This particular bus only ran every half hour and having stood shivering at the bus stop for a while, his feet like blocks of ice, it became apparent to Tom that the next bus was not coming. He turned away and resisting the temptation to Walk – you never knew who might be watching – began the half-hour trudge to school, the snow crunching under his feet. He felt his phone vibrating in his pocket; a text message had arrived.

He pulled out his mobile and found the message. It was from Andy.

'Pers says yes. Will go out wiv me,' it read.

Persephone had agreed to go out with Andy then.

'Great', thought Tom, kicking out at a heap of piled up snow. 'Life just keeps getting better!'

CHAPTER ELEVEN
THE THREE BROTHERS

The snow had all gone and daffodils were blooming when, several weeks later, Tom's mobile sounded an alarm.

The Hourglass I.T. department had downloaded an app to his phone configured to receive messages from the Institute. Different and very distinctive alarms would be sounded in different circumstances. This particular alarm was one that Tom had been both half hoping for, yet at the same time half dreading, because this one meant the Institute had detected another Time Cyst emptying its contents into the void. Another Titan, one of the companions of Iapetus or Crius, was about to emerge from aeons of slumber in captivity. Tom wondered when and where this next encounter would occur.

He looked across his English classroom to where Persephone and Andy were sitting. Since the episode at Waterloo, Persephone had pointedly avoided Tom. Indeed, she seemed to be going out of her way to spend time with Andy and was always busy when Tom tried to talk to her. As far as he was aware Persephone had not Walked anywhere since that incident, but he was anxious about her. He could understand that she was angry with him, but it was still his job to keep her under observation. In fact it had been rather embarrassing wandering after her at school or at weekends sneaking and almost stalking her at the shops.

On one occasion, not realising she was meeting Andy, Tom had followed her into the cinema and sat through a movie – not one he would have chosen to see – a few rows behind her. It was only when the lights came on and Persephone and Andy stood up that Tom had realised the two of them were together.

"Watcha mate, you following us?" Andy had asked.

"Oh no!" Tom forced a laugh. "Didn't know you were here actually."

"Sure you didn't, pal!"

Other similarly embarrassing encounters meant that life was getting quite awkward with Andy. Indeed, the last week or so Andy and Persephone had taken to sitting on the other side of the classroom from Tom. They had hardly spoken to him in days. Even whilst he and Andy were changing for rugby in the locker room and Tom had tried to start a conversation, Andy had brushed him off and run out the door without responding.

Now, as he felt the phone vibrating in his pocket, Tom considered telling Persephone about it. Then he changed his mind. To begin with he did not think the others would be very keen on him turning up with the Greek girl in tow. Then, as he thought about it, he realised he was getting rather fed up with Persephone and her attitude. Life had been a lot more fun before she was around.

"Oh, to hell with her," he muttered.

So, ten minutes later, when the dinner bell rang, Tom got up and without looking over at Persephone and Andy walked out of the door. He drifted along with the rest of his class as they headed towards the canteen and then veered off in the direction of the library. Finding a quiet place amongst the bookshelves, he Walked to the Institute.

Tom was in a grumpy mood and so, despite the previous

113

instructions not to do so, he materialised in Mr Phelps's office, but of Mr Phelps there was no sign. The door to the Professor's study was slightly ajar. Tom was about to push it open when he heard the rumble of voices within. Peeping through the crack to see who was speaking, he came to an abrupt halt. Even with their backs turned toward him, he instantly identified the two men sitting in front of the Professor's desk. Both were talking animatedly. The Professor, seated in his habitual place, was staring across his desk at them and looked unusually agitated.

Tom, not wanting to interrupt their conversation, moved back slightly and waited. As always it amazed him that the three men, so different in attitude were yet remarkably similar in appearance; indeed, their features were identical, so much so, they might have been mistaken for triplets. This was no coincidence and, as Tom knew, their relationship was much more complex than that. Before The Event, which Tom had witnessed in one of his dreams, all three men had been embodied in Titus. When The Event split Titus into three, each part of him had occupied a newly created reality and retained one aspect of his personality. Neoptolemas was kindly, if somewhat pedantic and academic. Colonel Thielmann, who had taken on the most ambitious part of Titus, was brutal and occasionally sadistic. In contrast, the Custodian, who had recently brought the vials to the Professor, was cold and calculating. He seemed almost hollow at times; a grey-suited individual without emotion, willing to take whatever steps he perceived were needed to keep the three realities in balance. Tom had learnt over the course of his previous adventures that all three men would take drastic actions at times, although they were not always in accord, and whilst he trusted the Professor he was both afraid and wary of the other two.

Mr Phelps was standing behind the Professor's chair, but was looking down at the floor and did not appear to have noticed Tom. Nor, apparently, had the brothers. It was clear that some sort of argument was taking place. Thielmann was holding what looked like an old map or parchment in one hand and kept waving it in the air and pointing to it as he spoke.

"Don't you see what this entry makes clear? We *must* lay our hands on this device."

The Custodian nodded. "If what the Colonel says is true, Neoptolemas, this may indeed represent our best opportunity to defeat the Titans once and for all."

The Professor shook his head. "What you are suggesting would require a sacrifice, one that I am not willing to contemplate."

"He is but one individual, brother. Surely the sacrifice of one is justified to save all. It is the basis of why men fight wars after all," the Custodian said, "for the greater good."

The Professor shook his head again.

Thielmann gave a cry of exasperation. "Knossos foresaw this. He was aware that what he and Titus were doing with the Titans was merely a temporary fix. We knew he was working on a permanent solution," the Colonel again jabbed his index finger at the parchment he was holding, "and according to this he eventually came up with one. It involved a device he called a *'Focus'* and he laid it all out in a manuscript. However, it is clear The Event happened before he was able to take matters any further."

Continuing to eavesdrop, Tom frowned. It seemed that whatever Knossos had been working on had now been found, yet nobody seemed very happy about it. Increasingly curious, he stayed where he was, hoping they would not notice him standing in the doorway.

"Now it appears that The Event flung Knossos' manuscript forward through the millennia, for in the early 1500s it came into the hands of the Conti di Rivoli. The Count was an avid collector of ancient writings, particularly those concerning early scientific instruments. As I said, what I have here is an extract from his diary. His notes indicate that he gave the matter a great deal of thought." Thielmann held up the parchment, "This evidence suggests that the manuscript, which he refers to as a Codex, will be found in his library in Turin. He records that monks fleeing Constantinople after its fall in 1453 carried it with them and that some half a century or more later it came into his possession as a young man. His diary shows that he not only studied it, but advanced Knossos' theory even further. I have reason to believe that either he located the Focus itself or he used the manuscript to construct a similar device. In his notes the Count refers to it only as 'the Artefact'. It seems he was convinced it could be used to deal with the Titans."

Thielmann paused. He glared first at the Custodian and then at the Professor, then said emphatically, "*Whatever* the cost, brothers, we must find it."

"Let's say for the moment that what you say is true, what do you suggest we do?" the Professor asked.

"Di Rivoli travelled through Europe extensively in his younger years and it will be extremely difficult to locate either the manuscript or the Artefact during that time. But we know that later in life, after he had married and had a child, he gathered all his treasured manuscripts and artefacts into his library, which became something of a spectacle at the time. We also know it was around then that he wrote his diary. So if we want to locate the Focus that surely is the period to target?"

The Professor fixed his brother with a severe expression.

"Why only the Focus? Don't we also need Knossos' manuscript?"

Thielmann hesitated, not meeting his brother's gaze. "I guess so, but with our knowledge I am sure the theoretical workings of di Rivoli's device will be understandable enough. I am convinced it is the practical application in the form of the Artefact that we need. With this device we can banish the Titans for eternity."

"Only by making a sacrifice that I am not happy to make," the Professor insisted again. "Besides, if this Artefact is so important – and assuming we will recognise it when we see it – why then don't you go and get it yourself, or at least send one of your people?"

The Colonel grimaced. "It is in *your* reality, brother, not mine. You know very well that it is a lot easier for those whom we control and command to travel in their own reality rather than in the opposing realities."

The Professor turned to the Custodian. "What about you? Do you not wish to take possession of this most valuable of artefacts?"

The Custodian shrugged his shoulders. "Not especially. I am certainly curious to see it, but you know my methods. I would prefer not to dirty my hands any more than I need to. My chief interest in this matter is to prevent the Titans from disturbing the balance of the realities. These creatures must be dealt with and what Thielmann suggests seems the best way to do it."

Tom, unable to contain his curiosity any further, chose this moment to step into the Professor's study.

"Do what?" he asked, striding forward. "What is this manuscript and device you are talking about, and what exactly do you mean by 'sacrifice?'"

Quick as a flash, his face red with anger, the Colonel jumped to his feet and swung round to face Tom, one hand moving automatically to his gun holster, the other still clutching the parchment. Meanwhile, the Custodian twisted round in his chair and regarded Tom's intervention without any sign of surprise or frustration. Had he perhaps known all along that Tom was standing there and if so, had he not cared? With the Custodian it was impossible to tell.

Relaxing slightly, the Colonel hastily rolled up the parchment and turned back to the Professor. "I will take my leave now, Neoptolemas. I advise you to think carefully about what we have said. As soon as you have recaptured the Titans we must be prepared to act. Those temporary cysts you're using will not hold them for long. Indeed, I doubt they will hold Kronos at all. He is the most powerful of the five. We don't have much time. My own specialists estimate that by summer the original Time Cysts will be empty and all five Titans will have emerged. Even before then you may find that Crius and Iapetus manage to escape the vials your Walkers used to trap them."

The Colonel cast a scowl at Tom then tucking the roll of parchment under his arm, nodded at the Professor and Custodian. "I will be in touch."

Without saying another word, he strode across the study, planted his feet on the Hourglass symbol that was woven into the carpet... and vanished.

"I would echo what Thielmann has said," the Custodian commented, getting to his feet. "However, I would advise caution, Neoptolemas. I am not saying our brother's suggested course is incorrect, only that I believe he has been less than fully open with us, although at this point I am not sure why. I suggest we gather more information before deciding what to do. It would be a shame to sacrifice anybody unnecessarily," he added, turning to glance at Tom.

Then he too was gone.

"What was that all about, Prof?" Tom asked, watching the old man, who had taken off his spectacles and was polishing the lens as he often did when discomfited.

Replacing them on his nose, the old man stared at Tom without replying. He seemed to be trying to decide how to answer. Tom was about to repeat the question when he felt a hand slap down on his shoulder.

"Well now, boyo, here we are again. Been a few weeks. Did you miss me?" Tom turned his head and saw that Septimus was standing behind him, Edward, Charlie and Mary materialising at his side.

The Professor cleared his throat. "Well, now that you are all here, shall we get on with the business in hand?"

"Do you need me to be here, sir?" asked Mr Phelps, who all this time had been standing to attention behind the Professor's chair.

"No, I'll call you if I do. Thank you Mr Phelps, you may go."

Septimus, clearly oblivious to what had occurred, threw himself into one of the recently vacated chairs then turned to Tom. "Come on, Tommy boy, we ain't got all day. Time and Titans wait for no man after all!"

There was a general outburst of groaning at the pun.

"Did you see what I did then?" the Welshman asked, grinning at Tom.

In spite of himself, Tom laughed. He pulled up a chair to join the others, who were now sitting down facing the Professor's desk. "Yes, Septimus, I saw what you did then. Unfortunately!" he added.

"Very droll, Mr Mason," the Professor commented, unrolling a map on his desk and looking around at them all. "Well then lady and gentlemen, let us begin."

Tom frowned. It seemed the old man was not prepared to explain what he and his brothers had been discussing - at least, not yet.

"The Time Cyst containing the Titan Hyperion is beginning to decay and has been located," the Professor said. "And this one is going to take very careful timing indeed..."

CHAPTER TWELVE
THE TUNGUSKA RIVER

Tom peered at the map. It appeared to show a heavily forested landscape split up by a few meandering rivers. There was little high ground; no mountains or coast and as far as he could see, no built up areas. It was not anywhere that he could immediately place. What was odd, though, was that several of the rivers had been labelled with a strange type of writing.

"This is Russian isn't it?" Edward commented.

"Don't tell me you can read Russian, Eddy boy?" Septimus asked.

Edward Dyson shook his head. "No, not really. I had an uncle who was with the 8th Hussars at the Battle of Alma – you know, in the Crimean war? He brought back a few books and tried to learn the language. When I was about ten he taught me a few phrases. I just recognise the letters that is all."

"So where are we going, Prof?" Charlie asked. "And when are we going?"

"You are going to the Lower Tunguska River, June 30th 1908—" Neoptolemas began, but got no further because Charlie let out a yelp.

"Oh my God!" he exclaimed, his face blanching.

"What is it, Charlie?" Tom asked. He glanced at the others, but from their facial expressions the date meant as little to them as it did to him.

121

Charlie, recovering from his initial shock, was now chortling. "Are you telling me that I actually know something about history that you folk don't?"

"Don't go on about it – had to happen sooner or later," Septimus said, feigning a yawn. "After all, you can read, can't you?"

"I suppose so, though I ought to confess it's not something I read in a book. I actually learnt it from a Russian chap back in… oh, let's see –'42 I guess."

"What were you doing in Russia in 1942?" Edward asked.

"Arctic convoy, mate. When the Jerries invaded Russia we sent some convoys to Murmansk to help out. You know: tanks, guns, ammo, fuel and so on. My first voyage after signing up in fact was on one of them – PQ 11 it was. When we got to port and were getting the ship ready to come home, the Ruskies took us for some drinks of that gut-rot stuff they drink. Anyways, turns out that one of the dockworkers was from some village in the middle of nowhere. Don't recall the name of the place, only that it was on the Tunguska River. His English was good – a lot better than my Russian anyway," Charlie grinned. "He told the tale of how, when he was a young lad, there was this huge explosion way out in the forest that made the earth shake and flattened every tree for miles. Him and his brother were tumbled out of bed by the force of it. He said it was in the summer of…"

Charlie paused for a moment to gather his thoughts. The others all stared at him in silence, hanging on his words, until Septimus, with a glance at the Professor, said, "I'm guessing it was the end of June, 1908? Go on Charlie."

"Well, apparently, just before the war the Soviets got interested and sent a survey team out to have a look. They took photos and measurements and interviewed all the witnesses. In the end they reported that a comet or something had blown up and

122

caused an earthquake."

Edward tilted his head and looked at the Professor. "Is this true?"

The old man nodded. "Charlie is quite correct that it was thought to be a comet or a meteor. Shortly after 7.15 a.m. on 30th June local inhabitants living close by Lake Baikali reported seeing a column of bright bluish light streaking across the sky. It was followed shortly afterwards by a flash and a boom. The accompanying shockwave knocked people off their feet and shattered windows hundreds of kilometres away. There was something that felt like an earthquake estimated at about five on the Richter scale. Years later, a scientific study discovered minute particles of dust and minerals consistent with the detonation of a comet or meteor in the high atmosphere. The explosion was vast – something like ten to thirty megatons in size – bigger than Hiroshima or Nagasaki. Had it not landed in such a sparsely inhabited area it would have been equally devastating."

"You mean like an atom bomb? You are sending us into an atom bomb?" Tom asked.

"Not exactly... there is no radiation as such," the Professor commented.

"Well that's a relief," Septimus said dryly. "Just one huge explosion!"

"Yes, Mr Mason, a big detonation. Over the years all sorts of explanations have been postulated. An asteroid, comet or meteor were the more likely theories. But there were other, much wilder ideas: a massive release of natural gas; a black hole passing by the Earth; a particular combination of minerals that somehow caused a nuclear explosion, and even anti-matter falling from the sky! But the Institute's I.T. department downstairs have detected that the next Time Cyst is decaying and will open at this location. The collapse of the Cysts we – that is Knossos and I... er, Titus – created could result in a showering of the elements we used to create them, which would look like a meteor shower."

"What about the explosion? What is the explanation?" Edward asked.

The Professor sat back in his chair and pressed his hands together, steepling his fingers. "Think about the nature of the Titans, Lieutenant."

"Are they not mortal men?" Mary asked.

The old man nodded. "At least, they began that way, but just as we can alter time they were able to manipulate other things, such as water or, in the case of Hyperion, light and heat. According to legends, the son of Hyperion was actually the sun, Helios. "

Charlie grinned weakly, "But that's just a legend, right Prof?"

Neoptolemas shrugged his shoulders, took off his spectacles, polished them and replacing them on the end of his nose, gazed over them at the Walkers.

"What can he do, this Hyperion?" asked Mary. Her voice was fearful and Tom wondered if she was thinking back to the night of the Great Fire of London. It was when they had first met. He had rescued her from the conflagration only in the nick of time and Walked her forward to the 21st. Century. Over time Mary had recovered from the shock, but she had never overcome her fear of fire.

"He can certainly create intense heat and use it to cause great devastation," the Professor said. "I remember how he set a fleet of warships on fire all those years ago..." his voice trailed away, his eyes distant.

"So what is the plan? How do we capture him?" Edward

124

asked. "Do we travel to this place," he gestured at the map, "the Lower Tunguska River, and wait for him to appear?"

Brought out of his reverie, the Professor shook his head. "You cannot."

"No, I agree, we can't," Septimus said. "If we go back and wait for him to appear we put ourselves at great risk. I do not think that even Mary with all her powers could shield us from an explosion of that force. We would be killed by the blast or at the very least seriously injured."

"What if we go back and prevent the explosion?" Tom asked.

The Professor's eyes appeared to bulge in their sockets. "You know better than that, Thomas! You cannot prevent a documented historical event. If you prevent the explosion you will change history and goodness only knows what the consequences of that might be."

"So, we have to appear just after the explosion and capture Hyperion then, don't we?" Charlie said.

"Well yes, but the only problem is we are not one hundred percent certain of the exact moment of the detonation. We do have some ideas from various seismic detectors that recorded the event. However, they might not be quite on the button. It is possible you could arrive a few seconds too late and find Hyperion has already escaped from the area."

Charlie grimaced. "Or a few seconds too early?" he murmured.

Septimus looked again at the map. "This dotted line marked here shows the limits of the immediate destruction, am I correct?"

The Professor nodded and Septimus continued. "So then, what we can do is return to the event but some miles away from the immediate area. Close enough to hear the explosion and probably see it, but far enough away to escape the devastation. The instant after the explosion we Walk to the epicentre and capture the Titan before he has a chance to escape."

Neoptolemas considered the plan and nodded approvingly. "That might well be the solution, Mr Mason." He opened a book, flicked through a few pages and found an entry, which he showed to Septimus.

The Welshman smiled and checked the map. "According to this entry, two brothers were disturbed by an explosion that could be clearly heard and lit up the sky in the vicinity of their log cabin in the woods, which was around here, about seven miles from the epicentre of the event." He patted a spot on the map where a small stream wound through the forest.

He glanced over at Charlie, "Your wartime buddy and his brother maybe?"

Charlie smiled. "Best not drop in on him. We don't want to cause any complications that change his future."

Septimus nodded. "Agreed. But the location is useful. I suggest we go there and we wait near the cabin until we too witness this explosion and then we act."

"OK, sounds like we might have a plan." Tom said. "Let's do it!"

"What a peaceful place," Mary said some ten minutes later.

Dressed in clothes appropriate for 1908, which were not a lot different to what they normally wore, they were standing on top of a grassy knoll. Below them a ramshackle little log cabin was just visible in the pre-dawn light. It stood in a clearing beside a small river, about one hundred yards away. All around the area was a dense coniferous forest. The fir trees stood tall and mighty and oblivious to the destruction that would be unleashed upon many of them in only a few moments.

"Oh yes indeed, we are about as far away from civilisation here as you would ever hope to be. We are right in the middle of Siberia," Septimus commented. "Good job it's summer!"

"Well it won't be peaceful for very much longer," Edward said, examining a fob watch which he now replaced inside his jacket. "Fireworks any minute now I should guess."

They stood for a moment enjoying the early-morning bird-song and the fresh air of the deep forest, which smelt of pine resin. Then Mary lifted her hand and pointed skyward. There, high above them, a spot of incredibly bright light had appeared. It was not the sun, which even now was climbing the sky to the east casting a red glow on the horizon.

As the bright light grew in intensity and became larger they became aware of a roaring sound coming from the light. Then, at the bottom of the light, it was as if a funnel had appeared and a tube of blue and white emerged. There was a brief, ominous pause and then the sky seemed to erupt into flames that were emanating out from the tube like an expanding supernova.

"Here we go!" said Charlie. "Block your eardrums!"

Even here, many miles away from the epicentre, the intensity of the sound was almost unbearable. A few seconds later they were hit by a shock wave of roasting hot air that knocked them off their feet. Tumbling down the slope Tom hit his head on one of the fir trees and for a moment all he could see was darkness and swirling white stars.

When his vision cleared he saw that his companions were slowly dragging themselves to their feet. Mary was sitting on a log and cradling her arm, which she appeared to have scraped, most likely on the bark of one of the conifers. Several branches had broken and crashed to the ground, but it could have been worse, for while some of the trees had been partially uprooted, because they grew so close together few had actually fallen and nobody had been crushed beneath one. Kneeling in front of Mary, Edward was applying a field dressing. It was the same arm she had wounded at Waterloo. Thanks to the Institute doctor's powers, healing had been rapid, but Mary would always bear the scar.

Septimus staggered over to Tom and helped him up off the ground. "Well, I tell you what boyo, I would not like to have been any closer to that blast!"

Tom, temporarily deaf, his ears still ringing, got the gist of what the Welshman had said and nodded in agreement. "I think we should go don't you? We don't know how long Hyperion will stick around," he said.

"Yes, no time to lose," Septimus agreed.

"Gather round everyone," Tom called.

It took only a moment to Walk to the epicentre of the explosion As they emerged from the void an intense heat assailed them. All around them it was as if a huge concrete wrecking ball had landed on the forest. As far as the eye could see, the tree trunks were shattered, splintered and flung outwards away from the blast. Everywhere they looked trees were on fire, as was the undergrowth. Beneath their feet the grass was scorched and smoking and the ground was quaking.

"We can't stay here for long. This heat is intolerable," Edward said undoing his collar buttons then putting an arm around Mary, who was visibly shaking.

"We don't need to," Septimus said. "I have spotted Hyperion. He's over there."

They all looked to where the Welshman was pointing. Only a few yards away a man was crouching in a clearing, his arms and hands splayed outwards as if he had just performed an acrobatic manoeuvre and landed on the mat in a gym. At first he was looking at the ground, his head tilted downwards, but now he slowly raised it. His hair was a nimbus of fire and his eyes, black as coal, focused upon them and fixed them all with a hostile stare. He was largely naked apart from a kilt-like skirt of leather. Slowly, with a ripple of the deeply tanned skin over his muscular form, he rose to his feet. He appeared to be unarmed, but having seen the devastation around them, none of them doubted for one moment that he could do them terrible harm.

Several words in what Tom assumed was Ancient Greek emerged from his mouth. Tom did not understand what he was saying, but the tone of voice was commanding and demanding; he would clearly not brook any argument.

Even so, Edward tried, replying in the same language. Hyperion glared at him and spoke again. To Tom's ears it sounded like a repeat of his first sentence.

Edward turned to the others. "He says he is the God Hyperion. He invites us to bow before him and swear fealty to him and he will then consider sparing our lives," Edward translated.

"Well that's nice of him," Septimus said. "Very considerate. I do like it when our enemies are polite too. It adds a certain classiness to the encounter don't you think? Who's got the vial?"

"You!" Tom and Charlie chorused.

"So I have," the Welshman said, tapping his pocket.

"Edward, tell the Titan we do not bow our heads to monsters and bullies," Charlie said.

"I just did, more or less," Edward replied, "but my Ancient Greek is a bit rusty. I'll try again." Another stream of gibberish issued from his lips.

As Edward finished speaking Hyperion raised his arms and

pointed at each of them, jabbing the air with his index fingers.

"Here we go," Charlie said, already on the move, "rumble-tumble time!" He whizzed away to flank the Titan, using that staccato movement that made the sailor look like a dancer caught in flickering strobe lighting at a disco party. By using repeated small jumps from one spot to the next he was able to move at a phenomenal speed. It was a good thing too, because the instant after he had begun moving a blast of fire erupted from Hyperion's outstretched hands and passed through the space Charlie had occupied only a second before.

The Titan frowned and then turned to the rest of them, drawing back his arms in readiness for another blast, or so it seemed.

"WALL!" Mary shouted, throwing up her shield of frozen time in front of them. The fiery blast hit the temporal barrier. The force of the impact was catastrophic and the Wall was shattered, but it had done its job and saved them – for the moment at least.

Edward Walked and materialised behind Hyperion. With the side of his hand the soldier attacked the Titan with a karate chop to the back of the neck, but as his hand touched Hyperion's skin, Edward screamed in agony. He leapt back clutching his hand, which Tom could now see had erupted into blisters.

"Try not to touch him!" Septimus shouted as he drew a revolver from inside his jacket and levelled it at the Titan's head.

Meanwhile, Charlie had circled far and wide through the shattered tree trunks and now nipped back on Hyperion's flank. He flung himself into the air feet first, aiming both his steel-capped boots at the Titan's chest.

Hyperion was too quick for him and twisted out of the way so that Charlie merely hurtled on by, crashing into a burning tree trunk that lay on the far side of the clearing. He lifted his head for a second then his eyes rolled up and he slumped down again, clearly unconscious.

Septimus fired two shots from his revolver. Tom was sure the bullets had hit the Titan but something about Hyperion's skin meant they merely ricocheted off.

"I think we're in trouble!" Septimus said as he moved nearer to the Titan, clearly intending to try his luck at close range.

"Mary, try to freeze time around Hyperion," Tom said. Remembering an experiment in the science lab at school, an idea had come to him.

"But that won't work. We just saw that he can blast his way through the Wall," Mary said, shaking her head.

Tom nodded. "Yes, but we don't just need to create a Wall, we need to freeze all of the air around Hyperion so that it encases him."

"I... don't understand Master," Mary said, reverting in her anxiety to her subservient nature; a nature fostered by the era into which she, a humble servant, had been born – a time when women were regarded as 'the weaker vessel' and dominated by men.

Tom placed a hand on her shoulder in an effort to calm her nerves. "Hyperion is a creature of heat and fire, Mary. Fire needs oxygen in the air to burn and heat needs the air molecules to be moving fast."

Mary looked doubtful at this. Clearly her seventeenth century grasp of physics was not going to be very helpful here. Physics, though, was a subject that Tom had just started studying at school and he found he understood it quite well. "Just trust me on this one, Mary. We need to surround Hyperion with frozen air and it needs to be very cold."

Still looking doubtful, Mary whispered, "I'll try, Mas... Thomas."

131

"Quickly, Mary! I will help you. You take the lead and I will make your barrier stronger." She nodded her head and closed her eyes in concentration. Then she opened them and pointed at Hyperion. He was staring at them, arms outstretched but motionless, a half-smile on his lips, almost as if he was deliberately holding back and savouring the moment, knowing the blast of Greek fire he was about to send like napalm from his fingertips would burn the upstart Walkers to a crisp.

"WALL!" Mary shouted.

Beside her Tom concentrated on the flow of time. He was beginning to understand that all things were connected. He had heard in his physics lesson only this past week that time and space were linked. So that meant all those molecules around Hyperion were present not just in space, but in time. They didn't just exist on their own either; they were constantly moving around. And so, Tom surmised, if he and Mary could freeze time around Hyperion then they would quite literally take the heat out of the situation.

The air around Hyperion shimmered and a puzzled expression appeared on his face. Clearly aware that something unexpected was going on, he prodded at the invisible barrier that surrounded him. Then he stepped back and clasped his hands together as if preparing to destroy it with his blast of fire.

Focusing on the Wall, Tom experienced a moment of revelation: he realised that he could now understand how Mary influenced time in the unique way that she did. He assumed this sudden clarity of mind was yet another manifestation of his potentate powers, which were starting to mature over time just as the Professor had told him they would – not that Tom was entirely sure exactly what being a 'Potentate' meant in his case, for he was neither a monarch nor a ruler, nor was he ever likely to become one. However, be that as it may, once he understood how Mary manipulated time to freeze it in a local area it was easy enough simply to enhance the effect, so that when Hyperion let forth a mighty blast of fire, this time Mary's Wall held.

Keeping his focus on the Wall, Tom shouted, "That's right, Mary, keep doing that; keep doing just that! Septimus, quickly, get the vial ready."

Septimus had reached the barrier of frozen time and stood outside it, his pistol levelled at Hyperion's head, but on hearing Tom's command he simply put the revolver back in his pocket and pulled out the vial.

Seeing the blue bottle, Hyperion's eyes widened. It was clear he recognised what it might be because his attitude changed and an expression of panic flashed across his face. He hammered his fists against the inside of the Wall, but with Tom continuing to strengthen it, the Titan's efforts had no effect. The air molecules within it slowed and slowed and finally halted – literally freezing around Hyperion.

Then Tom perceived that the hazy, almost transparent barrier, which was just discernible around the Titan, was gradually becoming opaque, turning into a wall of solid ice in front of their eyes.

Clutching the vial, Septimus swung round to Tom, "Will it work through the ice?"

"Try it and see," Tom said.

Septimus nodded and removing the stopper, pointed the vial at Hyperion. A moment later the device started to exert a pull on the Titan. Within the frozen white shell they could see him struggling, still trying to free himself, but in vain. The vial tugged at the Titan through the ice and the Wall bucked and bulged. An instant later it shattered and the Titan went tumbling

133

straight into the vial, shrinking in size as the powerful dimensional forces of the pocket universe took hold of him and began turning him into vapour.

"Three down and two to go," said Septimus with satisfaction, looking down at the vial in his hand.

He had spoken too soon. A blast of fire shot out of it and briefly enveloped him. Septimus dodged to one side with a yelp of alarm and hastily jammed the stopper into the neck of the bottle. Hyperion was finally gone.

For a moment the universe itself seemed to freeze. Nothing and nobody moved. Then Tom let out a deep breath and it was as if time came rushing back in, and all around them a forest fire was crackling, sparks and embers flying into the air, smoke stinging their eyes. The ground was shaking and trees being uprooted were creaking and groaning.

Edward ran across and crouched down beside Charlie, but laughed with relief when the sailor clambered to his feet, rubbing his head.

"Ouch that hurt," Charlie said. "How's the hand?"

Edward looked down at his burns. "They are stinging a lot actually, but I'll live and assuredly Dr Makepeace will sort me out in no time."

Mary approached Tom with a rather curious expression on her face. "Merciful heavens, Thomas," she said. "I am not sure I could have done that without your help."

Tom shrugged. "I don't see any reason why not. But you know, something has just occurred to me. Possibly something very important."

"What's that then?" Septimus said, walking toward them both as he popped the vial into his pocket and rubbed a hand over his singed eyebrows.

"The way we Walkers manipulate time... and the way the Titans control the elements..." Tom frowned in concentration, "...well I think these talents are linked and that maybe they are not as different as we first thought. Time comes into everything, you see."

"Deep stuff, Tommy boy!"

Tom laughed. "Yes it is a bit. I wonder what my science teacher would say if he heard me today."

"Not a lot, boyo. He isn't born yet!"

They all laughed, but Tom, feeling the ground suddenly move beneath his feet, held up his hand to cut their laughter short. "Oops!" he said. "Remember Alexandria, guys? Unless you want to witness another earthquake, it's time we weren't here!"

CHAPTER THIRTEEN
THE MANUSCRIPT

Back at the Institute, Edward, Charlie and Mary climbed the stairs to report to Dr Makepeace. A Walker like the others, Makepeace's talents lay in being able to accelerate the healing process significantly and within a couple of hours, Edward's burns, Charlie's cuts and bruises and Mary's grazed arm had been treated, leaving only faint scars. The three Walkers then returned to join the others in the Professor's study where Mr Phelps had just brought in mugs of tea and a pile of cheese and pickle sandwiches.

In the interim, Tom had actually returned to school, arriving in time for the end of lunch, so was able to sit through the afternoon lessons, one of which, as it turned out, was science with Mr Beaufort. On reflection, Tom decided to keep quiet about his theory that the physical world could be controlled by manipulating time, and although it was not so very far away from Einstein's theory of relativity and his famous formula $E=mc2$, Mr Beaumont had not gone into that in any depth yet. All in all it seemed a bit much for Year Eight Science, Tom felt. Besides, he preferred to keep a low profile.

Whilst Persephone was studying English and Maths with them she was not in their science group and so Tom had a chance to catch Andy on his own.

"Where were you at lunchtime?" Andy asked.

"Why do you ask?" Tom said sharply. "Thought you and Persephone would be together?"

Andy shrugged, "She was a bit funny when we got out of the lesson, kept asking where you were."

"Oh?" Tom said, hoping he sounded disinterested, but in fact surprised by how keen he was to know what Persephone had been saying.

"Said she was a bit upset that we'd all had a bust up and wanted to make peace with you. So where were you?"

Tom thought quickly. "Er… in the chess club."

"The chess club? Rubbish, you don't play chess."

"Yes I do!"

"Anyway, chess club is on a Friday. It's Tuesday today. Want to try again?"

"Oh, erm…"

"Fine, don't tell me," Andy said and stomped off to the other side of the science lab from where he flung dark looks at Tom for the rest of the afternoon.

After the double science lesson Tom had intended apologizing and coming up with a better excuse, but just before the bell rang the Institute buzzed his mobile. As Tom glanced down at the text, Andy shot off without looking back. Sighing, Tom lingered until the room was empty then Walked back to the Professor's study. He told himself he would give Andy a call later and sort it all out.

Sitting alongside the others in front of the old man's desk, he asked, "So then, what's the emergency, Prof? Do we have another Titan arriving so soon? I didn't get that alert on my phone."

The Professor shook his head. "No, not this time. We have

something else to consider and it concerns the instability of the vials. They were only ever intended as a recapturing mechanism and will not hold the Titans for long..." his voice trailed away and he directed a meaningful gaze at Tom.

Feeling his face flush Tom looked down at his hands.

"Thomas overheard a conversation between my brothers and me earlier today... didn't you, Thomas."

"Sorry, Professor," Tom mumbled. "I didn't mean to, but I heard you arguing and I didn't want to interrupt..."

"Yes, well, no matter," the old man said, turning his gaze on the others. "You all need to know what Thomas overheard. We were discussing the issue of the Titans and how Titus and Knossos had fought them and imprisoned them and then, realising the Time Cysts were only a temporary solution, how both Titus and Knossos contemplated a permanent answer. They were still on friendly terms at that time, but Titus soon became distracted by the fact that Knossos had established his own cult. Feeling threatened by this, I confess that I... that is, Titus, did not come up with much by way of solving the problem. Knossos, however, had given the matter more thought and had laid out his deliberations in writing."

"This would be the manuscript Colonel Thielmann spoke about?" Tom asked.

The Professor nodded, "Yes, exactly so."

"What happened to it?" Edward asked.

"I'm coming to that, Lieutenant. The manuscript was flung forward during The Event. It was lost for a while, but turned up in Greece at some point and was taken to a monastery within the Eastern Roman Empire. When Constantinople fell to the advancing Turks in 1453 a huge collection of manuscripts was carried west by monks fleeing the chaos. It was one of the causes of the

Renaissance, all that learned material hitting Western Europe – and in particular Italy – in a short period of time. In the hands of clever men it fired off a new age of learning and reason."

Septimus yawned. "Sorry, Prof, but what is the significance of all this?"

"The significance, Mr Mason, is that the Knossos manuscript was one of the documents saved by the monks and carried into Italy. To Turin in fact. Turin was becoming a significant city in the Kingdom of Savoy and a certain Fillippo, the Conti di Rivoli, had a Palazzo in the city—"

"Did you say Fillippo... di Rivoli?" Septimus interrupted, leaning forward.

"Yes, why do you ask?"

The Welshman shook his head. "No reason... sorry to interrupt... carry on, Prof." He sat back in his chair and waved at the Professor to continue. Tom noticed, though, that Septimus was now looking absently at the wall behind the desk, as if his thoughts were elsewhere. Then, as Neoptolemas cleared his throat to continue speaking, the Welshman's eyes snapped back into focus.

Tom frowned. There was something going on here, but what? A few moments earlier Septimus had looked thoroughly bored, which often was his manner when the Professor was talking about history, but now he seemed to be hanging on the old man's every word.

"Well, it appears that the Conti—"

"That's Italian for Count," Edward chipped in.

The Professor gave a slight frown, "Yes, thank you Lieutenant. As I was saying, the Count studied the manuscript and made additional notes of his own. We believe he even went so far as to experiment with a device that Knossos may have designed.

According to di Rivoli, Knossos' writings refer to this as a 'Focus'. The Count himself simply refers to it as 'the Artefact' – but whatever we call it, my brothers and I believe this device can be used to banish the Titans indefinitely. That being so, clearly we need to retrieve both the manuscript and this Artefact."

Tom looked intently at the Professor. The old man had made no mention of the sacrifice he had so strongly objected to when he and his brothers were talking earlier. To Tom it had sounded very much as if they'd had someone specific in mind. The Custodian's words came back to him: *'Surely the sacrifice of one is justified to save all?'* No names had been mentioned, but Tom had a nasty feeling that he was the *'one'*. It seemed to him that Neoptolemas was deliberately avoiding his gaze. *'Maybe he does not realise I heard that bit. Or maybe he doesn't care,'* thought Tom. Sometimes he was not sure how different the Professor really was from his ruthless brothers. In the end, just how far would he go to achieve his aims?

"How do you know about the manuscript and device, Professor?" Mary asked.

"Yes, sir, how do you know all that about the monks and everything?" Edward asked.

The Professor took off his spectacles, rubbed at the bridge of his nose and then replaced them. "It appears that the Count kept a diary. The Colonel came across it by chance in the Twisted Reality, but he says that apart from a few brief references to Knossos' work, it tells us little more than how the manuscript came into di Rivoli's possession."

Again Tom frowned remembering the Custodian's comment implying the Colonel was concealing something. Something to do with the manuscript? Tom would not trust Thielmann further than he could throw him.

140

"So what date do we go back to?" Charlie asked.

"Well, according to our research the Count travelled a lot in the mid- to late- fifteenth century, so it would be hard to pin him down. However, when he was about forty – that would be in 1485 – he married and retired to his Palazzo where his wife gave birth to a daughter. The Count died in February 1510, his wife shortly before him and his daughter inherited the Palazzo. Now, given that we need the manuscript with all his notes as well as the Artefact, I suggest a good time to go back to is shortly after his death."

"Before anyone has had time to clear out his possessions?" Septimus commented.

"Just so. Also, by then we know his research will be complete. You will be looking for a document in Greek with Latin annotations."

"Hah!" Septimus laughed. "It's not as if there will be very many Greek documents in Renaissance Italy!"

The Professor raised an eyebrow, "Yes, Mr Mason, I accept that does not narrow it down exactly. However, something about the document may make it obvious to you that it's the right one. Edward can read Latin and Greek of course, so that is a major asset in our favour."

"And the Artefact?" Mary asked. "What does that look like?"

The Professor held up his hands. "We don't know. We can but hope it is with the manuscript... or else that the manuscript will tell you what it is. I suggest Edward checks those Latin annotations carefully."

Edward nodded. "Very well, I guess there is no time like the present. If the Count died in February 1510, I think we should head for March."

The Professor nodded, but Septimus was shaking his head,

141

his breath hissing out in an audible sigh.

The others all turned to look at him. "What's wrong?" Tom asked, noticing that the Welshman's face had turned a delicate shade of pink.

"When the Prof mentioned Fillippo I thought we might have problems, boyo. Then, when he mentioned what it was we were after, I knew we did."

The Professor frowned. "I don't understand what the problem is with this, Mr Mason."

Tom, however, suspected exactly what the problem was. "The daughter of Fillippo di Rivoli... was she called Julia by any chance, Professor?" he asked.

The old man checked his notes. "Why yes, Thomas, she was. I did not see the relevance of the name so did not check..." He turned to stare at Septimus, "Now though, I believe the name of the Count's daughter is critically important. Would I be right, Mr Mason?"

"Julia?" Charlie asked, turning to Septimus. "Do you mean that Julia?" He grinned. "The one you and your erstwhile partner in crime, Rolf Lapace, had a thing about?"

Septimus sighed. "I never imagined it would be relevant to Institute business, but yes, that Julia. The manuscript and all the Count's notes were the items we were hired to steal in my last job with Rolf."

"You told me it was an heirloom," Tom said.

"Well in a way it was – even more than that to Julia. What happened was this. In the days when I was a mercenary, before the Prof persuaded me to work for the Institute, Rolf and I spent a lot of time in the fifteenth century. Can you imagine the wealth of works of art, as well as scientific and philosophical papers in Italy at that time – especially in places like Florence and Turin?

It was easy pickings as far as we were concerned. There are collectors who will pay a fortune for that material. We eventually took over a Palazzo in Turin and based ourselves there for a number of years."

The Professor was shaking his head. "Wanton ransacking of the past. Using your Walker's abilities in that way is strictly against the rules."

Septimus shrugged. "Heh! I wasn't a reformed character back then, Prof. As a mercenary I had no rules. It was a job and it was a lot of fun as well as being highly lucrative. Well, anyway, it was at that time we met Julia and Fillippo. We were guests at their place on many occasions. As you know, Fillippo was a collector himself and showed us his library and study. In pride of place was something he referred to as the '*Codex Eventus*'."

"'The Book of The Event?' Surely you must have realised its significance?" Edward commented.

Septimus shrugged. "I was more interested in the girl actually! I did look at the Codex, but I never dreamt it was originally written by Knossos, but rather that it was the philosophising of some ancient Greek. Not that I could read Ancient Greek and my Latin is not that great it has to be said. I did know that Fillippo had studied that manuscript for thirty years and had made copious notes, as well as writing extensive essays and theories of his own. After Fillippo died, his daughter spent several years collating and sorting all that material. To Julia it was as if her father was still alive and speaking to her through the documents. Well, you know the story... Julia eventually chose Rolf over me and I backed off..." The Welshman's voice trailed away, that distant look returning to his face along with a mournful expression.

"Go on," Edward prompted.

"Sorry, yes, where was I...? Soon afterwards, Rolf told me

143

about the job. We were to steal the manuscript – the Codex Eventus – along with Fillippo's diary. I refused to be part of it, but Rolf went ahead, as you know."

The Professor was polishing his glasses vigorously as he pondered what Septimus had told him. "This," he began as he replaced his glasses, "changes things. We cannot simply return to the Palazzo in Turin because if we go back before Lapace steals the Codex, we alter history to unknown end. Nor can we go back afterwards, because the manuscript will be gone."

He glanced at Septimus. "What about the Artefact, did Lapace take that too?"

Listening to the conversation, Tom was remembering that Lapace and Septimus had come under the influence of a nasty piece of work called Redfeld, a Nazi captain who had caused them all a lot of grief in the past. He inhabited the Twisted Reality – the Colonel's domain. Exactly how had Thielmann got his hands on the Count's diary? Had Redfeld had something to do with it? It seemed likely, thought Tom.

Septimus was shaking his head. "I don't think so. That was not part of the job and in any event I have no idea what it would have looked like."

"Think for a moment, Mr Mason. There can only be a few items in the Count's possession that it would be. Maybe an item he kept in his library?"

Septimus thought about this. "Well, he did have a number of devices for studying the stars, along with some engineering apparatus. Perhaps it was one of those? But all this is now irrelevant because, boyos, I am not stealing from Julia! I refused to do it then and I won't do it now."

"That is what the Colonel has asked us to do," the Professor pointed out.

"Since when do we do the Colonel's dirty work?"

"As I recall, it didn't trouble you before you fell for Julia," Tom said pointedly.

"That's as may be," Septimus grunted.

"The point is, Mr Mason," the Professor said, "this Artefact might allow us to banish the Titans forever. Surely you see how important that would be?"

Septimus thrust out his chin and made no answer, his expression stony and stubborn.

"In any event, surely we need the manuscript too? Without it we will not know how to work the Artefact even if we succeed in finding it," Edward suggested.

"Assuming it exists," Mary said quietly.

For a moment all they could hear was the ticking of the clock on the mantelpiece.

Finally, the Welshman nodded. "Accepted. There at least I may be able to help. If I contact Rolf he can tell us who employed us in our last job. Rolf never told me and I never asked."

"How will you locate Mr Lapace? Are you still in touch?" the Professor asked.

"Well, in years gone by we were hired through announcements placed in the personal columns of the Times newspaper," Septimus said, then he grinned, "But the world has moved on, Prof, and believe it or not we now use Twitter!"

CHAPTER FOURTEEN
LAPACE RETURNS

Barely fifteen minutes after Septimus had sent the message, his mobile let out an alert signal. The Welshman pulled it out of his pocket, read the screen and then gave a little grunt. "I tweeted that we wanted some information. Just got a reply. It's Lapace alright."

"How can you be so sure?" the Professor asked.

Septimus gave a wry smile, "Because he asked how much the knowledge is worth to us!"

Edward snorted at that. "Cheek!"

"Not at all; I would have been surprised if he did not ask." Septimus glanced at the Professor. "With your permission, I will get him here."

The old man nodded and Septimus proceeded to tap away on his keyboard.

Having alerted Mr Phelps to the imminent arrival of their visitor, the Professor unrolled an antique map of Northern Italy. While they waited, they gathered round his desk and Tom, who had never been to Turin, studied the map with interest.

Another fifteen minutes went by before there was a loud knocking on the front door, for no Walker who was not a member of the Institute could penetrate the sophisticated security system, but must enter the premises by traditional means. They

146

heard the rumble of voices in the hall and moments later Mr Phelps showed Rolf Lapace into the room.

As he entered he gave them each a broad smile, which Tom did not return. Lapace was of an age with Septimus, so in his thirties, and similar in height to Edward. His cropped red hair was covered by a black beanie. He wore combat trousers, army boots and a bright blue retro sweatshirt with a white collar, the chest emblazoned with a Chelsea FC badge.

"Well now, this is a surprise. Never thought to be back in such august company given the nature of our last meeting," he said, speaking in a pronounced London accent.

Stony-faced, Septimus vacated his chair and gestured that Lapace should sit in it, which he did. Then Septimus sat on the front edge of the Professor's desk and leaned forward, bringing his face close to that of his former partner.

Lapace beamed at him, "I have missed you too, my dear old friend," he taunted.

"Never mind all that waffle, Rolf, tell me who we were working for on the last job we did together. Who hired us to steal the manuscript from Julia?"

Registering surprise, Lapace shot Septimus a quizzical look. "Oh, that job. Now why do you want to know about that job all of a sudden?"

"Does it matter, Rolf?"

Lapace's face broke into a smile. "Trying to get on Julia's good side are you?"

Septimus reached out, grabbed Rolf by the collar and pulled him forward so that they were nose to nose. "What did you just say?" he growled.

"Heh, steady on there, pal. This is an expensive shirt. No need to be so touchy. Seems like I've hit a nerve."

"Mr Mason, please let go of Mr Lapace," the Professor said.

The Welshman pushed Lapace back into his chair and then stomped off to the corner of the study from where he glowered at his former partner.

Glaring back at him, Rolf Lapace straightened his shirt. "That's better," he said with a sniff. "Well now, you wish to know about my employer for the di Rivioli job, yes? You know I am a businessman, Sep. Make me an offer."

Septimus bristled with outrage. "You little toad, I was part of that job too. Whoever it was, he was my employer too."

Lapace shook his head. "Oh no. You walked out and refused to be part of it, remember?"

The Welshman took a step towards Rolf, but the Professor intervened. "Mr Mason leave him be. Mr Lapace, we will pay you a commission if you tell us who your employer was. Would a thousand pounds be sufficient?"

Lapace considered the figure. "Two thousand," he replied.

Studying him for a moment the Professor nodded and picked up his phone. "Mr Phelps, please transfer two thousand pounds to…" he turned back to Lapace, "What account?"

The Londoner rattled off a number, which the Professor repeated to Mr Phelps. As he was speaking Lapace pulled a mobile phone out of his pocket and Tom could see he was checking some sort of banking app. A few moments later the phone beeped and Tom caught sight of the message: *'You have got funds.'* Lapace smiled and replaced his mobile in his pocket.

"Well then, who was your employer, Rolf?" Septimus asked.

Lapace took a deep breath before replying. Of all the people in the room, only Tom was not shocked when he said, "Colonel Thielmann. He it was who paid me to retrieve the Codex and di Rivioli's diary. Which I did."

"What!" Septimus exclaimed. Even the Professor looked surprised.

"But that means—" Tom began, but the Professor held up a hand to stop him from saying any more and buzzed through to the outer office.

"Our visitor is leaving, Mr Phelps." Then turning to Rolf, he said, "Thank you Mr Lapace. Mr Phelps will show you out."

Looking disappointed, Rolf stood up and gave a mock bow to each of them, "Until we meet again," he said, then made his way to the door. Turning back he winked at Septimus, "Have fun Sep!"

As soon as the door closed behind him, Edward spoke. "What it means is that the Colonel already has the manuscript. So why on earth does he suggest we go back and get it?"

Thinking back to the brothers' conversation he had overheard that morning, Tom stared at the Professor. "He didn't though, did he, sir."

Neoptolemas shook his head. "No, Thomas, he didn't. He was more bothered about retrieving the Artefact, which makes sense now I know he has the manuscript already…" with a puzzled frown the Professor's voice trailed away.

Tom turned to the others, "The Colonel kept waving a page about in the air and saying it was from the Count's diary, arguing that he wanted us to go and find this Artefact… whatever it is. When the Prof suggested it was just as important to find the manuscript too, the Colonel looked kind of sly, as if he was hiding something. I thought so anyway and even the Custodian said you should keep an eye on him, Professor. It was like he didn't want us to know he had the manuscript already."

"Clearly that must be so, but why, Thomas?"

"He's *your* brother, not mine, Professor," Tom said, nettled.

149

The old man raised his eyebrows and there was an awkward silence until Mary spoke up. "Maybe there is something in the manuscript he does not want you to read?" she suggested. "When Edward does not want me to read a page of a book with rude or lewd words in it he sometimes skips them. Or else he covers them with his thumb." She smiled at Edward who blushed.

"Some of those words are not fit for a lady's eyes," he said.

"Oh Edward, you're a bit of a fuddy-duddy at times! I just go back and read them later anyway."

"Mary!" Edward exclaimed, in a fine example of Victorian outrage.

It broke the tension and they all laughed. The scowl even left Septimus's face for a moment.

"So then, if Mary is right," Charlie said, "for some reason Colonel Thielmann is not telling us the whole truth about this device and how we deal with the Titans."

Tom looked at the Professor, waiting for him to mention the 'sacrifice' part and explain what that was all about, but all he said was, "No, indeed, he is not. I must go and speak to him." He pushed back his chair and getting to his feet moved to the Hourglass symbol woven into the carpet at the rear of his study.

"Professor..." Tom began, intending to ask about the sacrifice before Neoptolemas disappeared, but before he could get the words out, the old man swung round to him and beckoned.

"Oh, Thomas, you are to come along with me." He then turned to the others, "You might want to go and get some tea while you wait for us?" His eyes twinkling, he looked principally at Charlie, "I believe they are serving doughnuts today. Come, Thomas," he said, stepping onto the Hourglass symbol, "we will use the conduit."

As they Walked through the portal to the Twisted Reality,

Tom thought about the last time he had been there and shuddered. It was not a pleasant place. His own familiar world had its share of madmen and evil dictators, terrorists and destructive wars, of course, but in the alternative dimension of the Twisted Reality there always emerged a much darker, more terrible version of history. In the Colonel's world the Third Reich had not lost the Second World War. They had defeated Britain and the USSR and gone on to conquer most of the rest of the globe, laying much of it to waste. Now, around seventy years on from the Second World War, Thielmann's Nazi overlords dominated the planet, putting down with ease and breathtaking brutality any rebellion. The twisted version of Britain had been turned into one huge industrial complex where the Third Reich employed slave labour to make the weapons it used to suppress its enemies.

The security for the occupation of Britain was at the command of a special force in which Colonel Thielmann was a high-ranking official. Its base was a massive fortress built in Trafalgar Square. It was to this complex that the Professor now took Tom. Last time he was here Tom had been on a mission of subterfuge fraught with danger. This time, however, the Professor took hold of Tom's hand and guided him on the journey deep into the interior of the Colonel's HQ.

They arrived in an outer office quite unlike that of Mr Phelps', materialising within a circular logo that bore the Nazi lightning bolt symbol of the Twisted Reality above a clock icon, embossed on the tiled floor. Here the clatter of keyboards rang out from the desks of two uniformed female clerks who were busy on one side of the room. They barely looked up from their labour as the two Walkers appeared, speedily returning to their work, clearly used to similar comings and goings. On the other side of the room a junior officer leapt to his feet.

"The Colonel has been expecting you, Professor. I will inform him you have arrived."

"Expecting us?" Tom asked in a low voice.

The Professor pointed at the symbol beneath their feet. "Since the incident with Knossos my brothers and I became aware that further challenges might lie not far ahead. We established a reliable means of communication and travel between our worlds. When I make official visits here I make sure I use this route. Each of us is aware when the others are using it. It is like making an appointment really. It avoids unpleasant surprises."

The officer replaced the handset of his phone. "The Colonel will be ready in just a moment, sir. Would you like to sit down or have some refreshment?" His tone was polite yet cold. Whatever the niceties of the brothers' means of communication, it was clear to Tom that the members of Thielmann's and Redfeld's time-travelling unit trusted the Hourglass members just as much as he and his friends trusted Thielmann and Redfeld!

"No thank you, Lieutenant, we will wait."

The officer nodded and returned to his work.

Tom took advantage of the wait to whisper the one question that was uppermost on his mind. "What did the Colonel mean when he mentioned a sacrifice that needed to be made, Professor... he was meaning me wasn't he?"

Neoptolemas turned and studied Tom for a moment, his expression serious. "Do you trust me Thomas?" he asked at last.

Tom thought about the question. "Yes, I do. But you don't always make it easy," he added.

The Professor laughed. "No, I imagine I do not. However, I have to ask you to trust me this time. Believe me, it will be alright."

152

Tom sighed in frustration. He was about to ask another question when a door behind the officer's desk opened and a familiar figure in Nazi uniform strode out. When he saw the pair standing inside the symbol, Captain Redfeld halted in his tracks, snapped his jackbooted heels together and smiled darkly at Tom.

"Well now, I have asked myself on many occasions what I would do if you, Thomas Oakley, appeared in my world once again and here you are in front of me. What delights I could construct for you downstairs in my interrogation chamber."

"Redfeld, let them be. They are here to see me," a voice called out from the room beyond.

The captain turned to look back into the room and sighed. "As you wish, sir," he replied and then stepped into the outer office and held the door for them.

"Another time maybe," he hissed as Tom and the Professor walked past him and he closed the door behind them.

The office walls of Colonel Thielmann's room were covered in maps of various parts of the world, all annotated with military symbols. Tom recognised New Zealand, South America, Central Africa and even Antarctica. The Third Reich here had conquered most of the world, but clearly there was still resistance to their regime in the more remote areas. More maps covered tables in the office as well as on the desk behind which sat Thielmann. He was studying Tom. Eventually he rose to his feet and waved them to a pair of chairs in front of him.

"Welcome to my office, Thomas Oakley. Do you like what you see? Your Professor here bothers himself protecting the history of your world, preserving what he calls the *correct timeline*. But here," he said with a wide sweep of his arm, "we define history. We change it to match what we decide it should be. That is how we won all the wars we have fought and will win those we fight

153

today, both here and one day in your own world maybe."

"Not if I have anything to do with it you won't!" Tom retorted.

"Impressive, Neoptolemas. Your puppy here does have teeth after all," the Colonel sneered.

"Indeed he does. But enough of that. I did not come here to bandy insults about," the Professor said.

"So why did you come?"

"To ask you why you did not tell me you already possess the Codex Eventus."

The Colonel frowned. "That little rat Lapace has told you this has he?"

The Professor did not respond.

"Well, is it true?" Tom demanded.

For a moment Thielmann seemed to think about his answer then he nodded, "No point in denying it I suppose. Yes, I have it," he said.

"Well then, will you let me see it?" the Professor asked.

Shaking his head, the Colonel turned to pick up a map, hastily unrolling it and spreading it out on his desk. Tom could see it was a map of Japan, which Thielmann seemed to be studying intently, yet there was something odd about his manner. The corner of the map began to roll up and he quickly moved a paperweight to hold it down. What lay beneath was visible for only a second or two, but Tom was certain he had spotted a brown sheet of parchment covered in handwriting. He had not recognised the language. Could it be Latin?

The Professor got to his feet. "Well, can I see it, Thielmann?" he repeated.

"No, not yet."

"Why not, may I ask?"

"Not until I am sure what we must do." The Colonel glanced

at Tom then back to his brother. "I do not believe you will take the right action when the time comes, Neoptolemas."

"What action is he supposed to take?" Tom asked. "It concerns me in some way, doesn't it?"

"It concerns us all, Thomas Oakley. Your family and friends as much as you."

"*My family*? What—"

"Enough!" the Professor interrupted. "Come with me, Thomas."

Tom stood up then he hesitated. "Colonel, what was that about my family?"

"What are you willing to do to save all that you hold dear, Oakley?" The Colonel said. "What are you willing to sacrifice?"

Tom froze on hearing that word again: sacrifice. "What do you mean?" he asked.

The Professor was at the door now. "Come along Thomas, we must leave," but Tom was still staring at the Colonel, who had fallen silent, a half smile on his lips.

"Thomas come!" the Professor repeated. "Now!"

Tom turned and stumbled after the Professor into the outer office, took up his position on the lightning symbol and prepared to pass through the portal back to the Institute. However, that word sacrifice was still running through his head. Just what was it that Neoptolemas was not telling him? More to the point, what was the Colonel hinting at but not saying?

As they appeared in the Professor's study, Tom turned to him to ask, but the old man spoke first "Thomas, I know you have questions about what my brother said and when I can answer them I will, but for now you will just have to trust me."

Tom sighed in frustration. Then he nodded his head, "Very well. I do have another question, however."

"Well, what is it?"

"What do we do now that the Colonel will not let us see the Codex?"

Stepping over to his desk, the old man smiled. "We take a leaf out of Messrs Mason and Lapace's book, Thomas: we steal it!"

CHAPTER FIFTEEN
THEFT

Hyde Park in the Twisted Reality at midnight was not an inviting place to be. Tom and his companions, were standing in a grove of trees waiting for a rendezvous. The park in Tom's world was an oasis of green in the heart of London. Here, the peaceful enclave still existed but Tom's understanding was that it was used for military parades and training exercises for the army garrisoning the city and was out of bounds for any civilian.

"He's late," Septimus said, checking his watch.

"I imagine that getting around London during the curfew is not easy," Charlie said. The sailor looked around and shivered. "To think that this might have been my London had the Jerries invaded like they did here."

"Do you think he has run into a patrol?" Edward asked.

"Well even if he has, he is a resourceful man. Give him a few more minutes," Septimus said.

They waited in silence for a little while and then Mary pointed out into the darkness. They looked that way and spotted movement in the bushes nearby, close to the edge of the Serpentine.

"Get down," Septimus hissed. They crouched, taking cover behind a park bench. A moment later a shape emerged from the bushes, studied them for a moment and then came jogging across the path.

"Hello Phil," Tom said, standing up, "we thought you might have run into trouble."

A big, beefy man, Phil had powerful muscular arms and a shaved head. In fact Tom might have mistaken him for some sort of football hooligan had he not already met him. When they had first met Phil, he had indeed been aggressive and by no means welcoming. That had been during Tom's first visit to the Twisted Reality a year or so ago when he and his companions had been captured by Thielmann's security force and taken to a prison camp at Newbury. Phil was a prisoner at the same camp having been similarly captured. He had been very suspicious and distrustful of them at first, but Tom, Edward and his other friends had helped to lead a breakout from the camp. Phil had been grateful and they had parted as friends.

Since that occasion, the Professor's agents had kept in contact with Phil, who was now in charge of a resistance force in Twisted Britain and trying to free the country from Nazi domination. Tom could only imagine how difficult a task that would be given the thousands of well-armed troops at Thielmann's disposal.

"Yes, sorry, I got a bit delayed." Phil beamed, "Well then, here you all are again. It's been a while."

"Thank you for responding to the Professor's request for help," Edward said, shaking Phil's hand.

"It is the least I can do. The Prof has been very helpful in supplying us with equipment and information. Of course, given who his brother is he has to be very careful, but I honestly think we would not have survived the past year without his help."

"Ah, that reminds me," Edward said, reaching into his pocket and pulling out two pairs of handcuffs. Each of the cuffs had the hourglass symbol stamped upon them. "The Professor asked me to let you have these. Said these are Walker restraint cuffs. Put them on one of Redfeld's men and they cannot Walk. He thought they might be useful."

Phil took them and tucked them into his trouser pocket. "Cheers, mate, they'll come in very handy. We certainly need a way to limit Redfeld or his thugs and their talents."

"Well, speaking of which, I gather you have discovered a few talents of your own, Phil?" Septimus said.

Phil nodded. "Yes. When we were in the prison camp and I saw what you and your companions could do, it opened my eyes. You see, when I was younger I experienced strange moments when I seemed to be reliving the same event more than once. It was more than just a feeling of 'déjà vu'; it actually seemed to be happening for real, but until I met you lot I thought it was just my imagination."

"That's exactly how it was for me," Tom said. "I thought I was going mad until Septimus appeared and told me I was a Walker."

"Turns out that I too am what you call a Walker. I am not particularly powerful, but I seem to be able to sense the ability in others. I have since discovered that many of the individuals imprisoned at Newbury were people with the potential to manipulate time in the way you do, though not all of them were aware of it. Eventually I found out that we were being targeted for pick up and arrest. Redfeld, Thielmann and their goons are afraid that if any resistance group could organise its own force of Walkers it would mount a serious challenge to Nazi authority."

Septimus nodded, "Makes sense. You could certainly run rings around any ordinary soldiers. I do hope you have been giving our friend Redfeld a hard time."

With a rueful grin Phil shook his head, "We've tried to, but it's not easy. He and Thielmann are so powerful with their tanks and artillery, planes, gunships, helicopters and specialist weaponry that we simply cannot obtain. They also have surveillance equipment and a sophisticated communications network than we can't set up. But... we keep trying. I am gathering my forces, stealing weapons and waiting for the right moment to strike a decisive blow... but enough of this chatting," he said, casting a glance around the park. "So then, how can I be of assistance?"

"What has the Prof told you about the Time Cysts and the Titans?" Edward asked.

"Enough to realise what a threat they are. The first three might have emerged in your world, but there is surely a chance of the other two coming here. I am well aware this problem is a threat to both our worlds, which is why I have agreed to help you. You need to gain access to Thielmann's office to steal a manuscript, right?"

"Right," Edward said.

Phil tilted his head and once more surveyed the park. "Come on, we had better be on our way. A patrol is likely to arrive at any moment," he said, setting off at a jog.

"Can't we Walk?" Tom asked, matching the big man's pace.

"Best not unless we have to. If they pick up any disturbance in the time flow they will be down on us like a ton of bricks."

They followed Phil across the park to the exit. Here he halted whilst he checked the dimly lit street outside. "All seems quiet," he said, then hurried them across to a truck parked in the shadows nearby.

"Get in the back," he instructed. "You will find some clothing. Put it on and leave your coats in the storage box there. I will

160

have the driver get them back to you later. You're going to pretend to be cleaners reporting for the night shift at Thielmann's headquarters. I have your passes up in the cabin. If the guards check you, I advise you keep as quiet as possible and avoid provoking them," he said.

They clambered into the back of the truck and Tom, switching on his pocket torch, soon found the pile of blue-grey overalls and caps Phil had left for them. Discarding their coats they began tugging on and zipping up the overalls.

Mary was swamped by hers. "It's too big for me," she whispered.

"Roll up the legs and cuffs," Tom suggested, giving her a hand to do up the zip.

A moment later the engine kicked into life and the truck lurched off down the road, throwing Charlie, who was still pulling on his overalls, sideways onto the bench that ran along the walls.

Edward pulled the cursing sailor upright and helped him get disentangled from his clothing.

"Don't care much for the driving round here, do you?" Charlie said when he had sorted himself out.

"I don't get it, why go to all this trouble?" Tom asked. "I mean, why couldn't we just have Walked into the headquarters straight from the Institute?"

"It's not as easy as all that," Septimus said shaking his head.

"Why?" Last time we were able to enter directly into the projection room."

Septimus shrugged. "Yes we were, but if you remember, we only got in because in Trafalgar Square there happened to be a portal open between our reality and the projection room. Thielmann's headquarters have significant protection, just like the

Institute does or for that matter The Office. The reason the three brothers have agreed to have a permanent conduit installed between the realities is that it is the only way past those barriers. We can enter the Institute because the Prof allows it to occur. However, if we tried to Walk into Thielmann's headquarters directly we would find not only that we would be detected, but most likely we would become trapped."

"So what is the plan then?" Mary asked, piling her hair on top of her head and covering it with a cap.

"Oh, it's not very complicated. According to Phil, we just have to walk in via the cargo doors. We're dressed as cleaners so we turn up and look ready to start mopping floors."

"Just so long as Redfeld or Thielmann don't turn up too and recognise us!" Edward commented, as usual the first to point out the obvious risk.

"Come on Dyson, show a bit of stiff upper lip: you are a Victorian officer after all," Septimus said.

The van drove on, turning this way and that as the driver navigated the streets of London. After about five minutes it lurched to a halt and they heard the handbrake being pulled on. A few moments later a harsh voice was interrogating Phil.

"Who are you and what is in the van?"

Phil's voice rang out in response. "Junior Manager Stanford, sir, escorting civilian workforce. Nightshift for the headquarters cleaning detachment in the back. Do you want me to open the doors, Sergeant?"

The answer must have been in the affirmative because they heard the passenger door slam shut and a few moments later the rattling of the locks on the rear doors. The door swung open and a beam of light shone inside directed at their faces, blinding them. As the torchlight flickered back and forth, Tom felt him-

162

self reaching out automatically to the flow of time, preparing to whisk them all away. He felt the squeeze of Septimus' hand on his wrist and the hissed words: "No, don't do that!"

Tom tried to relax, slowly letting go of that tentative connection with time. The light swung back and forth, but Tom could now make out enough to see the man standing beside Phil in the doorway. He was looking through papers – presumably the identification documents Phil had provided to the guard. He seemed to be taking a while and was obviously not happy about something.

"The identity papers are in order, but where is your Work Order Form?" the sergeant snapped.

"I am sure it's there somewhere, sir," Phil said.

"Do you take me for a fool? There is no work order form here. Without a W.O.F. I am not permitted to give access. You lot, out of the van. Now!" he barked.

"What is the problem here?" another voice broke in from somewhere out of sight. The torch light flickered away from the back of the van. For a moment it illuminated another officer before the sergeant dipped his beam.

"No problem, Lieutenant. I can deal with the matter. No need to bother yourself," the guard replied.

"It's no bother, Sergeant. It was getting stuffy in the Mess. I wanted to get a breath of air, I will deal with these workers. You and your men can take a break," the new voice continued.

Tom saw a figure step into view. Next to him he heard Mary gasp in recognition. He too had recognised the face they had last seen the year before in the woods near the Newbury camp. The man's name was Lieutenant Teuber, yet although he was an officer in the occupying forces, he wanted an end to the brutality imposed by the Colonel's regime. Teuber had told them he desired peace and wished for a better world than the dark one around them. For that reason he had not only helped them escape, but had agreed to meet with Phil after Tom and his companions had returned to their world, with a view to discussing possible cooperation in the future.

"They don't have a W.O.F. sir!" the guard persisted.

"Really? Well I will look into that. Off you go Sergeant."

The non-commissioned officer snapped his heels, saluted then marched off with his men, leaving Teuber staring at Phil.

"He was right you know, these papers are not in order," Teuber said. Then he smiled, reached inside his own field-grey jacket and with a flourish pulled out another document. Speaking in an undertone, he said, "Here is the W.O.F. I got it signed by the Junior Commissioner of Works just before he went back to Germany on three weeks' leave. Show it at the next security check and if the inquisitive sergeant asks about it later, the guards there will be able to confirm you had one. By the time they check it all out, hopefully the Commissioner will have forgotten about it and it won't come back to me."

"You and Phil are now working together then?" Septimus asked softly.

"Yes, we are. You started something when you introduced us. He now tells me this is important. All I can say is, it had better be worth the risk."

Septimus nodded. "It is."

"Then good luck. I must be about my duty," Teuber said with a nod at Tom. "Firstly, though, you will need these." He retrieved a set of keys from his pocket and passed them to Septimus, who was sitting nearest to the door.

"Good luck again," Teuber murmured then waved them forward and said loudly, "Carry on, carry on," so that any nearby

164

guards would hear. With that Manfred Teuber turned away and strolled off towards the guard post.

Phil, with a wink in Tom's direction, shut the doors and they set off once more. This time the journey was only a few moments and they seemed to be going down a steep hill. Tom, remembering that the cargo doors and parking lot of the headquarters were at basement level, knew they were almost there. When finally they ground to a halt and the truck doors opened, a dank smell like that of an underground multi-story car park, wafted in. This time Phil was alone, his face grey in the overhead lights. Behind him, about fifty yards away, were doors leading to stairs and an elevator, which gave access to the interior of the headquarters. Guards stood there on duty and Tom could see that he and his companions were being scrutinised as they disembarked from the truck.

Phil gave them a whispered pep talk as they gathered round him. "Try not to do any talking at all. Remember you are tired, put upon and downtrodden workers, you don't want to be here and you don't want to cause any trouble for yourself or your families. So you just turn up to do your shift and then you go home. Avoid making eye contact, don't engage the guards in conversation, and certainly don't try and joke with them."

"Where's the fun in that, boyo?" Septimus asked with a wolf-ish grin.

Phil turned round sharply on his heel. "Listen to me. I know enough about your world and you personally, Septimus Mason, to know that you go gallivanting around Time like it's some sort of amusement park. Let me tell you that this world is different. These guards will just kill you if they suspect we are spies, or we look at them funny, or even if they're just having a bad day. Their officers will usually just turn a blind eye or join in. This is not about fun, this is about survival. Mine as much as yours!"

For a moment Septimus looked taken aback by Phil's suddenly threatening demeanour. Just for a second Tom thought the Welshman was about to retaliate, but then he nodded. "You're right of course. I apologise unreservedly."

Phil grunted but said no more as he led the way towards the officers and guards. There followed the routine checking of documents and a brief inspection of each of them by the bored-looking goons. It seemed the additional paperwork provided by Teuber was adequate because in a few moments they were let in through the doors.

As they walked along the linoleum-covered corridor, the overhead strip lights buzzing and flickering, Septimus leaned across to the big man and said in a placatory tone, "Well done for getting Teuber on your side, Phil. He did a good job on those documents. "

"Actually, apart from the W.O.F. he did not do anything. I have the Prof to thank for them. They are Institute work. We don't possess sufficiently accurate scanners and printers to reproduce the security documents." He pointed at a door and opened it. They all trooped in. The room looked like a janitor's closet full of mops and buckets. In one corner was a sink and draining board, beneath it a drain and above it a shelf jammed with bleach, bars of soap and cleaning cloths.

"So then, we are in. What do you intend doing now?" Phil asked. "We are inside Thielmann's headquarters, but where is this manuscript the Professor wants?"

Tom blinked. Phil was right, of course. He might have got them inside the Colonel's heavily guarded headquarters, but where in all this huge building would the manuscript be?

Septimus shrugged. "I think, given how significant Thielmann feels the manuscript is, he would not give it over to anyone else, Tom. The most likely place has got to be his office."

Thinking back to his visit there with the Professor, Tom clapped his hand to his head. "Of course!" he exclaimed, recalling the brief glimpse of parchment that Thielmann had been at such pains to hide. So distracted had Tom been by what the Colonel had then said to him, he had forgotten all about it until now.

"Yes, you're right, Septimus, and I have an idea now where it might be. I think I might have seen it on the Colonel's desk when the Professor and I went to visit him, but I didn't get a good look at it because Thielmann covered it with a map."

"Well, it's a likely place for it," Septimus said. He looked over at Phil, "Any other suggestions?"

"The most secure rooms are in the basement. There are computer rooms and vaults down here. If you don't find it in the office we could check them out?"

"Very well, let's go," Septimus said, heading for the door.

"Wait up," Phil called out. "We need to look the part." He held up a mop and a brush and dustpan.

"It's all a bit antiquated isn't it?" Charlie said. "Even in my day they had vacuum cleaners!"

"No need to invest in machines when you've got a ready supply of slave labour," Phil said.

"No, I suppose not."

They each collected a variety of mops, buckets, brooms and dusters and set off.

"What do we do if the real cleaners turn up?" Mary asked Phil.

"They won't. I bribed them to stay away tonight. I had to promise we would clean around enough to cover their absence, though.

"Won't they talk?"

"Not likely. Right, are we ready? I suggest one of you comes with me and we make a quick... ahem... sweep of the lower floors. The rest go up to the top floors where the Colonel's office is, and don't forget to do some dusting on the way! Assuming you find what you're looking for, come back down. We've got about two hours before we need to be away from here or the guards will get suspicious. Hopefully it will be enough. We'll aim to meet along the corridor on the second floor, the one over-looking the statues in the entrance courtyard. You can't miss it."

"I think I know where the office is, it's where I first saw Thiel-mann," Tom said.

Phil grimaced. "We certainly don't want to run into him tonight."

"Suppose he's working late?" Edward commented. "I know the Professor often does."

"Cross that bridge if we come to it, Dyson," Septimus said. "Let's hope he is at his home and fast asleep."

"Can't we just Walk to it?" Tom asked.

"No, not possible in this building," Septimus replied. "We will have to use the lift."

They split up. Charlie accompanied Phil out into the corridors of the basement level whilst the other four went together to an elevator and stepped inside.

"Not sure which floor," Tom said, his fingers hovering over the buttons.

"25th," Septimus said straight away.

As Tom jabbed the button they all turned to stare at Septimus.

"How do you know that?" Edward asked.

The Welshman shrugged. "Oh, I stole a bottle of twenty-year-old whisky from the Colonel's room once. A single malt...

Glenfiddich as I recall. Definitely on the 25th floor."

No one replied.

"Heh! What's wrong with you lot? It was for a job, not just for fun," Septimus protested.

"Oh, that is alright then!" Edward said with a roll of his eyes at Tom.

Tom laughed and turned to smile at Mary, but then he noticed that she had her eyes tight shut. "What's up?" he asked her.

"I don't know if you have realised, but this metal box is moving," she said in a frightened voice.

"Poor old Mary. First time in a lift is it?" Septimus asked.

"It's alright Mary," Edward said, putting his arm around her. "I was scared the first time too. It's just a way of getting up through a building without using stairs."

"Well I don't much like it," she said.

The lift stopped, the doors opened and they emerged into a long corridor, this one thickly carpeted. They were at one end; doors lined each side of the corridor and at the far end was another set of lift doors.

"Middle door on the left, I believe," Septimus said, pointing down the corridor. They followed him to the door. He tried the handle. It was locked. He pulled out the keys that Teuber had given him and tried a few of them. The fifth key fitted the lock. With a soft click, the door opened. The room beyond was in darkness so Septimus felt around for a light switch. Once the light was on Tom recognised the room as the waiting room outside Thielmann's office.

"Look," he pointed to the emblem on the carpet. "That's the conduit. We can use it to escape back to the Institute," he suggested.

"No we can't," Edward said. "The Professor and his brothers

169

alone know how to activate it."

"Oh," Tom sighed. "Seemed too easy.

They trooped past the empty desks to the inner door. This too was locked, but succumbed to another key on the set they had been given.

"With all their sophisticated sensors and things, you'd think there'd at least be some sort of alarm or CCTV," Tom said, looking up and around the ceiling, but all he could see was the clock above the conduit. The room beyond looked just the same as it had when he and the Professor had visited, except that the map of Japan had been removed. Tom stared at the space where it had lain. "I think the manuscript was right here," he told the others.

Mary shook her head. "Well, it is not now," she said.

"Spread out: search the room," Septimus said.

They did so. Septimus and Mary went across to the large map table behind Thielmann's desk.

"My God, there are maps from all over the world here! Looks like they are even planning to invade Antarctica!" Septimus said as he and Mary lifted up maps and sorted through them. Meanwhile, Edward had gone across to the cabinet just behind the door. It had a metal shutter that was pulled down and locked. Edward retrieved a pen knife from his pocket and went about forcing the lock. In the centre of the room Tom searched the desk. The manuscript he was sure he had spotted was certainly not on the desk itself. He tried the drawers. One of them contained nothing more exciting than boxes of staples and pencils. In the other drawer, however, he spotted a cylindrical leather case. Could it be this easy? He took the case out of the drawer and shook out a brown-coloured, rolled up document. Completely absorbed, Tom unrolled it, instantly recognising the Latin hand-

170

writing that he had glimpsed before.

"Eureka! I've found it!" he announced, but no one replied.

As Tom looked up from the manuscript his smile froze. Standing in the doorway, revolver levelled at his chest, was Captain Redfeld himself!

CHAPTER SIXTEEN
ESCAPE

"Well now, Oakley, I am indeed a lucky man. I was so upset not to be able to continue our earlier conversation," Redfeld smirked. "And I also see that you have been so good to me, for you have even brought with you Miss Brown and Mr Mason. What joy. Three of you in my clutches. Indeed, as I believe you say in your world, it must be my birthday."

'He hasn't seen Edward,' Tom thought to himself. The lieutenant was still standing at the filing cabinet, which was just behind the open door, out of the captain's view.

"Now then, Thomas Oakley, before I deal with you and your companions, you will please give me that document. I do not believe it belongs to you."

"It doesn't belong to Thielmann either, or you, Redfeld!" Septimus said indignantly. "Indeed, I know to whom it belongs and I should take it back to the owner, who happens to be a lady of my acquaintance. Tom give it to me."

With the manuscript in his hands, Tom turned towards Septimus. As he did so, Redfeld took a step into the room, his revolver still pointing steadily at Tom's chest.

Edward lunged and brought his hand down in a karate chop action, which knocked the revolver out of Redfeld's hand. Edward seized hold of the captain's arm and tugged hard so that Redfeld came tumbling into the room and collapsed over the desk. As he struggled to regain his balance Edward followed up with a solid punch that connected with the Nazi's chin and sent him sprawling to the ground: out cold.

"Wow! Tom exclaimed. It had all happened in a blur of activity that left him feeling slightly short of breath. Mary was staring at Edward, admiration standing in her eyes.

Septimus was clapping. "Well, Edward, I must say I am very impressed," he mumbled.

Edward shrugged self-effacingly. "Oh, I used to box at school and then later, also for my regiment."

Right then, let us get out of here," Tom said, realising that where Redfeld was, other guards might follow.

"What about him?" Mary said, looking down at the comatose officer.

"Leave him. We just need to get away," Tom replied.

"Damn the Institute's rules! I wish we could just kill him and be done with it," Septimus commented.

"Well we can't," snapped Edward, "only in self-defence, which clearly it isn't while the man is unconscious."

They hurried out of the study, turned towards the elevator and piled in. Tom, who had rolled up the manuscript and tucked it into his overalls, pressed the button for the second floor and the lift rapidly descended.

"I don't like this mode of transport," said Mary, "it makes my stomach feel funny."

Exiting twenty or so floors down brought them out into a corridor that ran around the inner courtyard below them. Large windows looked down onto several life-size marble statues. "Those are the generals who conquered the world of the Twisted Reality in the name of Thielmann's Führer," Tom said with a grimace.

173

"Grim looking lot aren't they," Edward murmured.

On the opposite side of the corridor was a series of doors, some of which Tom remembered led to offices. One of the doors opened and Phil and Charlie emerged. Tom spotted a stairwell behind them; they must have climbed it from the basement.

"Well, have you got it then?" Charlie asked.

Tom smiled and gave him the thumbs up. He was about to reply when once again his smile froze. He had just spotted Redfeld stagger into view from the elevator, blood dripping from his nose. The Nazi captain was accompanied by two soldiers, both armed with submachine guns.

"You should have let me break his neck," Septimus muttered.

"Shoot: kill them all!" Redfeld bellowed an order.

"WALL!" Mary shouted at the same instant, turning to face Redfeld, her hands held upwards, the air already beginning to shimmer around them. "Run!" she shrieked as the first volley of automatic fire ricocheted off the barrier of frozen time she had created.

They all scampered around the corner of the corridor, which turned away at right angles from the courtyard and led towards the other side of the building. On their right, tall glass windows looked out over the city of London, but not the London they knew, for this was a city transformed for the purpose of industry and power. It was a frightening sight: all smoke and darkness with none of the bright city lights of their own world.

"Stop!" shouted Edward, pointing at three armed guards blocking the corridor ahead of them.

The Walkers skidded to a halt. Behind them the clatter of approaching boots heralded the imminent arrival of Redfeld and his guards.

"We're trapped!" Mary said. "And I can't hold the wall.

174

It's like something is stopping me!"

Tom reached out desperately for the flow of time but could not feel it. Then he recalled what Septimus had said about it being impossible to Walk inside the building. But perhaps there was a way.

"Everybody grab hold of me!" he instructed them.

"Tom, it's no use," Septimus said. "I told you before, we can't Walk in here."

"Not in here we can't, but how about out there?" Tom nodded towards the window.

"Are you insane? It's a fifty foot drop to the pavement below," Septimus said.

"Then I had better get my timing right," Tom said. "Hurry, Redfeld's goons are reloading!"

As they clustered around him he started moving. "Run at the window!" he yelled. "Keep your shoulders towards the glass and your heads down, and hang onto me!"

"Oh my God!" Charlie said, closing his eyes and shielding his face.

Clasped together like a rugby scrum, they hurtled towards the window and with an almighty crash of shattered glass hurtled through it. Then they were tumbling through the air, plunging down towards the concrete below.

Tom had mere seconds to react. Praying that he had been right, he reached out for the flow of time and this time, barely two metres from smashing onto the pavement, he felt it. Moments later, showered by fragments of broken glass, they all landed in a rhododendron bush. He had Walked them back across London to Hyde Park.

With a series of groans and curses, they picked themselves up and brushed off splinters of glass. Septimus shook his head.

175

"Thomas, You are the craziest boy I know, but even for you that was wild. Yet it worked and we are safe. Well done lad!"

Then he turned to Phil. "Well boyo, we have done it! All thanks to you of course."

Nodding, Phil pulled a large shard of glass out of his pocket along with a mobile phone. Throwing the glass into the bushes he rapidly tapped in a message. "Yes we made it, but that was a close call."

"A bit too close if you ask me," Charlie said, shivering. "I'll feel better when we're back in the Institute."

"Your coats are still in the truck," Phil said. "I've texted the driver. He should be on his way here if you want to wait for them." In the distance they could hear the wail of sirens approaching. "That'll be the security forces," he added.

"Best not hang about," Charlie suggested.

Septimus agreed. "Redfeld will be here in a moment I am sure. We will have to get our coats back another time."

"I hope Lieutenant Teuber and you don't get into trouble on our account," Mary said to Phil.

He laughed. "That rather goes with the territory I'm afraid. It is only a matter of time before one of us is caught, and you and I – as well as all my resistance chums – know exactly what that will mean. But it is a fight that needs to be fought."

"Maybe the Professor will allow us to do more to help you in your struggle."

Edward shook his head. "Afraid not, Mary. He is restricted in what he can do due to an arrangement the brothers made not to interfere in each other's worlds… though you could say the Professor has already done so by providing Phil with equipment," he added thoughtfully.

"So what!" Tom retorted. "It's an arrangement the Prof might

176

stick to, but Thielmann and in particular Redfeld, certainly do not!" he said indignantly.

"That may be so, but the Prof is in charge, so for now we have to do what he says. That means we can't do that much to help you, Phil," Septimus said, "though you have certainly helped us tonight."

"Well, what we did tonight was even more important perhaps than anyone will know," Phil said. "At least that manuscript should help you deal with this Titan threat. I certainly can't help much with that."

As he spoke, torchlights suddenly appeared near the Bayswater Road. They could hear a large dog barking and men running, their boots and equipment clattering.

"Well, time's up," Phil said. "Back to your world. I need to get away from these guys." He gave a final wave and was off south towards Kensington.

"Good luck!" Edward hissed after him.

"Good man that," Septimus said as he watched Phil vanish through the trees. A moment later a beam of torchlight flashed across them.

"You there. Stay where you are!" a voice rang out.

"Gather round Tom everyone," Edward said. "Right Tom, let's go!"

Walking within the Twisted Reality was different, as Tom had discovered last time he was here. Everything, including the clock, was back to front. Even more difficult was Walking from one reality to another and only very strong Walkers were able to do it. However, Tom had eventually discovered that although the map uppermost in his mind was of the reality he was currently in, a map of the opposing reality, which in this case was his own world, lay hidden beneath it. Once he had discovered

177

this, he found he was able to bypass the first map and focus on the second.

So, as the soldiers came into view, Tom, with the others holding onto him, Walked them between the realities, appearing in Hyde Park a moment later, but this was Hyde Park in his London, still at night, but with the bright lights of the metropolis all around them.

"We're back home," he said with relief.

CHAPTER SEVENTEEN
STAR IRON

A week later they were once more in the Professor's study. The manuscript was unrolled on the desk and a large magnifying glass on an extending stand was pulled across it. The Professor was staring intently at the lines of Latin text. As Tom walked in he saw Rolf Lapace sitting there, so he had clearly been invited too, but from the distrustful expressions on the faces of Tom's companions, none of them was particularly keen to see Septimus' former partner present at the meeting.

"So then, Prof, have you worked out what to do about the Titans yet?" Septimus asked.

Neoptolemas looked up and shook his head.

"Not entirely. But I now know that Knossos had done more than theorise. He had in fact created a prototype device designed to banish the Titans out of our reality forever."

"So this Artefact Thielmann wanted us to go and fetch was indeed built by Knossos?" Edward asked.

The Prof nodded.

"Yes, it is a device constructed from a rare metal found only in meteors that leave behind debris on the Earth's surface. *'Star Iron'* Knossos calls it. It is actually an alloy of several elements fused together by the intense heat created when meteors crash to Earth. It may originally have been formed in the hearts of collapsing stars where powerful gravitational fields distort the normal laws of physics and create peculiar elements."

"So, what can it do?" Mary asked.

"To put it in simple terms, it can create inter-dimensional conduits or portals to other realities."

"That's you putting it in simple terms is it?" Mary asked.

The Professor smiled. "I imagine it did sound confusing."

"You can say that again," Edward said.

"Well, basically it opens doors to other universes. It will then close the door permanently banishing these Titans forever."

"What about the people in these other universes? There could be worlds there. We can't just send these creatures through your magic door into a universe where they could rampage through new worlds."

"No, Edward, that would indeed be wrong. I'm talking here of freshly created pocket universes: new worlds if you like, with no civilisations, no cities, no people in fact. There will be the raw building blocks of the universe. The Titans will be able to create their own world, but they will never be able to return to ours."

Lapace coughed. "I am wondering why I am here, fascinating though all this is, of course."

"You are here because I need information from you: and do not worry, you will be paid," the Professor said.

"Well, that's all right then." Lapace smiled.

"I am hoping that you might have seen the Artefact without realising what it was, Mr Lapace. Is that possible?"

"Well, that depends. Do we know what it looks like?"

The Professor tapped the manuscript. "Yes, thanks to this we now do. The Artefact is triangular, about this wide," he held up his hands and spread them about a foot apart, "and this deep," he repeated the movement. "It would be of metallic appearance and gold in colour. Each limb is twisted slightly, relevant to the adjacent limbs: a little bit like an Escher drawing if you like. There are engravings in Greek down each limb."

The Professor looked at both Lapace and Septimus.

"So then do you recognise it and do you know where it is?"

Septimus shook his head. "I'm afraid not. I mean, the Count did own various pieces of scientific equipment but I cannot quite recall anything like that."

Lapace was smiling.

"Get ready to transfer the money, Prof, because I know exactly where the device is."

The Professor waved at Mr Phelps, who stood ready just inside the door with a tablet in his hands. He tapped on the screen, waited a moment then nodded back at the old man.

"So then, Mr Lapace," the Professor said, "two thousand pounds has just been transferred to your account. So, tell me where it is."

Lapace pulled out his phone and checked it. He then grunted and pushed the phone away.

"Where is it?" the Professor demanded, rapping the desk with his knuckles and glaring at Lapace.

"Hold your horses, Prof, I'm just about to tell you. It was once in the Count's study. I believe it was generally hidden away out of sight and under lock and key as it was an unusual artefact, which explains why Septimus did not see it. When the Count was alive I only saw it once. In fact he was closing a chest and locking it. I caught a glimpse of this triangular object. I didn't think much to it and would never have recalled it except that shortly afterwards the Count died and Julia took a fancy to the item – not only did it look as if it were made of gold, but I imagine it reminded her of her father. It was for this reason that she moved it from the Count's study to... ahem, a more personal location."

The Professor coughed. "Well, what location would that be Mr Lapace?"

Rolf Lapace looked across at Septimus and winked. "As you will no doubt swear," he said, "I am, of course, the total gentleman and as such I would never reveal how I came by this information, but I can tell you that in April 1510, the item you seek was in Julia's bedroom."

Septimus glowered and for the next couple of minutes there was an embarrassed silence. Then the Professor cleared his throat.

"Yes, well... so we now know where the Artefact will most likely be found. So then," he looked around at Tom and his friends, "will you go back to 1510 and retrieve it?"

Tom could see that Septimus was not at all happy with this plan. The Welshman had crossed his arms and was shaking his head.

"Count me out, Professor. I won't steal from Julia," he said stubbornly. "Nor will I enter her bedroom without an invitation!"

"You are still a sentimental old fool my friend, aren't you?" Lapace taunted him.

"You were her lover, Rolf, how could you steal from her? Call yourself a gentleman? You don't know the meaning of the word."

Lapace shrugged. "Julia was sweet, but it was work."

Septimus jumped to his feet and glared at Rolf. "For you perhaps. But Julia was always more than work to me." He turned to look across at the old man behind the desk. "Professor, I'm sorry, but I am going to have to ask that you do not make any attempt to retrieve the Artefact until I give the go-ahead."

Looking startled by this request, the Professor frowned. "Mr Mason, you are aware how urgent this matter is?"

Septimus nodded. "Yes I am aware. Just give me twenty-four hours. That is all I ask."

The old man considered this for a moment. Finally he nodded his head. "I have to assume your request is for a very good reason. Very well, Mr Mason, I will give you twenty-four hours, but not a minute longer."

"Thank you, Professor. I may not even be that long," Septimus said.

Rolf Lapace laughed. "You can't be serious! You are going to warn her aren't you? You are going to go and talk to Julia?"

"Yes, I'm going to ask her if she will give us the Artefact. I'm not going to lie to her, nor will I steal from her."

"Before you leave," the Professor said, "you'd best go and see Mrs Mackay."

"Yes, Prof. I'm on my way." Septimus strode to the door and hurried out, closing it behind him.

Lapace sniffed. "You should let me go get that gold triangle for you right now, Professor. Once that damned romantic Welsh fool has his little chat with Julia there's no telling what might happen."

The Professor shook his head, his lips set in a thin line. "Mr Mason may be many things, Mr Lapace, but he is not a fool. I have trusted him thus far and now he has called on yet a little more of that trust."

Lapace sighed and got to his feet. "I have to confess I was hoping for a job there," he said, with a sideways wink at Tom.

"Sorry to disappoint you, Mr Lapace," the Professor said with a tight smile, "but I have no further need of your services."

"Well, you have my number should you change your mind," Lapace said, and then he too was gone.

The Professor looked around at Tom and his friends then pulled the map of Italy over his desk. "You might want to familiarise yourselves with the topography," he said.

They crowded round him. After a few minutes, Tom felt the unmistakeable shift in the flow of time and knew that Septimus, having obtained a set of 16th Century clothes from the costume department, was now Walking.

"Well, I guess I might as well go home," Tom said, moving back from the desk. He was about to leave the room when the study door swung open and crashed back against the wall with a bang. Rogers, one of the I.T. team whose home was the basement level of the Institute, burst into the room.

"Sorry to interrupt, sir," the young man gasped, "but we have a problem."

"What is it?" Edward asked.

"It's about Mr Mason."

"He has just left."

Rogers nodded his head. "Yes, I know. It's where he went from here that has caused the problem."

"What problem?" Edward asked.

"Well, it appears that Mr Mason has created a fixed time point in a rather public way," the young man said, walking around the Professor's desk towards the rear of the study where, on one side of the fireplace a widescreen TV was fixed to the wall. In front of it was a set of easy chairs positioned for watching the telly, not that the Professor watched much, but once in a while some story related to historical events came on the news. Septimus had joked that it was also useful to check on the Test Match score, though for himself the Rugby Internationals were a lot more interesting than cricket.

"If you don't mind, Professor?" Rogers said, reaching for the remote.

"No, of course. Switch it on Mr Rogers," Neoptolemas said.

The screen came on to one of the news channels. The boffin flicked across to another one. It was an article about a newly discovered painting. Some art expert was talking enthusiastically in Italian. The translation scrolling across the bottom of the page read: *'Previously unknown Botticelli discovered in Milan. Experts confirm the brush styles and techniques match the master painter. Thought now to be his last painting – possibly only weeks before the painter died. Art experts are excited and speculating about the meaning of the painting they are calling 'The Invitation.''*

Now the painting itself was being shown. On it were two figures in Renaissance dress: a man and a woman. The man was clearly Septimus. The woman Tom did not recognise, but she was sitting down and holding on her lap a triangular device, which from earlier descriptions could only be the missing Artefact. Tom realised the woman must be Julia. She certainly was beautiful. Septimus was standing nearer the artist and holding an unrolled parchment. On it was written the word 'Invitatio', which Tom guessed was Latin. It was followed by a date: the fourteenth day of April 1510 A.D. The reporter went on to say that a heraldic device on the wall above the lady confirmed that she was the Countess of Rivoli. What was particularly exciting, he said, was that according to historic records, the Countess owned a Palazzo in Turin which was destroyed by fire on the fifteenth of April 1510. He concluded with the statement that the Countess and her mysterious companion were never seen again and the discovery of the Botticelli masterpiece was nothing short of a miracle.

"What! Is this new information?" Edward asked. "I mean, we would surely know if Julia had died in a fire?"

The Professor frowned. "I have certainly never heard anything about the Palazzo burning down." He turned to Rogers, "What do the sources say?"

"I'll just check, sir. The boffin tapped at his tablet then nodded. "Our internal sources stored here in Temporal Shift Resistant Vaults do not mention any fire at that date, Professor. However, all sources out in the world that refer to the history of Turin at that time do contain a reference to the fire. Because we maintain records here in such a way that they are generally immune to changes in the timeline we can track when a change occurs. So it does appear that an alteration to time has occurred.

"What did he just say?" Tom asked the Professor.

"He said that something happened that changed history in all the books and records that exist in all the libraries and museums in the world, except those we store here in special vaults that prevent them from being affected by a change in the past," the Professor said, his expression grim.

"So what are we saying here?" Charlie asked. "Are we saying that Septimus went back in time, arranged for this artist to paint him and Julia in such a way that anyone seeing the painting would know that the Artefact had to be in the Palazzo on that particular day, and then, on the following day, he started a fire? Why? For what possible reason would he do such a thing?"

As they were all taking in the remarkable image and its significance, the boffin's mobile rang.

"Excuse me sir. I need to get this," the young man said and then answered his phone. He spoke briefly, listened to the reply, grunted and then rang off.

"Sir, that call was confirmation of what I already suspected.

186

The expert being interviewed on TV is a certain Giovani Neo, who lives in Florence. He is an arts contact of Septimus Mason, known to us as a collector who would occasionally purchase Mr Mason's stolen artefacts, back in the days when—"

"Yes, yes, Mr Rogers," the Professor interrupted impatiently. "We are aware of Mr Mason's murky past. What about this Giovani Neo?"

"He is being very quiet about this, sir. However, it seems that Mr Mason arranged for this portrait to be painted and agreed with Botticelli that it would never be shown, but was to be placed in the safe keeping of a monastery near Bologna. We must assume it has been there ever since, until a month ago, when it was sent to this Neo. Apparently it was accompanied with instructions that he should confirm its provenance, but keep quiet about it until today's date and time. Accordingly, the Italian invited in reporters and made the press release fifteen minutes ago."

"Provenance?" asked Mary.

"Its authenticity," Rogers said, "that is, confirming that it really is a Botticelli and the date it was painted."

"Fifteen minutes ago is exactly when Mr Mason was leaving here," the Professor commented.

"He must have wanted to make sure we did not hear about this until he had got away," Mary observed.

The Professor nodded.

"Indeed, *had* the announcement been made and Mr Rogers and his department spotted Mr Mason in the painting and alerted me whilst he was still sitting here we could have had a paradox on our hands."

Tom was finding he understood these problems more and more.

"You mean it might have meant we stopped him leaving in the first place so that he could never have travelled back and had the painting made. But then if the painting was not made we would never have stopped him leaving meaning he would have been free to go back and make the painting ..." Tom trailed off realising that they were all staring at him.

"You've been around the Prof too long Tom. You are starting to sound like him."

Tom laughed.

"Any way, it seems he has sent us some kind of an elaborate message," Edward said, "but why?"

Tom too was puzzled. "But what does it all mean, Professor? Is Septimus saying he wants us to go back to the Palazzo on that date to get the Artefact?"

"More than that, Thomas. By putting the date on the painting, Mr Mason has established without question that the triangular device was there on that day."

"Does that matter?" Charlie asked.

"Yes," Edward said, glancing at the Professor, "it does."

"Why?"

"Well for one thing we can't now go back before the fourteenth day of April, 1510 and just pinch it. If we did, then it would not be there to be painted on that day. But it was, as is clearly shown. Were we to remove it, that would create a paradox and that gets so confusing and complicated that no one is safe."

"Quite correct, Lieutenant," the Professor said. "You are getting very good at understanding these issues. And yes, I believe that Septimus Mason is intending this as an invitation for ourselves, hence the Latin word 'Invitatio'. For reasons known only to himself he has forced our hand and obliged us to go to him on this particular date and none other."

He looked round at each of them in turn and pressed his hands together. "Well, gentlemen and lady, I suggest you change your clothes into something more in keeping with Renaissance fashion and visit Italy."

CHAPTER EIGHTEEN
JULIA

The Palazzo or Palace that the Counts and Countesses of Rivoli maintained in Turin was slightly away from the centre of the city in a rather elegant quarter. It was an impressive gothic structure with three stories. The lower story was built in stone whilst the upper two were made of brick, the top one crenelated. Tall arched windows populated every face and at one end of the building a bell tower with a clock stretched skyward and was twice the height of the main building.

Tom and his three companions had materialised outside the palace in a piazza or square, which was lined with similar grandiose buildings and fortunately was deserted. Above them the skies were just beginning to darken after what must have been a very pleasant spring day, for the lingering heat of the sun could still be felt in the early evening air.

"These tights are itchy!" Charlie complained, as he fiddled with his waistline. Like Tom and Edward he was wearing what Mrs Mackay had called 'hose' but which in Tom's view looked like a ballet dancer's tights. Over these they each had a pair of breeches or shorts, which stretched only as far as their knees. On their upper bodies they wore what seemed an excessively frilly white shirt with a high collar, and over it a padded jacket that Mrs Mackay had called a 'doublet'. Except for the shirts, all these items were brightly coloured: Charlie in blue, Edward in green and Tom mostly in red, which made him feel very self-conscious. Mary, meanwhile, looked elegant in a high-waisted gown of lilac with a tight bodice, a full-length skirt and long, wide sleeves.

"You look beautiful, Mary," Edward said.

"Thank you Edward, but I don't much like all the rolls of cloth in these sleeves. Makes it hard to wave your arms about," she replied.

"I don't believe a 16th Century Italian lady would do much waving of arms," he smiled.

Mary sniffed. "Maybe, but I do – you may have noticed."

This was true. Whenever Mary created her walls of frozen time she used a lot of arm movement.

"Well, maybe you can roll your sleeves up or something," Charlie said, still trying to adjust his hose.

"So, when do we go in?" Mary asked.

"The Professor suggested we wait until we see the artist, Sandro Botticelli, leave the Palazzo. We don't want to mess up Septimus' message to us," Edward replied. "Ah, see now, looks like we're right on time…"

The doors to the Palazzo swung open and a horse and cart emerged. The grey-haired, middle-aged man driving the cart leaned across and said something to the servant who had opened the doors and then the cart moved out onto the street. As it went past the four Walkers the man glanced at them briefly and then turned his attention to the road ahead. Tom noticed that in the back of the cart was a large, flat rectangular shape wrapped in a white sheet, together with an easel, several cases and an artist's palette covered in smears of various colours. Then man, horse, cart and what Tom assumed was the Invitatio painting rounded

191

the bend in the street and were lost from view.

"That's our artist, I guess," Tom said.

Edward nodded. "Certainly looks like the portrait of Botticelli I have seen. Right then, come on."

They followed him across the road to the Palazzo and Edward knocked on the door. After a moment it opened a crack and the servant peeped out. He was now carrying a lantern, which he held up to Edward, who spoke some words in Italian. The door opened wider. The servant looked them over once and then, gesturing that they should follow him, strode ahead.

"What did you say?" Tom whispered.

"I told him that we had an invitation from the Countess and her companion to call upon them this evening. If you think about it, that's exactly what we do have."

Tom considered this a moment and then smiled. "I see your point."

They were led through an archway and into a paved court-yard that lay at the centre of the palace. Opposite them were two huge doors. Lanterns hung on either side, their flickering light attracting a flurry of moths. It was to here that the servant now took them. The doors opened up onto an impressive entrance hall paved with black and white tiles, a bit like a huge chess board. By the light of an enormous chandelier full of lighted candles Tom could see that all the walls were covered with murals; decorative paintings that mostly depicted biblical scenes. One appeared to be of Jonah and the Whale; another of Daniel in the Lion's Den, and a third of the People of Israel being led by Moses through the Red Sea. Still others depicted more mythological subjects: Greek and Roman gods, sea creatures and battles. Glancing up at them, Tom decided not to look too closely for any images of Titans.

From the hallway a curving stone staircase ascended to a landing area, which it appeared led off to various state rooms. The servant paused at a set of gilded doors, knocked and then entered. Tom and his friends followed.

There, sitting on a chair looking exactly as she did in the painting, was the lady they had all heard so much about, the Countess di Rivoli: Julia. Standing, leaning on a mantelpiece over a low fire, was a very elegantly dressed Septimus, his doublet made of dark red velvet and his white shirt even frillier than theirs. They all entered and lined up in front of the Countess. Uncertain of how to behave, Tom thought it best to bow. Beside him Mary bobbed a curtsey.

The Countess inclined her head in response but remained silent. Septimus studied them all quite intently for a moment before speaking.

"Well now, it's been a good ten minutes since the artist left. What took you so long?" he said. Then he laughed and moved over to them. He gave Tom a huge bear hug, planted a wet kiss on Mary's cheek, and then grasped both men by the hands.

"I have missed you, Tom boyo. All of you in fact," he said.

"Steady on, old chap," Edward said. "It's not been two hours since you left the Professor's study!"

Septimus was shaking his head. "Not for me."

"What do you mean?" Charlie asked.

"Guys, I have been here in Turin for the last nine months!"

"What? Why?"

The Welshman was about to answer Charlie's question, but glancing at Julia, Edward spoke first. "I imagine you would prefer we discussed this elsewhere, Septimus."

"Discussed what?" Julia asked in strongly accented but perfectly clear English. "You perhaps refer to Institute affairs? If so

193

you can speak freely."

"You know?" Tom asked.

"I know everything about all of you, Thomas Oakley."

"Septimus, it would have been wise—" Edward started to say, but the Welshman interrupted him.

"What? What would have been wise? To lie to Julia like Lapace did? I told you I would not. Never again. I have told her everything."

"*Everything?*" Mary asked him, but it was Julia who replied.

"Yes, Miss Brown. For example, I know that you were rescued from a fire that will not happen for one hundred and fifty years and will destroy the heart of the great city of London. I know that Edward here was a soldier in battle in the wilds of distant Africa and I know that Charlie was also rescued when about to drown on a ship that can sail under the seas. I know that you can all transcend the bounds of time."

Edward's eyebrows shot up in surprise. "You seem to have accepted it all rather easily."

Septimus laughed. "Who said anything about it having been easy? Her father, Filippo, brought Julia up to be curious and to ask questions. She is literally one of the first children of the Renaissance. Even so, it took some persuading and not a little proof before she accepted what I told her. I did say I have been here nine months."

"It's amazing how persuaded a person can be when she sees a man disappear and reappear thirty feet away!" Julia said. "When you see that happen you tend to accept everything else at face value and seeing you all here today, exactly as Septimus described you, just reinforces what I had already accepted." Suddenly she trilled with laughter. "You all look very uncomfortable. There is no need to stand on ceremony with me, please sit down." She gestured to the various brocaded seats dotted around the room.

"Thank you, Countess," Edward gave a little bow.

"And you may call me Julia," she added with a smile.

Warming to her, Tom could see why his Welsh friend had fallen so deeply in love with her. "So then, Septimus, I imagine you have a story to tell," Tom said, moving to a chair and sitting down.

"Stories are best when accompanying dinner I always think," Julia said before Septimus could reply. Rising gracefully from her chair, she walked to where a cord dangled from a nearby wall and gave it a tug. Somewhere far away in the house a bell could be heard ringing. A moment later the doors swung open and a manservant stood there.

"Ah, Alfonso. We will eat at once," the Countess said.

"Un momento, Contessa." The servant bowed and retired. Julia then led Tom and his friends through the double doors and along a corridor into a dining chamber. Brightly lit by numerous candelabra, the room was mostly taken up by a long oaken table surrounded by high-backed chairs. The table was laid with various plates, wine goblets and items of silver cutlery.

As they took their places, a succession of servants carried in silver trays bearing bowls of soup, freshly baked bread and platters of roasted meats. Realising how hungry he was Tom proceeded to devour everything that was placed in front of him, but he avoided the wine which was served to the others. Instead he drank something that Septimus called 'small beer'. It tasted a little like the lager shandy Tom's father had let him try at Christmas time.

Whilst they were eating, Septimus took a sip of wine and started talking. "When I got here I first had some work to do

195

simply to get an audience with Julia. As you know, she believed I had stolen the manuscript from her and wanted nothing to do with me."

"But it wasn't you. It was Rolf Lapace," Charlie said.

Julia nodded. "Yes, I know that now."

"Then I had to convince her of the importance of the Artefact and how I needed to retrieve it," Septimus continued. "That required me to explain what it was, what it could do and so on. In the end the entire story of what we are and what we can do came out and eventually..." he paused and directed a loving smile at Julia, "...she agreed to help us."

"My father spent years working on that triangle and making notes. I thought it was just a pretty ornament he had made..." Julia's voice broke on a sob. "I still miss him so dearly. Now I find that the work he did is vitally important and the Artefact could make a real difference to the world and... well, what daughter would not want her father's legacy to have meaning?"

"Your father must have been a remarkable man," Mary said.

"He was a genius," Julia smiled.

"So once Julia had agreed to give you the Artefact, Septimus, why did you not simply come back to the Institute?" Tom asked.

"Ah, well. There lies the problem. I discovered that whilst I was holding the triangle, I could not Walk. In fact I cannot Walk more than a few yards or moments in time when I am within several hundred yards of it. It must be something to do with how the device works. It almost seems to act like an anchor. I am hoping that you will be able to Walk with it, Tom. You are so much stronger than the rest of us."

A thought occurred to Tom. "So, why not move a greater distance away from Turin and try to Walk from there?"

"Well yes, that thought did occur to me, but if I'd succeeded that would have left the Artefact and Julia here in Turin."

Charlie scratched his head. "So? It would only have taken you an hour or so to come back to the Institute and fetch Tom."

"True, but even that would have been too long. You see, soon after I had tried to Walk away I became aware that the Palazzo was being watched. There have been two attacks on it in the last month and Julia's agents around the city have discovered that someone is hiring hit-men, perhaps with a view to another attack very soon. I am fairly sure they are after the Artefact and I think I know who is behind the attacks. Clearly I could not risk leaving it even for a moment. So far the palace guard has been able to fight off the attackers, but the last time several of Julia's men were wounded and apart from half-a-dozen servants, she now has only two guards left who are able to fight."

Julia nodded her head. "This is so, and I am determined that no enemy takes hold of my father's golden triangle. I have made secret preparations to evacuate Turin and have bought a small town house in the city of Vienna. If you and your friends had not come, Tom, our plan was to leave for Austria with the Artefact first thing tomorrow."

"So you sent us the message by way of the painting to get us here?" Edward asked.

Septimus nodded. "It was all I could think of and it took some organising I can tell you. It had to be something that would attract the attention of the media and so would get back to you. Fortunately, I have friends from when I was here before: Sandro Botticelli for one and Giovani Neo for another. He, incidentally, is a Walker."

"Well of course; we'd gathered that," Edward said. "You realise you have changed history? The Institute is not best pleased."

Septimus shrugged, "It was a risk I had to take. They will be

197

even less pleased if we don't get rid of the Titans!"

At that moment their conversation was disturbed by shouting from outside the Palazzo, followed a few seconds later by the crash of broken glass from one of the downstairs rooms. The door to the dining chamber opened suddenly and a man dressed in armour stood in the doorway.

"Contessa, we are under attack once more! We must get you away from here."

"A moment, Riccio," she said, turning to Septimus. "I must take the Artefact!" Without another word she strode past the guard and out of the door.

They all leapt to their feet and followed her. Julia was already halfway across the landing when Tom spotted three men charging up the stairwell towards her. One had a cumbersome-looking firearm of some sort – an early musket maybe. The other two were armed with swords. The gunman halted, rested his musket on the bannister, took careful aim at Julia then touched the top of his weapon with what looked like a length of smoking string. There was a huge bang. Smoke poured out of the barrel and seemed to envelope Julia. Yet, as the gunman had fumbled with the fuse, Mary had acted fast. Her sleeves shoved back to her elbows, she stood with her arms raised. The musket ball sped towards Julia and smacked into the shimmering wall that had appeared around her, leaving her unhurt.

The two swordsmen charged up the stairs. Julia's guard engaged one of them whilst Charlie and Edward headed for the other. The swordsmen were soon joined by the gunman who, now using the musket as a club, was chasing after Charlie. The sailor was leading him a merry run around, phasing in and out of time and finally appearing behind him to land a kick to the back of his knees. As the man's legs gave way Charlie shouted up to Tom and Septimus.

"Get the Artefact!"

Tom ran with Julia and Septimus into what appeared to be a bed chamber. Without pausing, Julia headed to another door leading off it. Flinging it open she stopped dead in the doorway, let out a cry of alarm and backed away.

Tom and Septimus stared past her into the small, windowless room that lay beyond. By the light of a single flickering candle they saw a man standing before a low table. He was bent over it, examining an object that stood on its polished surface. It was a triangle, its gold-coloured metal glinting in the candlelight.

It could only be the Artefact... and the man was none other than the Custodian!

CHAPTER NINETEEN
THE CAPTAIN'S FEARS

"So you are the one behind the attacks!" Septimus said. "No doubt designed to give you cover so you could seize the Artefact? Whose side are you on? Apparently not ours!"

The Custodian did not respond. Rather, he picked up the Artefact, brought it close to his eyes and studied it carefully. He was swathed in a long, black, hooded cloak, but beneath it Tom spotted the grey suit the man always wore. Julia was staring at him, her eyes wide with shock.

"Are you listening to me, Custodian?" Septimus said, raising his voice. "I don't think the Professor will react positively to these attacks, do you?"

Now the Custodian looked up at them. "Attacks?" he said, vaguely.

"That triangle belongs to me," Julia insisted. "Give it to me!" Moving into the small room she thrust out her hand and stamped her foot, her anger outweighing her fear.

The Custodian regarded her in silence for a moment then passed the Artefact over. "Take it. I have found what I needed to know," he said. Without another word, he simply vanished.

Julia gawped at the space where the Custodian had stood. "Blessed Virgin, he was one of you as well?"

"Not exactly," Tom replied, wondering what it was the

Custodian had needed to know.

Shaking her head in astonishment, Julia turned and passed the triangle to Septimus. "There you are. Take it and use it well... my love," she added softly.

Grasping the triangle, Septimus gazed into her eyes and nodded. He looked as if he was about to say something, but just then Mary, Charlie and Edward rushed into the bed chamber.

"We all need to get out of here. Someone has started a fire in the kitchens. There is a lot of smoke coming up the stairs. Those hired thugs are running mind you," Charlie said breathlessly. "We gave them a bloody nose alright and we've beaten them off, but I don't think we can put out the fire."

A sudden thought occurred to Tom. "Maybe we are not meant to," he said, glancing around at his companions.

"What do you mean?" Julia asked him and Tom hesitated. Seeing his discomfort Edward stepped in.

"Countess, I'm sorry, but history records that this very night there was a fire here that destroyed the Palazzo. Neither you nor Septimus were ever seen again. It was assumed that you died in the fire. Don't you see? It is the perfect cover. You can vanish and start a new life and the Custodian or whoever is behind this will not know about you surviving."

Julia's face went pale. "But my family's home... all my things..."

"...will be lost and I am sorry, but it comes down to what is more important: the Palazzo or your life?"

Julia nodded. "So be it," she said weakly, glancing round at her beautiful home, tears coming to her eyes. Septimus squeezed her shoulder and then turned to Tom and passed him the Artefact.

"Right, Tom," he said. You take this back to the Professor.

Tell him I will join you all soon."

Tom took the golden triangle from Septimus. It felt cold and heavy in his hands. Then he realised what his friend had said and that Septimus was not coming with them.

"Join us soon? Why, where are you going?"

"To Austria. As soon as you have taken the Artefact away from here I will again be able to Walk. I will take Julia to her new house in Vienna and make sure she is safe under a new name before I return to the Institute."

"Alright, but I don't know if I can. If you can't Walk anywhere near the triangle, maybe I can't either."

"That is true, but you are much more powerful than I am. You are a Potentate, remember?"

Tom shrugged. "Maybe."

"Well, boyo, there is only one way to find out," Septimus grinned.

Tom nodded. "Very well. We'd best say our goodbyes in case this works. Good luck, Julia. I am glad to have met you." He gestured to Edward, Charlie and Mary, who chorused their goodbyes then gathered around Tom.

As usual he reached out for the Flow of Time, imagined the image of his clock and the map in his mind and tried to Walk. Usually the sense of movement was immediate, but this time it was like a slow motion replay of an athlete making a long jump. It was as if he was trying to move them all through treacle. The Artefact felt suddenly incredibly heavy and he had to fight to keep hold of it. He gritted his teeth and threw all his energy into the effort and then, at last, he was away. Released from the anchoring effect, he hurtled them forward to the present day and popped out of the void in front of Mr Phelps. It was then that the fatigue hit him and he slumped down in a chair in Phelps' office, gasping for breath. Even Mr Phelps, who had looked as if he were ready to scold them all, bit his lip and held back his tirade.

"Are you… alright Mr Oakley?" he asked.

Tom, still catching his breath, nodded. "Yes… I am now. It was just… exhausting."

"So you have the Artefact, Thomas?" the Professor asked from the door to his study.

Tom nodded.

"Good, you have done very well."

"Sir, there is something we need to make known to you concerning your brother… and also about Septimus," Tom began, but the Professor held up his hand.

"You need to rest, Thomas. Edward can fill me in. Change your clothes then go home and get some sleep. We will study the Artefact and be in touch."

Too tired to argue, Tom did as he was told and went home.

An hour or two later, sitting at table eating the evening meal with his mum, dad and sister, Emma, Tom found himself enjoying the family's mundane conversation, mostly what was going to happen next in his mother's favourite soap. So dramatic were his adventures that he sometimes found relief in plain, ordinary life; it helped him keep a perspective. Wishing a distraction from the concerns on his mind he agreed to watch a movie with his father before going to bed. The events of the last two days had taken their toll and when the film ended he was so tired he could hardly drag himself up the stairs. So it was that he was stifling a yawn as he opened his bedroom door. What he saw then made him stop and stare, for there, sitting on his bed, was Captain Redfeld!

Tom found that his gaze went automatically to the officer's hands.

He was relieved to see that the captain was not armed.

"Do not be alarmed, Oakley, I am not there with you in your bedroom, I'm in the projection room," the captain said, as if reading his thoughts.

Tom let out the breath he had been holding back. Now that he studied the captain further he could see that this was in fact a hologram; a projection of the Redfeld's image. If you knew what to look for there was something almost cinematic about his appearance: like an image being thrown onto a screen. It was a 3D image, but an image nonetheless.

"I'm rather glad to hear that," Tom mumbled, entering the room and shutting the door. "So then, Redfeld, are you and the Colonel planning something you wish to tell me about?"

Redfeld waved a hand. "Oh, I am not here to pass on a message from Colonel Thielmann. In fact the Colonel knows nothing about this communication. If he did he would be... unhappy."

"Interesting, so what are you up to?" Tom asked crossing the room and sitting down on the chair at his desk. "Last I heard you wanted me dead, so why the chat now?"

"The Colonel has discovered the theft of the Codex. Needless to say, he is angry with you all, although that anger is to an extent reduced by the news that the Artefact has been retrieved."

Tom smirked. "Yes, thanks to us, despite the fact that the Custodian tried to steal it by organising an attack on the Palazzo while we were there."

"The Custodian?" Redfeld asked in surprise.

Tom gawped. "You are saying it was not the Custodian?"

"Never mind," Redfeld said, ignoring the question. "Whatever happened it is retrieved... alas."

Tom frowned. "Wait a mo. What do you mean 'alas'? I thought Thielmann would be happy we got the device."

Redfeld nodded. "He is. I am not!"

Tom laughed and scrambled for a notepad and a pen and then held them up like a reporter making notes on a story.

"Oh really? Sounds like a nice bit of gossip here. I must make a note of it. Trouble with the master race is there?"

Redfeld scowled at him. "If you really want to know, there are aspects of this Artefact I am not happy about. Aspects that I feel put both our worlds in jeopardy. I believe that the Custodian, the Colonel... and the Professor for that matter, are not telling us the full truth."

The image of the three brothers talking in the Professor's study flashed into Tom's mind and he frowned, but said nothing.

"Ah, I see from your expression that you too have concerns, Oakley."

"No," Tom shook his head. "The Professor always acts for the best and I trust him." Even to his own ears this sounded hollow and unconvincing.

Redfeld gave a mocking laugh. "That old man will do what he feels is best for the preservation of his precious timelines. That does not mean it is necessarily best for you, young man. A time always comes when you, Thomas Oakley, have to ask yourself this question: are you fighting on the right side?"

Tom glared at him. "You really think I can believe you came here out of some concern for my safety? We both know that given half a chance you would kill me."

"Perhaps, but at least I am honest about it."

Tom yawned. "Look, I need to sleep. Just tell me what you've come here to say."

"There are two aspects of the manuscript that you need to know about. Neoptolemas understands the first, but does not fully comprehend the second. Nor will he until he has fully deciphered what is written."

205

"Go on, I am listening."

"Well, the reason the Colonel is so keen on getting hold of the Artefact is that by using it, a Potentate can banish Titans permanently into a pocket universe of their own."

"I think we understood that already," Tom said in a tired voice.

"Maybe. But did you understand that the temporal power needed to drive the device would consume the Potentate who used it?"

Tom felt his heart thumping in his chest. "What?"

Redfeld's image nodded at him. "Oh yes, indeed. And only you are a powerful enough Potentate to drive that Artefact. That is why the Colonel wanted it found. He would not have any qualms if the Titan problem was solved and you died at the same time. He knows that you are coming to the height of your powers when you will be more powerful than he is. That is the last thing he wants. Oh yes, make no mistake about it. He wants you obliterated before that can happen. If you use the Artefact to banish the Titans, Thomas Oakley will no longer exist!"

Tom stared at him. "The Professor wouldn't ask that of me..." he mumbled, faltering as the word Sacrifice came flooding back into his mind.

"Are you certain of that, Oakley?"

"You... you said there is a second aspect to the manuscript," Tom said hurriedly. "What is it?"

Now it was Redfeld who seemed worried. He glanced behind him at the unseen door to the projection room before replying.

"The other is that the manuscript contains notes added by the Conti di Rivoli. In these notations the Count reveals knowledge of The Event. Moreover, he developed a theory of how the three realities could be reunited, thus undoing The Event."

"Really? Is that possible?"

Redfeld again checked behind him. "The Custodian came to see the Colonel," he said quietly. "He seemed attracted by the idea."

"I am not surprised by that. The Custodian likes balance and order. If he could undo what happened during The Event I think he would be happy. But why are you telling me this?"

"I am concerned that the brothers might try out this plan for unification."

Tom shook his head. "The Custodian would. The Professor might even do it if he felt the world would be better for it. But, the Colonel... what would he gain?"

"The Colonel's main aim is to gain power. Can you imagine the feeling of power he would get if he could change reality? If he believes he could mould the result into a world he can control, I think he would do it for a chance of that... in fact I am certain he would."

Tom frowned, "Even if that was the case, Redfeld, I ask again, why are you telling me this?"

"I like my world, Thomas Oakley. I like the Reich my people have made and the domination we wield here. I enjoy the powers I have and the chance to use them. I do not wish my own reality to be lost. So... I implore you: destroy both the manuscript and the Artefact – for your own sake and for the sake of our realities. You surely don't want your own world to disappear?"

Tom considered this for a moment. "Suppose I agree with you, what about the Titans? Without the Artefact how would we deal with them?"

Redfeld shrugged. "Maybe 'deal' is the right word here."

"Eh? I don't understand..."

"Deal, Oakley. You said it. Why not cut a deal with the Titans?"

Tom was already shaking his head. "No, Redfeld, we can't..."

Redfeld's image thrust a finger at Tom. "Listen to me, Thomas. If you will bring the vials to me then together we will go to the Titans, offer them the vials and swear allegiance to them if they will allow us to rule the worlds under them. It is... the only sensible solution."

Tom laughed. "You seriously think I would do that?"

"Boy, listen to me. You don't really have any choice. You either do this or let the Professor and his brothers, banish the Titans, destroy you in the process and create whatever world they want. You are to be sacrificed for their own ends, can't you see that?"

The Nazi captain seemed genuinely frightened and Tom, if he was honest, knew he was afraid too, but he had had his fill of this conversation. Right now he was too exhausted to think. "I have heard enough, Redfeld, it's time for you to leave. Please, just go."

"Thomas, I implore you again. Do not let them carry out this plan. For both our sakes."

Tom just glared at him and Redfeld nodded. "Very well. I will go. But think it over."

Then the image flickered and vanished, leaving Tom alone with his thoughts.

CHAPTER TWENTY
A DREAMWORLD

When Tom had first discovered he had the ability to Walk through time, his talents had shown themselves erratically and sometimes they had manifested via his dreams: dreams in which he would become another Walker or at least witness events involving other Walkers. During the adventure surrounding the Crown of Knossos he had learnt how to go beyond merely being a witness and had found that he could direct his dreams to visit significant moments in history. Now, as he pulled back the sheets of his bed and settled down to sleep, he cleared his mind of mundane thoughts and focused instead on just one. That thought was: what exactly did the Professor know and just how far would he go to get his way?

Despite the confrontation with Redfeld, Tom was so exhausted that he did not find it hard to sleep and had not long closed his eyes when he felt sleep take him. As he drifted into slumber he kept thinking of the Professor, his study and the manuscript. To begin with there was darkness. Then a jumble of shapes began to form: Edward bending over and reading something; the Professor polishing his glasses; a manuscript in swirling Latin script floating into view; Mr Phelps with a diary in one hand and a pen in the other. Then the shapes came together and formed a scene that was taking place in the Professor's study. For Tom it was as if he was actually there, standing just inside the study door.

Looking across the room he saw the old man was sitting in his usual place and was indeed polishing his glasses. Edward was standing at his side, leaning over the desk, and there at its centre was the manuscript. Of Mr Phelps there was no sign. It was a few moments before Tom realised this was because he was viewing the room through the eyes of Mr Phelps. He had in fact become Samuel Phelps and was looking down at the diary he held in his hand.

It was rather an unusual diary because it listed not only appointments that the Professor and other Institute members had on the current day, but also ones that they had to attend in the past, with the dates and times of those as well. This was necessary because it caused endless confusion – not to mention paradoxes and occasional disasters – if a Walker turned up for a meeting with an individual prior to one that had already taken place. As the Institute's senior administrative officer, Mr Phelps kept on top of all of that. He also maintained detailed records of the various Walkers' visits to the past, gleaned from the debriefing sessions the Professor held with each of them. All this was helpful because there were some individuals, like that irritating Welshman, Mr Mason, who never filed any reports on their temporal excursions, which full members of the Institute were supposed to complete. That Thomas Oakley was another exception to the ordered existence of the Institute. Exceptions bothered Samuel's similarly ordered mind, but the Professor saw something in the boy and trusted him and Mr Phelps trusted the Professor, so he did not argue when Neoptolemas instructed him to leave the boy out of the usual paperwork. This did not stop the administrative officer from grumbling and tutting about it, however. He was tutting under his breath now because the Professor had an appointment due and he was late. Mr Phelps glanced down at his diary once more. The time of the appointment was 23.30 hours. The annotation read: Meeting, Custodian and Col Thielmann, The Office. Samuel checked his watch. It was gone half past. He tutted again. If the Professor heard the noise he did not react. Instead he popped the glasses back on his noise and looked at Lieutenant Dyson. He and Dyson had just spent three hours poring over the manuscript. Close to it was a notebook with scribblings of the translation. The Victorian officer was looking at it and then across at the manuscript. Finally, he looked up at the old man, his expression grim.

"You have a question to ask, Lieutenant?" the Professor said.

Dyson nodded and straightened up.

"Sir, I am concerned about what this manuscript implies about young Tom."

"What does it imply?"

Dyson now looked frustrated He gestured at the manuscript.

"Sir, you know the meaning of this section: that a Potentate at the height of his powers could use the Artefact to banish the Titans for ever, but in so doing his own life energy would be consumed. Like… er,"

"Like a catalyst in a chemical reaction, Lieutenant?"

"Indeed, sir. You know that Tom is the only Potentate of sufficient power. It cannot be that you are considering this plan – a plan that would consume him?"

The Professor sighed. "The times are dangerous. Sometimes a sacrifice must be made."

"But Tom… he is so young," Dyson said. "His whole life is ahead of him. You cannot simply wipe it out."

"I feel that you have not completely understood the full implication of this manuscript and why I must consider this plan."

The lieutenant frowned and once more bent over the notes. "I … I don't understand," he mumbled.

Neoptolemas, now looking more like an impatient headmaster than

an absent-minded professor, tapped the manuscript. "Here and...
here," he said.

Dyson's frown remained as he studied the indicated section. Then
it was as if some understanding flooded his mind. Mr Phelps could
see nothing other than swirling writing and notes in the margin. To
Edward Dyson, however, they clearly had meaning for he stared up at
the Professor, eyes wide.

"You... you would go that far?" he asked.

The Professor nodded. "If it needs to be done I will do it, yes."

Dyson said nothing for a moment then he nodded his head. "So be
it!" he said finally.

Tom woke up with a start. It was around midnight and as always
when he had been Walking in his dreams he was at first disori-
entated. For an instant in the light of the glow from his radio
alarm he saw his bedroom as Mr Phelps might see it: untidy and
with clothes strewn about. He tutted and muttered to himself.

"This room needs tidying up, I will make a note in my diary!"
he said, and reached out for the same notepad he had used earlier to taunt Redfeld. Seeing it, he instantly recalled who he was
and the sudden realisation brought him back with a bump, banishing the feeling of being Mr Phelps.

He fell back onto his bed and lay there for some time staring at
the ceiling as the memories of that scene in the Professor's study
passed through his mind. Redfeld seemed to be telling the truth.
The manuscript described a way to be rid of the Titans, but the
method would destroy the Potentate who used it; namely himself, Tom Oakley! Edward had at first seemed hesitant, but then
clearly had changed his mind and agreed with the Professor.
What was it Neoptolemas had pointed to in the manuscript?
Whatever it was, Tom was doubly shocked. Firstly by the fact

that the Professor would entertain the idea and secondly by the knowledge that Edward accepted it too.

'A time always comes when you, Thomas Oakley, have to ask yourself this question: are you fighting on the right side?' Those had been Redfeld's words. Tom had trusted the Professor and Edward but now... could he continue do so? Would they really sacrifice him? The old man often had a secret plan. Did he have one now? Thinking of the Professor reminded Tom of the meeting Mr Phelps had recorded in his diary. The Prof was due to meet his brothers in The Office any time now. That would be worth listening in on, Tom thought, if he could just direct his dream to another time and place...

He closed his eyes. With thoughts still whirling around in his mind it took a while for sleep to come, but eventually Tom felt himself sinking once more.

'The Office', he told himself. *'Take me to The Office.'* Images of a tall tower came to him. A concrete fortress complete with dark windows reflecting the moon's glow; an office that had surfaces of polished marble.

Standing around the room were men in suits, motionless like a president's security team or the bodyguard of a rock star. It was through the eyes of one of them that Tom was now viewing the scene. In the centre of the room was a long table covered with sand whose surface rippled and swirled like a stream. Sitting at the table were three men: the Custodian, the Colonel and the Professor. It was the Colonel who was now speaking.

"How dare you raid my Headquarters? We are supposed to be working together on this matter," he said, gesturing violently towards the Professor.

The Professor laughed.

213

"What is so amusing?" the Colonel demanded.

"It is ironic that you should be so angry given the fact that you already had the manuscript and were withholding it from us."

"Yes, well I did not wish for you to get distracted from the job at hand. The choice here is simple: use the Artefact, sacrifice the boy and banish the Titans. There is no need for further discussion."

"That is not a decision for you to make alone, Thielmann. We need to know all the facts so we can make the right choice," the Professor replied.

"There is no other choice to make. In wars sometimes sacrifices must be made. My armies have lost thousands of men. Oakley is merely today's sacrifice."

The Professor shook his head. "Easy choice for an officer to make, sending his men out to fight, selecting who will die whilst he stays behind safe in the headquarters."

Thielmann bristled. "Are you calling me a coward? If I needed to make the sacrifice I would do so!"

"Would you? Would you really?" the Professor asked.

The Colonel leapt to his feet, anger etched onto his face.

"Brothers please!" The Custodian intervened, rattling his knuckles on the table. "Arguing amongst ourselves will not help the situation. We must make some decisions. We do not have much time. The other Time Cysts are disintegrating as we speak."

The Colonel appeared to calm down, nodded at the Custodian and then turned back to the Professor. "Exactly so!" he said as he sat down.

"However, the Professor is correct that we do need to consider all the options," the Custodian continued.

The Colonel's eyes narrowed again. "What do you mean?"

"The manuscript contains more than just the method to banish the Titans does it not, brothers? The Artefact that Knossos so carefully constructed can be used for more than just that."

214

"How do you know about that?" the Professor asked.

"I keep an eye and an ear on travel between the realities, brother. Just this evening Captain Redfeld visited Thomas Oakley and revealed to him—"

"He did what?" the Colonel interrupted. "The traitor!" he shouted. "I'll have him stripped of his captaincy and sent to the front in Antarctica!"

"Do not change the subject, brother. The point is that according to the manuscript, the Artefact can be used not only to banish the Titans but also to unite the realities. If we could do this we can create a new, balanced world. This struggle between realities would be over." The Custodian clasped his hands together and for the first time that Tom could recall he actually smiled. "To me that is good."

"Or we could create a world in which the Reich truly dominates all. A world of order and strength," Thielmann said.

"A world of oppression and malice you mean. No freedom, no liberty," the Professor said.

"Maybe it need not be like that," the Custodian said. "Maybe we can have the best of all worlds. Justice, order, peace and stability. Moulded right it could be perfect. A Utopia."

"Whatever the world is, we still need to banish the Titans. Are we agreed that a sacrifice must be made?" the Colonel asked.

"There seems to be no other way," the Custodian replied. "Brother what do you think?"

The Custodian and the Colonel now turned to look at the Professor. The old man hesitated.

"Do you agree?" The Colonel said, pressing him again.

Now, finally, the Professor nodded.

"Yes," he said. "Yes, I agree!"

CHAPTER TWENTY-ONE
THEFT

When Tom woke, the early morning light was streaming in through his bedroom windows. His dream-Walking had taken up the entire night, yet physically he actually felt quite rested. Mentally though, he was reeling from what the Professor had agreed to. It was clear to Tom now that Redfeld had been right and that in order to achieve his goals the Professor was willing to sacrifice him.

'What do I do now?' Tom asked himself. He gazed around his bedroom, unable to think beyond the questions that were bombarding his brain. 'What should I do about it? How should I react? Is the Professor right? Should I be prepared to make this sacrifice for the good of all mankind?'

Tom was still asking himself these questions when his mobile phone rang.

"Hello," he answered.

"Tom, it's Septimus.

"Oh, you're back. Good. Is all well with Julia?"

"Yes, thanks. Tom, the Professor wants a word. We think the fourth Titan is emerging soon."

Tom did not reply at once.

"Tom, did you hear me?"

"Yeh, sure. I'll be there as soon as I can."

He rang off, leapt out of bed, dashed to the bathroom, came back to his room and hunted for his jeans then remembered it was a school day and tugged on his school uniform. Finally, he scribbled a short note for his parents saying there was a pre-school meeting about a new cricket team he wanted to try for so had left early. Sometimes he felt bad about deceiving his mum and dad, but he could not allow them to know about the double life he led. He sometimes caught his mother eyeing him with a suspicious, worried look in her eye, but so far she had never said anything. Tom was not sure how he would deal with it if she did. Would she even believe him, he wondered, or would he be marched off to a psychiatrist like before?

By the time he had Walked to the Institute Tom had just about made up his mind to take the bull by the horns and calmly ask the Professor what he was thinking of doing with him. There was no point losing his cool, Tom told himself. The Professor was a sensible old man. All he had to do was come straight out with it and ask, and then they would talk it out nice and calmly.

That was the plan, but what happened next, Tom had not planned at all.

He Walked into the old man's study and found Edward and the Professor on their own in almost the same spots they had occupied in his dream. In front of them on the desk were the manuscript and the Artefact. The golden triangle was shining, caught in a shaft of early morning sunlight that fell across the desk, the engravings along the three sides clearly visible. Tom had not noticed until now just how ornate it was; no wonder Julia had wanted to keep it.

Edward looked round as Tom entered the room. Suddenly, without any warning, something clicked inside Tom's head and it seemed to him that he was back in one of his dreams observing the scene from a distance, and that what might occur in the next few seconds was totally out of his control.

"Ah, Tom, that was quick—" Edward began, but Tom interrupted him.

"What?" he shouted. "Bit too quick was I? No time to cover up the evidence, eh?"

"Tom!" Edward gaped at him. "Whatever do you mean?"

"You know what I mean. Plotting with the old man to sacrifice me, that's what I mean."

"Thomas!" the Professor exclaimed, shaking his head. "You have it wrong, I assure you—"

Tom did not give him the chance to finish. "Don't lie to me, Professor. I saw you. In fact I heard you. Both of you. First you talked Edward round and then you allowed yourself to be persuaded by your brothers. What was it the Colonel said? That I am to be today's sacrifice!"

His face turning suddenly pale, the Professor made no reply.

"Tom, you don't understand—" Edward tried again to explain, but by now Tom was boiling mad.

"I am fed up with having to save the day all the time. But now it seems that you, Edward, and you and your brothers, Professor, have all decided that killing me is the easy answer to all your troubles."

"No! Wait!" the Professor cried out, but Tom was not listening. He strode forward and with a wide sweep of his arms seized the Artefact and the Codex from the desk.

"Well, you can't do it without these!" he snapped. Then clutching them tightly to his chest, he Walked away from the Institute. The last words he heard were Edward's, shouting for him to wait.

As he moved through the void Tom's mind was in a whirl. He

still felt so angry, but scared too. *'So much for not losing my cool,'* he thought, and then, *'oh my God, what did I just do? And more to the point, what do I do now?'*

He was just wondering where to Walk to when he felt something running through the Flow of Time. Like a note vibrating down a guitar string or water rippling across the surface of a pond. Something was happening to time, something huge. He followed the vibrations as they grew more powerful and almost seemed to be echoing through his mind and then, a moment later, he was materialising in the art room at his school.

He stumbled to a chair and threw himself down. Letting the Artefact and the manuscript drop to the floor he sat there panting to catch his breath. He gazed around the room, searching for the source of the disturbance he had felt. Yet the room was empty and quiet. The only sound was the clock on the wall ticking softly as the hands turned to 9:15 a.m.

'I must be going mad,' he thought.

Just then he heard the school bell ring and out in the corridors the bedlam of twelve hundred kids rushing from form rooms to the first lesson of the day. The door burst open and thirty year tens hurtled into the room.

"What you doing here, squirt?" one huge boy said as he bumped past Tom. "Heh what is this?" the oaf added, kicking the golden triangle across the room.

"Oh… er nothing," Tom answered and hurriedly scooped up the manuscript, scurried over and grabbed the Artefact then doubled back towards the door. He narrowly dodged Mr Blunt, the art teacher, who was just about to enter the room.

"Sorry sir! Got confused. Wrong room!" he gabbled and vanished into the swirling maelstrom of children milling round the school corridors. It wasn't exactly a lie; he was confused.

'What day is it? Monday? Where am I supposed to be this morning?' he asked himself.

Just then Andy, followed closely by Persephone, pushed past him, English text books clutched in their arms. *'Oh yes, English first period... and I left my school bag and homework at home. Dad will kill me if I get another detention,'* Tom thought as he set off in pursuit towards the Modern Languages corridor. On the way he passed his sister going in the opposite direction. She glanced at him, rolled her eyes and handed him his rucksack.

"Mum says you'll forget your head one day," she grinned, then ran off into the French classroom at the beginning of the corridor.

"Thanks Em," Tom called after her, pushing the Artefact and manuscript into his bag, slinging it over his shoulder and hurrying on.

The classrooms on the right were the languages ones, those on the left, science labs. He was halfway along the corridor when the ground started to shake. This was accompanied by a roaring sound that built in volume. Children in the corridors on their way to lessons stood stock still and stared about them in confusion, younger ones started to cry, but as quickly as it had started, the shaking and roaring stopped and everyone started moving again. Then, just as Tom was passing the window in the door of the Chemistry lab, it shattered, spraying fragments of broken glass across the corridor.

He flung his arm up to deflect the glass from his face and peered into the room. A desk came hurtling across it and slammed into the white board at the front. Two chairs followed the desk, one of which smashed the monitor of the teacher's computer and sent the printer crashing onto the ground. A shower of sparks sprayed upwards. Tentatively, Tom craned his neck to look at

220

the rear half of the classroom.

At first he saw nothing, then another desk hurtled in the air, this one directed at him. Ducking, Tom stared at the muscular form of a young man who was uncurling from a crouch and standing up. Like his brother Titans he was wearing old-fashioned clothing, in this case a blue tunic girded at the waist by a belt with a big bronze buckle. Over the top of the tunic was a cloak fastened at the right shoulder by an elaborate broach. The young man reached out with one arm, pointed at another desk then flicked his arm sideways. The desk spun into the air, smashed through the classroom window and out onto the playground.

Tom was in a quandary. Septimus had called him to the Institute to discuss the imminent arrival of the latest Titan to break free from a Time Cyst. Clearly this creature was it – for surely this had to be a Titan – and it had emerged right here and now in his own school right in front of his eyes. It could only be a coincidence.

The creature moved across the room towards the long white tables that lay end to end against the side wall. They had gas pipes built into them to carry gas to nozzles for plugging in Bunsen burners. He studied the nozzles and then tore the taps off the benches. From where Tom was crouching in the doorway, he could clearly hear the hiss of escaping gas.

The Titan looked around the room, his gaze settling on the teacher's desk. Sparks from the printer must have landed on a sheaf of paper there, for it had ignited and was beginning to smoulder. Smiling, the creature strode across the room, picked up the paper and brought it close to his eyes. As if enjoying the glowing flames and rising smoke he stood there watching it, then still smiling he looked back at the hissing gas pipes.

221

Tom bit his lip. If there was an explosion there could be carnage. He couldn't just Walk away leaving hundreds of children to be hurt or even killed. He had to act fast. Somehow, on his own, he had to trap the Titan and get the kids out of school. But how?

He glanced down the corridor and spotted a fire alarm embedded in the wall near the door. Without hesitation he leapt towards it, smashed the glass and pushed the alarm button. A bell started ringing straight away, the sound of it echoing round the corridors. Tom knew it would alert the fire brigade and within minutes fire engines would be arriving at the school. Almost as soon as the bell rang out, doors opened and children poured out into the corridor. First to emerge from a nearby room was Persephone. She spotted Tom.

"I felt… something was wrong…" she said, nodding her head in the direction of a wall clock. Tom knew she meant 'wrong with time'.

"There's a Titan right here," he said quietly. Persephone's eyes widened, but before she could say anything, more children emerged from the classrooms and began pushing around her, Emma among them.

"What's going on, Tom?" his sister asked, hanging back.

"No time to explain, Em. Just get outside with the rest," he said urgently. Emma looked ready to argue, but her own class teacher was now herding the French class towards the fire exit at the end of the corridor.

Just at that moment there was a massive explosion and a huge crack appeared in the corridor ceiling. At the same time smoke started billowing out of the chemistry lab. Almost immediately there was another ear-splitting bang and the wall and ceiling started to fall on them. Persephone ducked, whilst Emma screamed as the debris tumbled towards her head. Acting instinctively, Tom instantly threw up a dome of frozen time. The shimmering air of his barrier was hidden by the smoke as concrete blocks, planks of wood and reinforcing metal bars bounced off the dome and clattered harmlessly to the floor in a cloud of masonry dust.

"I think it's a gas explosion! Quick everyone, outside," one of the teachers shouted, running along the corridor towards them.

Tom hurriedly dissolved the barrier as the teacher came dashing over to help Emma to her feet and send her dazed and stumbling towards the exit amongst a group of her own class mates. Then, with a glance at Tom and Persephone to make sure they were unhurt, he hurried back to his own classroom to check that it was empty.

Another teacher emerged from a nearby room and looking about him, spotted Tom. "You, Oakley is it? Get a move on and get out of here." Then he too was waving his own class along the corridor. The moment his back was turned, Tom grabbed Persephone and pulled her into an empty classroom.

There they waited a few moments to be sure everyone had gone. In the aftermath of the explosions Tom could hear more masonry collapsing into the corridor and was suddenly afraid for his sister.

"Quick, Persephone," he instructed. "We have to do something. Come with me. The Titan's in the lab."

Tentatively they stepped over the rubble and through the hole in the wall into the chemistry lab. The scene was one of utter devastation. At one end the ceiling was hanging down exposing the roof timbers. The white tables were on fire; desks had been thrown about and glass vials and jars cast to the floor. Some of them had contained flammable chemicals and it was these that

Tom surmised were causing the rainbow of colours erupting out of the torn gas pipes. Some quick-thinking teacher must have turned the gas off at the mains, however, for there were no more big explosions.

Judging by the mayhem, the Titan had clearly been enjoying the destruction of his immediate surroundings, but as Tom and Persephone entered the lab he stopped what he was doing and studied them. Tom was about to erect another frozen wall, but the creature made no immediate move to attack them, in fact he seemed almost curious about the new arrivals.

"What do we do now? Do you have a vial?" Persephone said out of the corner of her mouth.

"Er, no..." Tom replied.

"Why not?" She glanced at Tom and then looked around as if realising for the first time that he was alone. "Where is everyone else?"

"Long story..." he started to say, but at that moment Edward, Charlie, Septimus and Mary materialised in the classroom.

Edward was scowling at Tom. "Why the blazes did you run off with the manuscript and Artefact like that?" he snapped. "What were you thinking of?"

The Titan's eyebrows shot up as he observed their sudden appearance then he started to laugh. The booming sound of gleeful mockery, with which they were all too familiar, filled their ears.

Persephone stared at Tom. "A long story, Thomas?"

He shrugged, "Well, maybe not that long!"

He was about to try and explain when the Titan spoke.

"Who are you puny creatures and what age is this?" he growled, looking directly at Tom.

It took a moment for Tom to realise that the Titan had spoken

224

in English. "Hold on. How come you know our language?" he asked.

"It is always best to study one's enemies before one attacks them," the creature said in a boastful tone. "So I cause some mayhem and I hear the shouts and cries of terror. Then I listen to the myriad voices and I study them, and thus do I learn."

"You must be a quick learner," Septimus observed. "May I ask your name?"

"Do you not know, mortal? That explains why you are not on your knees. I am Coeus," he boomed and then cast his gaze across them all as if waiting to see how they would react. Clearly he thought that having heard his name they would fall to the ground in worship. When there was no such response Coeus sniffed dismissively.

"So then, ignorant mortals, where am I and when is this age? How long have I lain entombed?"

"This land is called England and it is the year—" Tom began, but Edward interrupted him and shook his head.

"That will mean nothing to him, Thomas."

Sir," he said, turning to the Titan, "this land is called Albion and maybe five thousand years have passed since you were imprisoned."

Coeus seemed shocked, for a moment almost lost. Then he recovered and looked at them each in turn.

"Truly? Five millennia have come and gone whilst I lay in my prison? Albion you say? So I have returned to the ends of the earth?" He shrugged his muscular shoulders, "So be it. These wild lands on the edge of the Northern Ocean is where my Empire will begin."

"I don't like the sound of that, mate," Charlie said. "Others have tried to conquer us in these 'wild lands'. We don't tend to

225

take to it that well."

The Titan's eyes narrowed. "What is this? Resistance? Do you mean to pit your feeble selves against me? I am a god!"

Charlie clenched his fists so the joints cracked. "Too bloody right we do, mate!"

Coeus thrust out his arm at a group of desks to his left. They lifted from the floor and like moons orbiting a planet circled around him. The Titan smiled at Charlie. A nasty smile that bared his teeth; a smile intended to intimidate.

But the sailor was already on the move. He flickered to the left, circling beyond the spinning desks.

Plainly taken aback, Coeus frowned. Then, with a spiteful flick of the wrist he sent one desk hurtling sideways.

Mary stepped forward and thrusting out her hand threw up a barrier. The desk smashed into it and disintegrated. Meanwhile, Charlie flickered on round and like a rugby forward launched himself at the Titan's knees. He and Coeus collapsed in a heap on the floor and Edward, holding up a vial in his hand, started forward towards them.

With a great roar, Coeus leapt back onto his feet, sending Charlie spinning away with such force that the sailor went hurtling through the shattered windows and out onto the playground beyond.

Edward un-stoppered the vial and directed its mouth towards the Titan, but before the temporal forces contained within it could take effect, Coeus sent another of the desks straight at him. It slammed into Edward with such bone-crunching impact that the vial flew up out of his hand and he went crashing into the whiteboard mounted on the front wall of the classroom. The board shattered around him and he, with blood trickling from his nose, slid down the wall and collapsed on the floor.

"Edward!" Mary screamed, rushing to his side.

The vial went looping towards Septimus, who threw himself sideways, hands outstretched, and caught it in one palm before it could shatter on the ground.

"How's that then?" he said, and tossed it in the air like a fielder on a cricket pitch. Then, flicking it around with his fingers, he pointed it once more at Coeus.

This time Coeus felt its pull. "What is this?" he roared. "How dare you?"

The tug got fiercer, lifting the Titan towards the vial. He became longer and thinner until his features began to dissolve. Coeus flung out an arm and latched onto the window frame, but soon the pull was too powerful and with a final scream of outrage, he was sucked into the vial.

"Got you!" Septimus said. Then his face fell and he looked all around on the floor where Edward had fallen. "Where's the stopper?" he asked, keeping his thumb over the top of the vial. "Mary, have a look in Edward's trouser pockets will you?"

Somewhat pink in the face, Mary did as he suggested and pulling out the stopper handed it to Septimus, who jammed it into the neck of the bottle.

There was a groan from outside. Charlie had dragged himself upright and was heaving himself back through the window.

Inside the lab it was getting too hot for comfort, the fire spreading rapidly as the greedy flames fed on the upturned desks and benches. Smoke was billowing out through the broken windows and bits of ceiling were falling, showering them all with lumps of plaster. It looked as if at any moment the entire lab was going to collapse in on itself.

"If we don't get burned to death first, we're likely to be crushed under a ton of rubble," Septimus cried.

"Yes, we need to get out of here right now," Tom said. His chest felt tight and his eyes were streaming from the smoke. Outside he could see all the children of the school were gathering in the playground and being herded by their teachers to line up in their classes ready for a roll call. The strident sound of the fire bell could still be heard ringing out across the compound and now two fire engines were speeding towards the school gates, blue lights flashing and sirens wailing.

"They'll panic when they notice we're not there, Tom," Persephone said, following his gaze.

"Can't worry about that just now." Tom rushed over to Edward. The officer was coming round and struggling to sit up, blood still trickling down his nose and also from the back of his head.

"Why did you snatch the Artefact and run away, Thomas?" Mary asked, her eyes hard and accusing as she helped the soldier to his feet. "Edward insisted on coming to find you. He and Septimus used up a lot of energy getting us here. Now Edward is hurt. Is that because of you?"

"Yes, why did you do that, boyo?" Septimus said. "Not like you at all."

Unable to look his friends in the eye, Tom turned his head away. How, when he could barely understand it himself, could he explain the red rage that had boiled up inside him and made him do what he did?

"Come on," he said instead, "let's get back to the Institute while we still can."

He reached out for the Flow of Time as they closed in around him.

"But why did you run, Thomas?" Mary repeated as he Walked them away.

CHAPTER TWENTY-TWO
TODAY'S SACRIFICE

Tom did not get a chance to answer Mary and when, having Walked them all back to the Institute and placed his rucksack with the Artefact and manuscript on the Professor's desk, he turned to face them all, she was still glaring at him, waiting for his explanation.

Mary had always been so trusting – even subservient to him at times, although he had never wanted that – and now, seeing her staring at him with that furious and hurt expression, he was cut right to the bone. He wanted to explain, but he wasn't sure how and at the same time he was far too worried about Emma and his school friends to think about anything else just now. Or so he told himself. Were they all alright? Had the gas explosions injured any of them – or worse? Much as Mary's expression made him want to explain, he could not linger here. That was understandable, surely? Or was it rather the case that he felt uncomfortable about being here right now and his sister and school friends were a convenient excuse?

Torn by conflicting emotions, Tom shuffled his feet and looked down at the floor. "I…" he began, but before he could say anything more, Edward groaned and slumped back against Septimus.

"He's concussed. Get him to the doctor – quickly!" Neoptolemas ordered and suddenly everyone was huddling round Edward and trying to help. Then, whilst Mary and his other friends were taking the injured officer upstairs, Tom turned to face the Professor.

"Thomas... we need to talk," the old man said, but Tom did not let him get any further.

"Look, I'm sorry I bolted like that, Professor," he said hurriedly, holding up both hands in a gesture of surrender, "but I can't talk now. I need to check on my sister and friends. Make sure they're OK." Quickly, before the Professor could say any more, Tom Walked. He felt guilty for leaving so quickly because while it was true that he wanted to check on his sister, it was also true that he did not want to face the others right now. Mary in particular was blaming him for Edward's injury and Edward himself had seemed hurt and upset with Tom for storming out as he had. On the other hand, the Victorian had agreed with the Professor that Tom must be sacrificed and thinking about that still made him angry and resentful. Before he faced them, he needed time alone to think about everything that had happened.

He materialized behind the goal posts at one end of the playground and stood for a while watching what was going on. From there he could see the shattered windows of the classroom where less than twenty minutes ago he had fought a Titan. Two firemen were directing a steady stream of water at the roof of the chemistry lab, from which a thick plume of smoke was still pouring. Outside, the smashed remains of a desk and a heap of glittering shards of glass lay on the ground surrounded by police cones. Fire engines, ambulances and police cars were parked all around the school and even as he watched, the blare of a siren heralded the arrival of yet another ambulance. The vehicle parked and its crew opened the doors and pulled out a stretcher. Meanwhile, half a dozen firefighters carrying axes and breathing apparatus jogged past them and entered the school.

Scanning the excited children for a sight of his sister, Tom moved a little closer. He could hear them gossiping about what had gone on. The talk was of gas explosions; some problem with the central heating; how long the school would be closed, and whether that meant no more lessons or homework this week! Greatly relieved he spotted Emma standing with her year group, which was a year below his own. She appeared to be cradling her left arm and he could see that it was smeared with blood. Despite his efforts she must have hurt it when the ceiling collapsed. The thought of her lying crushed under the rubble made Tom shiver. His own form group was lined up next to Emma's. Panicking slightly, he searched for Andy and smiled with relief to see that his mate was there, talking animatedly with his other friends. They were safe. Yet it could have all been so different. Had he not been there and had the other Walkers not arrived in time, Emma may now be dead, maybe some of the others too. Titans were violent, destructive and malevolent. They clearly had little appreciation of the value of human life. It was only by chance and due to the speed with which his friends from the Institute had dealt with Coeus that someone at the school was not dead.

This thought brought Tom up short and made him feel even more guilty. He had been so concerned about his own life, so bothered that the Professor and his brothers and even Edward were plotting against him, that he had not given much thought to the other people in his life. Now, as he looked about the school it was all real, too real: his friends and his sister had been in harm's way. They were still; the rest of his family too, although they did not know it. But Tom did. He had once agreed to become

Tomorrow's Guardian. He had vowed to protect his world's own history and its future. Now that his powers were developing, Tom realised he had the ability to do far more.

No, more than that, he must do more. His companions and he had temporarily recaptured four of the Titans, but surely not for long. Unless he acted they would one day break free of their bonds, and from what the Professor and his brothers were saying, that day would be soon. Only a Potentate could stop them. Only a Potentate had the power to banish them for ever. Tom sighed, but it was not a sigh of despair. He alone could make the difference. It would mean his death, but looking around at the havoc of the smouldering school, he knew that this was needed.

With the decision made, Tom's anger and resentment fell away and he felt at peace. He would stand up and do the job required of him. He had not asked for this, but this was the hand he had been dealt. He, Thomas Oakley, would be *Today's Sacrifice*. He took one more look at Emma and his friends. He wanted desperately to join them, to hug his sister and laugh with his mates, but that he could not do, for in order to do what he must, he had to remain missing. Eventually they must think he had died in the explosion and was buried in the rubble. After he was dead, the Professor could no doubt add his body to the rubble where it would be found. His parents and Emma would be devastated, but in time they would move on with their lives, as would be the case with his friends. Hopefully they would remember him... at least for a while. Swallowing hard, Tom dashed his hand across his face to wipe away the tears that had gathered in his eyes. *'Stop feeling sorry for yourself and get on with it,'* he told himself. It was time to leave before he changed his mind – or was spotted.

He Walked to the Professor's study to find that Mary, Septimus and Persephone were there with the old man, but Edward and Charlie were not. They all looked up at Tom as he materialised, but no one said anything. He threw himself into a chair and for a few moments there was an awkward silence. He cleared his throat and was about to speak when the door opened and Rolf Lapace walked in and sat down.

"What is *he* doing here?" Tom asked.

"I have engaged Rolf's services again, Thomas. Over the years, both with and without Septimus, he has led many missions to the Twisted Reality and has developed a means of tracking Walkers travelling there from our reality. He has offered to help the I.T. department keep a good grip on us during this trip."

Tom frowned. "The Twisted Reality? So is that where—" he began to ask, but was interrupted by Charlie bursting through the door.

"Edward's going to be alright. Doc says he cracked a couple of ribs and his nose, but he is fixing it." Grinning round at them all, Charlie sat on an empty chair by the desk. "Oh, hello Tom. Back with us are you?"

They all looked expectantly at Tom, perhaps about to ask him what he had been thinking of, storming off as he had, but before any of them could speak he jumped in first.

"Mary, you asked me why I ran. I know you were angry with me and I understand why. Maybe my running out like that led to Edward's injuries, maybe not, but I was wrong to do it and I am sorry." Tom glanced at the Professor, then added, "As to why I did it, I can't explain just now, but—" he was again interrupted. This time by the old man.

"You were upset, Thomas, perhaps even a little afraid? Afraid of what I plan to do and of what Lieutenant Dyson agreed to?" The Professor tilted his head toward the door and smiled.

Tom glanced over his shoulder and saw that Edward was

standing in the doorway. Doctor Makepeace had done a good job; there was barely a sign of his injuries. Relieved, Tom nodded at him then turned back to the Professor. "Yes, I was upset. If you want the truth, Professor, I was boiling mad. That is why I seized the manuscript and the Artefact. They're in there," he said, pointing at his rucksack still sitting where he had left it on the corner of the Professor's desk.

The old man nodded, "And now?" he asked.

"I trust you to do what's right, Professor. Whatever happens I will be ready for it."

"That's good," said Edward, moving across to the desk, "because I fear we don't have much time for lengthy explanations." He handed to the Professor a piece of paper and a long cardboard tube. "However, I will tell you what we were discussing... what you presumably overheard in one of your dreams?"

Tom nodded.

"Well, as I say, I will explain as quickly as I can what we have planned—" he broke off as Tom raised a hand and pointed at Persephone.

"Er... I take it by her presence in the room that this time you mean to include Persephone in your plans?"

Edward grunted. "We all doubted her after the incident at Waterloo, but at your school when she could have aided the Titan she risked her life to help us trap it. She clearly has some talents and right now we need all the help we can get. She also knew Knossos. The Artefact is his construction and that knowledge could be useful."

Persephone smiled. "I hope so," she said. "Indeed I have been thinking about it."

"You know how it works?" Charlie asked.

"Not exactly, but I do know one thing."

234

"What is that?" asked Edward.

"Knossos's strongest power was his will. His Crown was designed to focus that will."

"Yes, go on," the Professor urged her, sitting forward in his chair.

"Well, I can't see him changing his method with other devices. I think the Artefact is controlled by the force of the user's will in much the same way as the Crown was."

The Professor slowly nodded his head, "Yes... I believe you might be right, Persephone."

"What about the words engraved on the arms of the triangle. Are they relevant?" Edward asked.

"Probably not," the Professor said. "Knossos had a major failing: he believed everyone was weaker than he. The words are merely incantations – magic spells if you like – intended to focus the mind of the user, but a user of sufficient power, that is to say, one with sufficient force of will, would have no need of them."

As he spoke, the Professor directed his gaze at Tom. *'Is he again suggesting that I must be the one,'* Tom wondered, meeting the old man's stare, *'or is there something else behind it?'*

The Professor cleared his throat and looked down at the long tube he still held in his hand. "Now, according to the I.T. Department the last of the Titans will emerge in the next hour." Standing, he opened the tube, tipped out the rolled document and spread it across the desk, weighting each corner with a book from the pile that always sat on his desk. The document proved to be a map of a huge city, one with a river running all along its eastern edge. It was covered by odd-looking letters, which Tom thought he now recognised.

"Russia again?" he asked. The Professor nodded.

"Where exactly will the Titan appear and on what date?" Septimus asked, squinting in puzzlement at the map.

"The date line is the present," the Professor said. "I mean quite literally within the next hour."

"Where then?" Mary asked. "What is this city?"

It was not the Professor who answered, but Charlie. "Stalingrad!" he exclaimed. "I recognise the shape of the city and the river from newspapers. When I left Britain the fighting there had not long started, but the reporters thought it an important battle and covered it extensively."

The Professor nodded. "Stalingrad was the city on the Volga River where the Russians stopped the Nazi juggernaut and altered the course of World War Two in Russia, much as El-Alamein had done in Africa a few months before, and also Midway, in the Pacific. Each of these hard fought battles turned the war in favour of the Allies." He paused then added, "All this is true in our reality, of course."

"In our reality?" Edward asked. "Did I hear you correctly, sir?"

"Indeed, Lieutenant," the Professor nodded. "In the Twisted Reality history played out differently. The Germans had defeated the RAF during the Battle of Britain and invaded England, knocking this country out of the war. So there never was a desert war, there never was an El-Alamein. At Midway the Japanese sank all the US aircraft carriers and having destroyed the Pacific Fleet, moved on towards the US West Coast. Then, at Stalingrad, Hitler's armies, with no need to keep strength back in France or send troops to Africa to counter Britain, were able to break through and cross the Volga."

Following all this closely, Tom's eyes widened. More than ever it came home to him how one event led to another and another and another, like when you threw a pebble in a pond and watched the rings in the water getting wider and wider.

He remembered thinking how everything in time and space was connected and was about to remark that this must be so in all realities, but the old man was now pointing at the map so Tom kept the thought to himself.

"Once over the river the Germans rapidly seized Stalin's oil field in the Caucasus and used that fuel to destroy the Soviet armies west of the Urals. However, in both realities the battle at Stalingrad was fierce and a great many thousands of people died fighting over a few city blocks." With these sombre words the old man fell silent, his eyes distant and unfocused.

"You were saying, sir?" Edward prompted after a moment.

The Professor came to with a start and focused back on the map. "After the war in Europe was over in the Twisted Reality, the Germans made Stalingrad a symbol of their struggle. It was left alone. The corpses were buried, but no rebuilding was permitted. Burnt out tanks, rusty old guns, half sunk boats: they were all left where they stood when the fighting finished. Now, seventy years on, the city remains a huge museum and a memorial to Nazi valour and Nazi victory. School trips are made from towns all over Germany and Nazi rallies are held there every year."

"Creepy," Septimus said.

"Yes, but it's important to remember the sacrifices people made," Tom said. "Last November, our school did a trip to the Menin Gate at Ypres in Belgium to hear the last post. Guess it's the same thing if you think about it."

Septimus shrugged. "Maybe," he said.

The Professor now pointed at a large structure towards the north of the city and not far from the river. "That is the Tractor Factory where they produced tanks and other military equipment for the war effort. In both realities it was one of the hot

237

spots of the fighting. It is right there that the last Titan, Kronos, will emerge."

"Sir, what powers does Kronos have? We have met Titans that can drive the seas, create fire, inspire men to fight or just have tremendous strength and intelligence. What about this one?" Edward asked.

The Professor took off his glasses and began polishing them. This was usually not a good sign and they all waited with bated breath to hear his answer.

"He is the most powerful of them all. When Knossos and I fought the Titans Kronos was the most difficult to capture and subdue. He is capable of manipulating time in ways similar to ourselves and I am not even sure the pull of a vial will be strong enough to trap him." The Professor replaced his glasses on the end of his nose and added, "It is for this reason that I am coming with you this time."

"You, Prof? Are you sure? It is likely to be dangerous," Septimus said.

"Yes, Mr Mason, it will be dangerous, extremely so. That is why I have made this decision," Neoptolemas answered, sliding open his desk drawer. He pulled out the wooden chest containing the vials and lifted the lid. Inside it was subdivided into compartments and standing upright in each one was a small blue bottle; a miniature pocket universe. The Professor selected one and holding it up to the light he studied it. Tom could see a dark swirling mist inside, which he thought was red but it was hard to be sure through the blue glass. The Professor replaced the vial and picked up another. This one was empty. Placing it on the desk he closed the chest and looked up, directing his gaze at Rolf Lapace, who had sat in silence throughout.

"Mr Lapace, will you tell the scanners downstairs to commence the trace on us please."

Rolf nodded, stood up from his chair and walked to the door. "Good luck. See you all soon, I hope," he said and was gone.

Looking round at the others, Neoptolemas got to his feet. "Are we ready?" he asked.

Each of them nodded.

Tom clenched his jaw. He knew that if he was to act to spare the others from danger he had to do so soon. There would never be a better moment than this. His companions gathered around him. He waited until each of them was close and then he focused on the Flow of Time. This time, though, he did not use it to Walk them all. Instead he used the connection to slow down the molecules and atoms all around him, both in the air and within the bodies of his friends. He used the trick he had learnt from Mary – a trick he had since perfected – to create a band of frozen time. A polo mint shape shimmered around him, occupying much of the room. He acted so quickly that they did not know what had hit them. Nevertheless, Tom saw the Professor's eyes narrow for an instant before he too was frozen. It left the old man unmoving but staring with surprise and anger right at him.

"Sorry, Professor, but it is for you that I am doing this. For all of you, in fact."

Reaching for the chest of glass vials, Tom recovered the empty one and dropped it back into its compartment. Closing the lid he took a searching look at the map of Stalingrad still unrolled on the desk, then picking up his rucksack, he shoved the wooden chest inside and felt it clunk against the Artefact. Finally, he took a long look around at his frozen friends thinking that this would be the last he ever saw of them. He then realised with a jolt that Persephone was not among them.

"Just what are you up to, Tom?" She was standing near the window outside the belt of frozen time.

239

"How did you do that?" he asked, ignoring her question.

She frowned. "I... I am not sure. I just knew what you were going to try and got myself out of the way. It's like I could feel what you were doing to time."

"Nice trick," Tom grunted.

She scowled at him. "You have not answered my question."

"Look, I just have to do this," he answered. "It is too dangerous for anyone else. I can stop the Titans but I must do it alone. That is what the Professor discovered in the manuscript." Hoping to catch her unawares, Tom reached out while he was still speaking and froze the time around her. Even so, Persephone reacted too quickly and almost escaped. With a cry of alarm she tried to Walk away, but a ribbon of frozen time caught her right arm and pinned it. She shouted out in frustration and fought to free herself, but her arm was trapped and she could not move it.

"Help!" she shouted, struggling to tug her arm free and at the same time calling out to Mr Phelps.

The door opened and Mr Phelps stood in the frame. He took in what was happening and moved swiftly towards Tom.

"I am sorry, but I must do this!" Tom said, and before Mr Phelps could reach him, he Walked away.

Crossing the boundaries between one reality and another was far from easy. It took all of Tom's concentration to focus on the image of the Twisted Reality that lay beneath the map of his own world. He left London and drifted into the void across the Europe of that alternate reality, until he reached his target: the city of the Volga. The city of Stalin: Stalingrad.

CHAPTER TWENTY-THREE
STALINGRAD

Tom materialised in a huge structure that towered high above him. More massive than the largest English cathedral, the Tractor Factory's tall walls supported arches made of steel girders upon which rested the roof. Looking up, Tom saw that much of the roof was missing, the remaining jigsaw-like pieces separated by gaping holes through which sunlight flooded the interior. In some places where it had been hit by wartime artillery, the roof had collapsed completely and tumbled inside to lie in heaps on the ground. Each one a mass of tangled girders, iron bars and corrugated tin sheeting, looking rather like some long dead giant insect, its rusting legs and wings thrust skyward.

The collapsed roof had joined the symbols of industry that filled the factory: an unfinished Russian tank, turret-less and with no tracks, stood where for sixty years it had waited in vain for the factory workers to return and complete it. Adjacent to the tank there was a conveyor belt on which lay forever the components intended for it. Wrecked and shattered machinery dotted the building: here some device with huge cogs and rubber buttons; there a chain swinging gently from a pulley suspended from a girder protruding from the wall.

Tom walked along, winding his way between the decaying apparatus until he reached a low-lying wall made of sandbags all heaped up to create a dugout. On the top was a tripod-mounted machine gun. He imagined the German soldiers who had once used it, fighting the Russians for every inch of this strong, strategic point. The gun seemed remarkably serviceable despite the passage of sixty years. The belt of bullets that hung down from the breech glittered in the sunlight and showed not even a spot of rust. Moving on past it, Tom looked around the vastness of the factory, wondering where Kronos might appear and trying to decide where to hide.

Suddenly, he heard an ominous click behind him; the click of the machine gun being cocked in preparation for firing.

"Stay where you are, Oakley!" a voice rang out.

Tom recognised the harsh tones of Captain Redfeld and was about to dive for cover, but the Nazi captain called out, "Don't move a muscle, boy. I would hate to have to give the order for the *Unteroffizier* to open fire. At this range the bullets would cut you clean in two."

Tom froze. Tentatively he reached out for the Flow of Time.

"Do not try that either, please," Redfeld shouted. "This is my reality, Thomas. I can sense it if you try to Walk. Trust me, if you do you will arrive in your beloved Institute perforated. Now, turn around slowly."

Reluctantly Tom did so. Redfeld was standing next to a soldier who was manning the machine gun. Tom now knew why the weapon had seemed so pristine and new. It was in fact a modern weapon occupying the ancient dugout – a weapon brought here by Redfeld and his men. The Nazi captain himself was armed with a Luger pistol. This he levelled at Tom's head as, moving out from behind the sandbags, he sauntered towards him.

"Give me that bag you carry, boy."

"Why should I?"

"Because if you do not I will shoot you and take the bag anyway," Redfeld sneered, cocking the Luger.

Sighing, Tom pulled the rucksack off his back and handed it over. "Handle it with care," he warned.

Redfeld looked inside. His eyes widened and he glanced sharply up at Tom then wandered over to an abandoned piece of machinery with a flat top. He upended the rucksack onto the metal surface and rooted through the contents. Pushing the golden triangle and manuscript to one side he opened the chest of vials, picked one out, looked at it closely then stared back at Tom.

"What is your game, boy?"

Tom shrugged. "You were the one who proposed I bring the vials to you, why are you so surprised I am here?"

Redfeld tilted his head to one side and considered Tom, who was briefly reminded of a blackbird eyeing up an earthworm before pulling it out of the ground.

"Somehow, Oakley, I do not believe you were really planning to do that. As a matter of fact you seemed rather surprised to see me here."

Tom nodded. "Well that is true. Just what are you doing here? How did you know Kronos would be emerging in this place?"

"Do you think yours is the only organisation that can track changes in the time line, boy?"

"I suppose not."

"As it happens, though, we have the advantage of inside information." Redfeld smiled and stepped back.

From behind a nearby machine, Rolf Lapace stepped into view."

"Rolf, you sod! You've betrayed us! I knew it was a mistake to trust you," Tom hissed.

243

Lapace scowled. "I did no such thing. I merely maintained a pretence of cooperation whilst I gathered information for the captain here. I was able to keep him updated regarding your progress in collecting the Titans in those little vials. When the Professor sent me to the I.T. Department to put a trace on you, I came here instead and located Captain Redfeld.

"But why?"

"Well, partially for the money naturally," Lapace smirked, "the pay's better here. But even more than that, I felt Septimus was owed a defeat. He's got the better of me one time too many and I seem to have developed this burning desire to get even."

"So it's all about money and revenge," Tom spat. "That's all you care about isn't it."

His contempt rolled off Lapace like water off a duck's back. The traitor merely nodded and said with a smile, "That does seemed to summarise my personality rather well, Tom. How perceptive of you."

Redfeld tapped his knuckles on the top of the machine to draw their attention.

"Enough! Answer my questions, Oakley. We were expecting your entire group to arrive. Yet you come alone. Why? What are you planning to do here?"

"I don't think you would understand even if I tried to explain," Tom replied.

Redfeld's face twitched. "Maybe not. Don't bother to tell me. I imagine it would be something needlessly heroic and sickeningly self-sacrificing. So then, here we are again with you standing in front of me and me with a gun. This time, however, there is no Colonel to intervene on your behalf. I gave you a chance to come in with me and you turned me down. Well you've run out of chances now, boy."

He levelled the Luger once more and began squeezing the trigger. "Goodbye, Master Oakley," he sneered.

Instinctively, Tom flinched away. At the same moment there was a blur of movement off to his right and a rusty iron bar came flying through the air. Spinning end over end it struck Redfeld's arm and the Luger went off, the bullet flying wide and ricocheting with a metallic clang off a machine several metres away. The captain yelped, clutched his arm and let go of the pistol, which flew under the nearby tank.

It had all happened in less than a blink and Tom, still reeling from his imminent death, looked all around seeking his rescuer. Seeing Phil running forward, dressed in combat fatigues and armed with a revolver, he breathed a sigh of relief.

"Shoot them!" Redfeld screamed, diving out of the way of the machine gun behind him. The gunner heaved on the gun, swinging the barrel round, but Phil reacted quicker, letting fly with a couple of shots. The second one hit the gunner in the chest and he fell back. Phil then looked for Redfeld, but the captain had taken cover behind the tank so Phil pointed his gun at Lapace.

Rolf stuck up his hands. "Heh, I am unarmed. Don't shoot!"

Before Phil could react to this, the ground beneath their feet began to shake and a tremendous boom echoed throughout the huge structure. Immediately after this a high-pitched whistling started up near the tank Redfeld was sheltering behind. Tom could now see that an intense white light had appeared in the air above the vehicle. As the light expanded so the noise level rose in pitch.

"Take cover!" Tom yelled. Running for the dugout he hurtled head first over the sandbags. A moment later Phil and Rolf both dived in beside him.

Phil carefully edged upright to peer over the parapet. "Oh my

God! Is that what I think it is?"

"If you think it's a Titan, the answer's yes!" Tom said.

As he spoke there was another ear-splitting boom followed by an even brighter burst of light, and now Kronos, the greatest and mightiest of the Titans, stood on top of the obsolete tank and glared down at them all. Plainly dressed in a green tunic, which was belted at the waist with a golden belt and did nothing to conceal his bulging muscles, he rested his hands on his hips and stood with his legs apart, his feet encased in golden sandals. Here was the Titan who according to myth had killed his own children in case they grew up to defeat him.

It was not hard to believe, thought Tom. The creature's stance was arrogance itself, his face curled into a sneer that suggested he regarded them all as mere insects of little worth. What need had he for armour or weapons amongst such as they? The other Titans had each had a presence and something about them that confirmed they were far from being mere mortal men, whether it was mastery of the elements of fire or water, power over men's desire to fight and kill, great strength and supreme intelligence. It was no wonder the Greeks and Macedonians and their ancestors had just accepted these beings as gods. Yet with Kronos it was something even more than that. With such a force of will as he possessed, coupled with other powers that Tom could sense but had yet to see, the Titan exuded an aura of majesty, of divinity almost, such that Tom felt the urge to bow down before him, to worship and obey. It was almost overwhelming in fact.

Tearing his gaze away from Kronos, Tom saw that at his side Phil's face had gone blank and his knees were bending as he did indeed fall to the ground. Rolf Lapace seemed to have vanished and Tom, looking all around, could not see where he had scuttled off to. Redfeld's guard was slumped down behind

246

them clutching at his chest, blood oozing from between his fingers, face screwed up in pain. As for Redfeld, where was he? Tom wondered. He glanced back at the tank. Kronos appeared to have lost interest in the puny mortals below him, no doubt already having dismissed them all as insignificant. He appeared to be studying the tank itself, running one hand across the rivets and armoured plating.

At that point, Tom spotted Redfeld emerging from behind the tank. He was lifting something up in one hand and fiddling with it: something small and… blue. It took Tom a moment to realise that it was a vial the Nazi captain was holding and now pointing at the Titan.

As soon as Kronos felt the tug of the temporal forces upon him his head turned and he stared at Redfeld with a mix of anger and surprise. He jumped down from the tank and rather than attempt to escape the pull of the vial, he actually advanced directly towards the captain.

Grinning in expectation of victory, Redfeld himself took a step towards Kronos, perhaps believing that the Titan was already ensnared. In this he made a grave mistake, for unlike his brothers, Kronos seemed immune to the forces of the vial. As Tom watched, the Professor's words came back to him: *'Kronos was the most difficult to capture and subdue. I am not even sure the pull of a vial will be strong enough. He is capable of manipulating time in ways similar to ourselves…'*

By moving closer, Redfeld had brought himself within reach of the mighty being and Tom, despite his loathing for Captain Redfeld, felt obliged to warn him.

"Redfeld, watch out!" he shouted.

Whether the captain heard he could not tell. At that moment Kronos disappeared and reappeared behind Redfeld. In a blur of

247

movement one muscular arm swung up and the Titan brought his clenched fist crashing down on the German's head. Redfeld's eyes rolled into his skull, he tottered backwards and fell full length on the ground behind the tank. The vial he had been holding rolled out of his hand and clattered across the stone floor, coming to rest near Kronos's feet. The Titan brought up one sandaled foot and stamped it down, smashing the vial to pieces as he might crush a beetle.

There was a loud boom and Kronos was thrown a few feet backwards. Tom felt a blast of cold air as the contents of the bottle emptied into the factory. Then the air reversed and was drawn toward the remains of the vial. Finally, there was a huge pop and the shattered blue glass, along with a chunk of stone from the factory floor, was sucked inwards and vanished.

Kronos's eyes widened when he saw this and then his gaze fixed on the open chest of vials lying next to the Codex and Artefact close at hand. With two huge strides he reached the vials and snatched them up.

"No!" Tom yelled. Suspecting what the Titan would do next he moved out from the dugout, focussed on the Flow of Time and prepared to Walk. If he could only seize the vials from Kronos and get away from here... But before he could move, Kronos had tossed the vials and chest to the ground and was lifting his foot once more, preparing to smash them.

Knowing what was about to happen, Tom dived for cover behind the sandbags. There were four huge detonations followed by a mighty outburst of air that knocked the sandbag embrasure over on top of him, Phil and the moaning gunner. For a moment the world went black. Stunned, shaking his head to clear it, Tom found that he was buried. With a grunt of effort, he pushed one of the sandbags off the top of his head and peered out. The detonation seemed to have ruptured several water pipes, which were spraying a fountain of water across the factory. Somewhere they must be in contact with a heat source because clouds of steam now seemed to be filling the whole area.

As the steam slowly dispersed four shapes emerged from the mist; indistinct at first, but growing clearer all the time. Tom swallowed hard as he recognised the four Titans that had cost him and his friends so much effort to recapture. Coeus, Iapetus, Crius and Hyperion were stretching their limbs and glaring across the factory. Finally, a fifth figure was among them. As Kronos stepped into their midst the other four inclined their heads and bowed to their master.

Five of the most powerful beings ever to walk the face of the Earth were free. And united. And standing in the ruins of Stalingrad!

Tom gazed at them with a terrible sinking feeling in his heart.

"Oh my God, what have I done?" he said.

CHAPTER TWENTY FOUR
THE TIME HAS COME

Turning away, the five jubilant Titans completely ignored Tom; Redfeld's inert body lying on the ground, and the worshipping figure of Phil, who had scrambled out from the collapsed dugout and was back on his knees gazing in awe at the demigods as if in some kind of hypnotic trance. Redfeld's wounded gunner was still buried, all but his feet, which stuck out from beneath the sandbags. He had stopped moaning and Tom assumed he must now be dead.

"*Phil!*" Tom hissed, but the big man took no notice.

The Titans were striding away through the factory complex. They appeared to be exploring their surroundings, glancing about them at the machines and rubble like a party of sightseers on a day trip! Tom could hear the low rumble of their voices as every so often they stopped to examine a machine more closely.

Watching them through the sprays of water and steam that continued to cloud the factory, Tom suddenly realised there might still be an opportunity to complete his task. Stalingrad in this twisted reality was a museum. It was not a living city. So rather than the hundreds of thousands or even millions that might live in a modern city, here there would be only the museum curators and security staff and whichever visitors were here on this day. With luck he might deal with the Titans without anyone else getting involved.

Creeping across to the tank where Redfeld had emptied the rucksack Tom searched the pitted ground. Straight away he found the smashed remains of the small chest that had contained the vials, but he could see neither the Artefact nor the manuscript. Sick with disappointment he thought they must have been sucked into the void along with the shattered vials, but as he turned away he spotted a gleam of gold. The triangle was lying partially concealed by rubble beneath the tank.

"Yes!" Tom whispered.

Falling to his knees he scrabbled in the debris to free the Artefact, relieved to see it did not appear to be damaged. The manuscript was there too, a bit crumpled but still in one piece. Clutching hold of both, Tom got to his feet, cast a last glance back at Phil then set off after the Titans, whose enormous strides were carrying them rapidly through the factory into the distance.

Tom had gone barely fifty yards when he felt a disturbance in the Flow of Time. Somebody was Walking and they were about to arrive here at any moment!

Glancing back the way he had come Tom saw his friends materialising near the sandbags and his heart sank.

"Go back!" he shouted, turning to face them. "I know what I'm doing. I know what I have to do. There is no use you lot taking any risks!"

Septimus cupped his mouth with his hands and shouted something in reply, but Tom did not hear what he said. Clearly agitated, the Welshman was waving his arms about and pointing at something behind Tom.

Swinging round, Tom gawked and froze. The Titans must have Walked back up the factory while he was looking the other way, for they now stood only a few paces away from him and all five were staring at him.

"It is *you*, boy!" Coeus said in English, then switching to an archaic language he pointed at Tom and said some words to the others. They each considered first Tom and then his friends, grim recognition appearing on their faces as they stared at their former captors.

"My brothers and I are delighted that you are here this day," Coeus said. "Lord Kronos has released us and destroyed the vials you used to capture us. We are free and you no longer have the means to stop us." Once again, for the benefit of his brothers, he laboriously translated what he had said.

While Coeus was speaking, Tom looked hastily down at the manuscript in his hand. He could not read the Latin script, but the drawings were easy to understand. A person dressed in old-fashioned clothes was holding up the Artefact so that the opening of the triangle faced a group of what could only be Titans, their shape and form exaggerated such that they did appear to be gods. There were five of them, one larger than the other four and each one accompanied by a thumbnail sketch illustrating his power. Tom, knowing at first-hand what these powers were, easily recognised Crius, Hyperion, Iapetus and Coeus. The largest figure had to be Kronos.

The triangle felt cold and heavy in Tom's hand. He was sure he could feel its power, but how did he release it? Were there some words he needed to say to make it work? If only he could read the ancient engravings. He recalled what Persephone had said about the device, that having been designed by Knossos it had been made to obey the will of its wielder in the same way as the Crown had been.

Then, in a blinding flash of intuition Tom realised he did not need to understand how the Artefact worked. He may not be a Titan, but he was a Potentate. He had strong and powerful will.

He was in contact with the Flow of Time. No, much more than that: he dominated the Flow of Time and could command it. All the Artefact did was to focus the powers of the person who wielded it and magnify them, which must be why Knossos had named the device a 'Focus'. Tom could not read Latin and could not understand the inscriptions Knossos had written, but that did not matter. He knew instinctively that this triangular device would enhance his will and focus the power of his mind: he needed merely to command it and it would obey him.

He became aware that Coeus had finished translating and was looking at him, lips lifted in a menacing smile.

"You hear me boy? I say again, you no longer have the means to stop us!"

"I think I have," Tom said quietly.

"Have what?" Coeus snapped.

"A means to stop you. To defeat you forever… and the time has come."

Tom lifted up the Artefact to frame the Titans in the triangle and focused his will on the Flow of Time.

"*Tom!* Look out!" he heard Persephone shouting, but not from fifty yards away. She had Walked the short distance and come right up beside him. With both hands she shoved him bodily to one side.

Taken completely by surprise Tom tripped, stumbled and ended up in a heap behind the wreck of an adjacent tank, at the same time he lost his grip on the Artefact, which spun out of his grasp and ended up under the same tank.

"What did you do that for?" Tom said. He glared up at Persephone and was just in time to see a blast of fire hit her in the belly, setting light to her clothes and sending her tumbling away. Hyperion had been aiming his fire ball at Tom, but Persephone's ability to sense a Titan's or a Walker's action before it happened had come to his rescue. She had acted without thought and her intervention had saved him, but at what cost to herself? Tom looked at her and swallowed hard. Her clothes were blackened and smoking and she did not seem to be moving.

Another blast of fire zoomed past him, this time directed at Charlie, who was zig-zagging in and out of time toward the Titans. Edward and Septimus, in an attempt to out-flank them, had moved round to the far side of the tank near the sandbags, past the still form of Captain Redfeld and into the tortured mess of bent iron and steel pipes beyond.

Mary was standing in plain view just in front of the collapsed dugout. Her arms were raised and around her a shimmering Wall had appeared. Coeus pointed at a nearby girder then clenched his hand into a fist. As if of its own volition, the girder rose up from the ground, cartwheeled in the air then flew at Mary. It hit her Wall, ricocheted off and crashed into a nearby pile of wreckage.

'Well done, Mary,' Tom said to himself, sending her an encouraging smile. Then he noticed that Iapetus had moved away from his brothers and was striding swiftly to the factory entrance. As Tom watched, the Titan stopped in the doorway and stood looking out at the city beyond. Then he laughed, a loud, booming laugh, and raising his arms high, swept them round in a wide arc that encompassed the city. It was the same movement he had made at Waterloo and with a sinking heart, Tom knew what to expect.

Nothing happened immediately, but moments later people began emerging from between the ruined buildings and running towards the factory. As they approached he saw that many wore uniforms similar to Redfeld's men and were armed with pistols or submachine guns. Tom reasoned that these were the security forces stationed here in Stalingrad, but among them were people in civilian dress. Were these simply visitors to this city-wide museum? Soon, around fifty had gathered. As they ran, the civilians picked up lumps of concrete, sticks of wood and pieces of iron – anything that would serve as a weapon. They had been summoned by the Titan God of War and under his control had become an army boiling for a fight, and just like the soldiers at Waterloo, they were marching to battle. Entering the Tractor Factory they spread out and began closing in on Tom and his friends.

Meanwhile, Charlie had reached Kronos and using his staccato style of movement was circling the Titan, trying to take him by surprise so he could get in a punch or kick. Seizing an opportunity when Kronos appeared to be looking the other way, Charlie lunged forward, but as he moved, Kronos vanished, reappearing a few yards away.

"Charlie, it's no use. He can manipulate time like we do!" Tom yelled.

The sailor spun round, frustration showing on his face. For a moment his gaze met Tom's and Tom knew they were both thinking the same thing: 'If this Titan can do all that Walkers can do and more, what hope do we have?'

Septimus now jumped out from behind the tank and tried to seize Crius, but the Titan had seen him coming. With a circular gesture of his wrist Crius summoned a swirling whirlwind. It seized Septimus, lifted him off the ground and carried him high above them, held him suspended there for a moment and then flung him toward the side of the factory. Tom saw fear on the Welshman's face as with a cry he crashed into the wall, slid down it and disappeared into the pile of rubble at its base. As with Persephone, Tom could not tell whether Septimus was dead or alive.

At that moment Edward fired his revolver at Crius. The bullet struck the Titan squarely in the chest and he staggered back a few feet. Edward smiled with satisfaction, but an instant later his smile froze, for Crius was climbing back onto his feet and where the bullet had struck him there was hardly a mark. The Titan gave a shout of anger, thrusting out a finger to point at a metal hatch cover embedded in the ground.

At first Tom was not sure what Crius was trying to do, but it soon became clear. A rumble of sound thundered beneath the ground; it grew louder and suddenly, the metal cover burst upwards. A spout of water shot out of the opening and fountained high into the air. Crius rubbed his hands together as if he was warming himself on a cold winter's day. As he did so, the water changed shape, swirling and looping round itself until finally it took on the form of a man. Now it was a mighty creature of water that charged towards Edward, pummelling at him and finally, with a contemptuous swipe of its watery arm, tossed him across the factory to land with a thud against a tank. Edward collapsed to the ground and did not move again.

Kronos, the most powerful of them all, appeared to be content to leave things to his brothers. Legs apart, hands on hips, he stood and watched what they were doing, a smile on his face.

Tom was in despair. Of all his friends only Mary, alone in her bubble of frozen time, was left standing, but Iapetus's angry army was rapidly converging on her. Would she be strong enough to hold up her Wall against them all? 'It's no good,' thought Tom. 'The Titans are just too powerful.' He and his companions could not hope to defeat them in battle. This, of course, is what Titus and Knossos had realised all those centuries ago, which is why they had trapped each Titan in a Time Cyst and banished them. From where he lay, Tom could see the golden triangle lying where it had landed beneath the rusty old tank. Constructed by Knossos, the Artefact was the only device capable of banishing the Titans forever. Tom knew he had to try, no matter what the cost to himself.

He scrambled under the tank, reached out and grasping hold of the triangle pulled it toward him. It felt cold in his hand and he shivered. It was not the chill of the metal making him shiver, though. It was a sudden wave of fear. Frightened by what was about to happen, Tom lay there under the tank for what seemed like a long moment, reluctant to take the next step.

Then an image came into his head of his sister and their mum and dad sitting in a woodland glade. It was a day last summer when they had gone on a family picnic. They were all laughing because he had just opened a bottle of coke. It must have been shaken up in the hamper because it had exploded, showering him in coke and forcing him to change his top.

Now, knowing he would never see his family again, Tom felt an ache in his chest and his eyes filled with tears. And yet, seeing their faces in his mind had stiffened his resolve. He knew he had to take this next step; he had do this to protect them. Not just them – Andy and his other school friends deserved the chance of life too, just as did Septimus, Charlie, Edward, and Persephone, if indeed they were still alive. And Mary, who was staring in his direction, tears streaming down her face.

He, Thomas Oakley, was a Potentate: he alone could give them all that chance. He took a deep breath, wiped his eyes, crawled out from under the tank and prepared to do what he knew he must.

It was time to use the Artefact and take the action that would protect all the worlds from the Titans for ever.

It was time for Today's Sacrifice.

CHAPTER TWENTY-FIVE
THE MAN I WAS BORN TO BE

Emerging from under the rusty old hulk Tom knelt in its shadow waiting for the optimum moment to leap up and use the triangle. There seemed to be a lull in the fighting; all he could hear was water splashing and steam hissing. Iapetus's army appeared to be taking stock, preparing to sweep up what remained of Tom's friends. It seemed the Titans had forgotten about him, either that or they thought him too insignificant to worry about. Kronos was leading his brothers forward. Passing Tom's hiding place they strode on through the ruined factory.

Adrenalin surged through Tom's body. He figured that he had to get this attack just right, because the Titans would surely counter-attack as soon as they spotted what he was trying to do. He needed to get them all in his sights at the same time.

Taking a deep breath he prepared to move, but before he could get to his feet a shadow loomed over him and a hand seized the triangle pulling it out of his grasp. Startled, he looked up in panic, terrified that Kronos or one of his fellow Titans had doubled back and now had possession of the Artefact. So it was with considerable relief and not a small amount of surprise that Tom saw the Professor looking down at him.

Behind the old man, both the Custodian and the Colonel were materialising and taking cover at the rear of the tank. How had he not felt them Walking? Tom wondered. Had the Artefact dulled his senses? Then his eyes widened, for behind Colonel Thielmann fifty or more grey-uniformed soldiers had arrived and were spreading out. The Colonel must have brought them with him.

A shot rang out. It was followed by a volley of gunfire as the new arrivals engaged the rag-tag army Iapetus had created. Three of the Colonel's men ran past Tom and hastily set up a machine gun at the corner of the tank. Within moments it was pouring bullets at Kronos and his fellow Titans, who recoiled from the attack and, for the moment at least, retreated.

His eyes filling with tears of relief, Tom saw that Edward was struggling to his feet. Then he saw Charlie emerging from behind a heap of rubble. Both of them alive! Mary had spotted them too. She had let down her Wall and was running over to join them. Encouraged by the reinforcements, the three Walkers advanced together on the Titans and began to attack. Tom knew they were simply buying him time, for it would not be long before the might of the Titans destroyed them all. He needed to act quickly. He got to his feet and shouted over the din of gunfire.

"Professor, I am sorry about what I did, but I need to use the Artefact. It can only be activated by a Potentate and as I am the only one alive it has to be me. He held out his hand for the triangle. "I am the sacrifice, I know that now."

The Colonel looked with approval at Tom then turned to the Professor. "You see, brother, the boy understands. He realises now. He does it willingly too. What more is there to say? Do as he asks. Give him the Artefact!"

Still hanging onto it, the Professor shook his head. Thielmann reached out to take it from him, but Neoptolemas did not let go, so now they each held a side of the triangle.

The Colonel frowned and tugged at it in an attempt to wrest it from the Professor's hand. "Let go, brother. If you will not give it to the boy then let it be me."

"No!"

Thielmann scowled at him. "Let me have it, Neoptolemas!"

"Please Professor, we don't have much time," Tom said, but both the brothers were now engaged in a battle of wills and ignored him.

At this point the Custodian stepped forward and reaching out took hold of the third side of the triangle.

"Let me try my way, both of you. Let me merge the realities so that we can bring all back into balance as it should be, as it was always meant to be."

The Professor made no reply. Instead he smiled at Tom. "You are right, Thomas, you are the only Potentate alive, but that was not always the case. Once, when we three," he nodded his head at his brothers, "were one, we were the most powerful Potentate that ever lived." Still smiling, Neoptolemas looked first at the Colonel and then at the Custodian. "We shall be so again," he said, closing his eyes.

The Colonel gasped in alarm. "What are you doing brother? Stop it at once!" He began to struggle, trying desperately to let go of the triangle, but it was as if his hand was in some way glued or welded to it and he could not release the Artefact.

The Custodian, although not panicking like Thielmann, was also trying to free his hand. "Brother, stop – this is not what we agreed. We agreed to use the triangle to merge the realities. You are using it in a way it was not designed to be used and in such a way that even its creator, Knossos, did not envisage. I am not sure if it can be made to work like that."

Looking from one to the other of the three determined old

261

men, Tom bit his lip. All around them a furious battle was raging: the machine gun near them rattling away; Iapetus's vengeful army returning fire. Bullets were zipping and whining past the tank where Tom and the three brothers were sheltering. He could no longer see his friends and feared for their lives, for now the Titans had come back into view and had moved to stand behind their soldiers. Grouped together they were directing the battle, occasionally stepping forward to shoot fire or ice at the Colonel's men. Only Kronos stood aloof, a bored expression on his face as he watched the proceedings.

For a short time after the arrival of Thielmann's soldiers the enemy had paused to regroup, but now, egged on by Iapetus, it seemed they were gaining ascendancy. The Colonel's grey-uniformed men had begun to fall in greater numbers and Tom could see it was only a matter of time before they were defeated.

He turned back to the three brothers and shouted, "Whatever you are going to do, I'd urge you to make your minds up quickly!"

None of them appeared to hear him. The Professor seemed oblivious to what was going on around him. He was nodding his head, still looking at the Custodian. Now he said, "You are wrong, brother. The device can be used to work like that. I have studied the Codex of Knossos together with the diaries of the Conti di Rivoli. The Count understood The Event: he understood how the Crown of Knossos shattered and divided the realities. Don't you see? It is significant that the realities were divided into three. The triangle was born of the same material as the Crown. Both were made by the same being: Knossos. He alone knew how the Artefact could be used to focus the wielder's will and merge the realities once more, but the Conti di Rivoli had gone a long way toward working it out."

262

"Exactly, Neoptolemas. Now you are talking sense. Merging the realities is precisely what I want to do," the Custodian said.

"Yes, I know. However, I am no longer sure we should do that, brother. Our worlds have been separate for thousands of years. Generations have lived their lives. Kingdoms and Empires have risen and fallen. Can we undo all of that? Not everything that has happened in my world is good, not by a long way. Indeed, not everything that has happened in Thielmann's world is bad. Events there have given the chance for some men to show courage and others a reason to risk all for a better future. I would not do away with that. We do not have the right to alter history; to toss away billions of people's lives. Your longing for orderliness and balance blinds you to what is right."

The Custodian's eyes narrowed. "I think I see now what your plan is, brother. You mean to merge we three again to become Titus once more. You intend that the Custodian, the Colonel and the Professor will vanish and the most powerful Potentate that ever lived will once more exist in place of us. But what then? You mean to sacrifice Titus? You intend that we three as one will die to banish the Titans?"

The Professor nodded. "Yes brother, I do."

The Custodian considered this for a moment, seemingly not bothered by the prospect of his own end. "We three would once again be united…?"

"Yes we would… but only briefly."

Looking down at their three hands clutching each side of the triangle, the Custodian nodded. "I would never have previously admitted this, least of all to you two, but I have always feared death if it happened whilst we were divided from one another. It would be regrettable to die as separate parts. But to become again the man we once were, even if then we would die? Yes, I

263

think that would be acceptable."

"What!" the Colonel shouted, "Are you mad? Listen to what you are saying. If we three are destroyed who will look after the realities and protect them? It is our duty to guard these worlds. We took on that role a long time ago."

The Professor shook his head and opened his mouth to respond, but his words were lost in a great boom of sound. Hyperion had tossed a ball of fire at the machine gun and its crew, which had been shielding Tom and the three brothers. The fire ball had detonated, consuming the gun and wiping out its screaming crew. The next moment, four of Iapetus's soldiers ran around the corner of the tank and raised their guns at the brothers and Tom.

Without pausing to think, Tom flung out his hands and froze time in a globe centred on the wrecked machine gun and encasing all four soldiers before they could fire a shot.

The Professor chuckled. "No, Colonel, as I was about to say and as you can see, it is our job no longer. That role has been passed on. As Titus it was our duty and our battle all those ages ago to defeat the Titans, but because we were distracted by our power struggle with Knossos we did not finish it. Let us be done with it now and leave to others the task of protecting time. They will be the guardians of tomorrow."

Thielmann was shaking his head, still tugging at the triangle. Neoptolemas placed his free hand on the Colonel's shoulder. "Brother, you only recently said that if the moment came to make a sacrifice, you would do it. Do you remember that? Have you changed your mind? Have you already forgotten?"

The Colonel stopped struggling and looked long and hard at the Professor. "No, I have not forgotten," he replied quietly.

"Well then, right here and now is the chance to make that sacrifice," Neoptolemas said.

As he spoke, another of Iapetus's men poked his head around the tank, his eyes widening as he saw the soldiers trapped in Tom's bubble of frozen time. In his hand he held a grenade – one of the old, German style hand grenades that looked like a tin attached to a wooden handle. He tossed it at them then ducked back.

Letting it land, Tom threw up a Wall around himself and the brothers. The explosion impacted on the Wall but could not penetrate it. After a moment, Tom let it drop and tried something new. He pointed a finger at the man who had thrown the grenade, who was again peeping round the tank, and accelerated time around him. The air became suddenly unbearably hot as the air molecules speeded up. Suddenly, the man's sleeve caught fire and he screamed. Whimpering and clutching his arm, he backed away then turned and ran, his clothes smoking.

The Professor and his brothers looked at Tom appraisingly. The old man chuckled again and nodded to himself as if this had confirmed something he already knew.

"As I said, brothers, Thomas has grown into his strength as a Potentate. There is little left to teach him. All he needs now is belief in his power and there will be little he cannot do."

The Custodian nodded. "I agree. The realities can be left safely in his protection… so long as he remembers to keep them in balance.

"And does not alter history," Neoptolemas added with a smile.

The Colonel, though, was looking at Tom with an expression approaching greed on his face. Finally, he turned to the Professor.

"You try to appeal to me by talking of causes and sacrifice.

265

If truth be told, sacrifice for a cause does not appeal to me," he said.

"But, Colonel—" the Professor started to say, but Thielmann silenced him.

"Wait," he said, raising his free hand. "I have not finished. No, I do not feel the same motivation a good cause inspires in you, brother. But power such as this boy has… that power is what I seek. That is what motivates me. As Titus we had power all those thousands of years ago. Indeed, we had more than anyone before or since. I have missed not having it. Ah, how much I desire to know that power once more…" Again the Colonel's gaze fell on Tom.

"Thielmann, there is no greater foe, no more powerful enemy than the Titans," the Professor said. "Let us have that power once more and use it as we could not before."

The Colonel turned his gaze back to Neoptolemas and was obviously considering what his brother had said. Yet doubt still remained on his face and Tom, with sudden insight, understood what Thielmann needed to hear.

"Colonel, take the power and use it. Destroy the Titans and you will prove that you are the most powerful man that has ever lived. Even more powerful than I am or ever will be. Be that man, Colonel: be Titus again!"

Biting his lip, the Colonel stared at Tom. "Yes, to be the most powerful man ever… even if only for a moment. Then to use it to win our ancient battle… yes, that is good." Slowly the Colonel nodded his head. "So be it," he said. "Let us begin!"

All three of the brothers now closed their eyes. A few moments later a low hum began to emanate from the Artefact. The humming grew louder and louder until it was the only sound Tom could hear. Suddenly there was a blinding flash of light, so intense that Tom was forced to avert his gaze for a few seconds.

When he looked back, the three brothers were no more. Instead, towering over him was one immense man. He stood holding the triangle, one edge held against his muscular chest, his powerful hands grasping the other two. He looked a little like each of the brothers. He studied Tom in a way that the Custodian would often do, as if weighing him up and assessing him. Something about his face was sterner than the Professor's kindly features, more like that of the Colonel really, yet in his eyes there was the hint of something softer than Thielmann had ever shown. It was strange how this one being somehow was at once a blend of all three brothers and at the same time something new, something different, something more than the parts that made him up. Even his clothes had changed – he still wore a suit but it was darker than that of the Custodian, more formal than the Professor's and a tighter cut: rather like a uniform, but it bore none of the regalia and symbols that the Colonel's had.

He studied Tom for a while and then swept his gaze around the factory, taking in the battle still raging around them. Then he looked down at the triangle in his hands.

"It is time," he said. "I am ready to do what has to be done." His voice was different from any of the brothers: stronger, more confident, Tom might even say arrogant.

'Yes,' thought Tom, 'I remember all that. I remember how it felt to be Titus.'

"The Professor has gone then?" he said sadly.

The figure shook his head. "No, Thomas Oakley. He is here, as are the Custodian and the Colonel. I feel them inside me: they are my compassion, my logic and my will. All are part of me but I am once again the man I was born to be. I am Titus."

He turned away from Tom and still holding the Artefact

267

strode out from behind the tank to where the Titans could see him. Tom crept past the men still held captive in his bubble of frozen time and peered around the corner of the tank.

Iapetus's army had spread out mostly to the sides of the factory and were engaged in a bitter struggle. Automatic weapons rattled; grenades detonated and men were shouting and screaming. Thielmann's men were trained soldiers armed with assault rifles backed up with machine guns and a full complement of support weapons, including modern hand grenades and a mortar. They knew battle tactics; they were part of an army that was victorious all around the Twisted Reality. By contrast, Iapetus' recruits were civilians or security guards with few weapons. Even so, the Colonel had brought only fifty men with him and few of those remained standing, whilst Iapetus had by now managed to summon hundreds to his call. Under his influence they seemed willing to sacrifice their lives without care, fighting with a fury that was barely human, so that although dozens were being wounded or killed, surely and steadily they were overwhelming their foe. Now, with one final charge, Iapetus's army overran the last of Thielmann's men, leaving Titus, Tom and what remained of his friends to face the might of the Titans alone.

Iapetus stood in the centre of the factory from where he had been directing the battle, whilst Hyperion, Crius and Coeus were shooting balls of fire, chunks of ice and various iron bars and bits of wrecked metal at Mary, Charlie and Edward, who Tom now saw were sheltering behind machinery near the collapsed sandbag embrasure. His friends were doing their best to dodge the attacks whilst occupying the attention of Kronos, who looking decidedly irritated, was flexing his muscles and clenching his fists as if he now intended to wade into the fray and with his superior strength finish the Walkers for good.

The moment Titus stepped boldly out into the centre of the factory to face his enemies, Kronos's attention switched. The other four Titans stopped what they were doing and stared at the new arrival.

Suddenly there was silence. It reminded Tom of a scene in an action movie, with Titus some sort of super hero preparing to take on his enemies, or else maybe a gunfighter in an old fashioned cowboy film, about to shoot it out with five crack shots.

"You cannot be here now," Coeus said, finally breaking the impasse. "You lived and died millennia ago."

Titus nodded. "If Knossos and I had done our job properly nor should you be here. Yet, here am I and here are you. Five thousand years have passed since we met in battle. Now it is time to end it all and rid the worlds of your menace for eternity. "

Coeus laughed. "Look around you, old man. Your allies are scattered and defeated. We are united once more and we have won! When you met us before and captured us with your trickery, Knossos was with you. He is not here today. What can you do alone?"

Titus brought up his arms so that the triangular Artefact now faced the Titans. They looked at it suspiciously. Coeus tilted his head.

"What is that you have there, old man? A golden trinket is it?"

"You will see," Titus said. As he spoke the Artefact began to glow brightly as it had before, but this time the sound was different: a high-pitched whirring sound, rather like that of a jet engine, which began to grow in volume.

"What are you doing, Titus?" Coeus asked, a hint of worry in his voice. "What is that thing?"

When Titus did not answer, Kronos took a step towards him,

hands held out as if ready to tear him in two, his lips rolled back in a snarl, revealing his teeth. He stepped to within five paces of Titus and looked prepared to rip him apart. Then, suddenly, an expression of disbelief came over Kronos's face. He was struggling to move closer, but it was as if he had walked into a solid, invisible wall.

The other Titans now moved to his side and tried to reach Titus, but not one of them could move any nearer. Reacting to their immobility they roared in frustration and then began to scream in terror. The triangle glowed even more brightly and now it seemed that heat was radiating from it, because Titus's hands were blistering. Then he too began to cry out – but in his case it was with pain.

Tom ran towards him, instinctively wanting to reach him and pull the Artefact from his grasp, but Titus shook his head.

"No! Keep back, Thomas," Titus said, gasping as the pain wracked his body. "It... will not... go on much longer."

Now, in the space between the Titans and Titus a pinpoint of darkness had appeared. As the sound emanating from the triangle continued to increase in pitch, the darkness expanded until it looked like a hole leading from the Factory to... whatever lay beyond. It reminded Tom a little of the portal he had passed through into the Projection Room in Thielmann's headquarters, or the one that had appeared at Tintagel when he and his friends had been in a fight with Captain Redfeld. In both those cases, however, Tom had caught a glimpse of what lay on the other side: the machinery of the Projection Room; the buildings and flags of Tintagel in the Twisted Reality. Here though, the opening showed only the darkness of space with a few distant stars; a tiny part of the separate universe into which Titus was sending the Titans.

"Now, we are ready!" Titus said through gritted teeth. The pain seemed to subside a little and he turned and smiled at Tom. "Goodbye Tomorrow's Guardian," he said. "I have been privileged to know you. Goodbye, Thomas Oakley!"

The noise had now risen to an intense whine and the triangle was incandescent. Iapetus screamed in agony. His body seemed to collapse in on itself and finally vanished through the opening into the world on the far side. After Iapetus was gone Crius followed him into oblivion, and then Hyperion.

"No, stop this! You must stop!" Coeus implored, before he too vanished through the portal and into the void.

Finally, only Kronos remained. The most powerful of the Titans he struggled to be free of the Artefact's power. With a gargantuan effort he managed to take two further strides towards Titus. Then he fell to his knees and, like his brothers, the last of the Titans was sucked away into eternity.

There was a final burst of intense light from the Artefact and with a great boom of sound both it and Titus vanished. The huge blast threw Tom, the other Walkers and the remnants of Iapetus's army onto their backs. Then, with an ear-shattering crack, the portal slammed shut and it was over. Titus, the greatest Potentate the world had ever known was gone, along with his enemies.

Today's Sacrifice had been made and the worlds were safe once more.

CHAPTER TWENTY-SIX
THE NEXT STEP

For several minutes there was utter silence in the factory. Then the Walkers, security guards and museum visitors staggered groaning to their feet. For several more minutes they stared at each other, at the devastation around them and at the spot where the Titans and Titus had stood. There was no sign of the portal; no mark on the floor; nothing to show they had even been there, if you didn't count the many dead soldiers lying about the place; the chunks of ice melting into the widening pool of water still leaking from the pipes, and the flicker of flames where Hyperion's fire balls had landed on something flammable.

Nobody spoke. Finally, one of the museum guards turned and ran back out of the factory doors. As if this was a signal the other guards and all the museum visitors dropped their weapons and followed his lead. In only a few moments the Walkers were alone.

Gradually, one by one, Edward, Charlie and Mary staggered over to Tom. In silence and with a deep sense of dread they all stared at the pile of twisted scrap metal into which Septimus had dropped earlier in the battle. Fearing the worst, Tom sighed.

"We should go and find his body," he murmured.

Not looking to see if the others were following he set off toward the pile of scrap, but had taken only a few steps when he heard someone coughing inside it. Then he saw bits of metal begin to move and a rusted piece of tank turret slid off the top of the pile and fell with a clang to the floor. A moment later, still coughing, Septimus crawled out from beneath the tangled heap of iron.

Tom's face split into a wide grin of relief as the Welshman stood up, dusted himself down and limped over to him.

"I… I thought you were dead, Septimus," Tom said.

Septimus smiled. "Ah now, boyo, you should know it would take more than mortal combat against the most powerful creatures in history to do for a Welshman."

"I guess so," Tom said as the other three Walkers clustered around them.

"All present and correct then," Septimus said, looking round at their relieved faces.

"No!" Tom gasped. "Where's Persephone?"

Splashing through the pool of water and scanning the factory floor he rushed over to where he had last seen her. She lay where she had fallen, wisps of smoke still rising from her clothes.

"Oh no, Persephone!" Tom cried in anguish, throwing himself to his knees beside her still body. Yet, as he knelt by her side he saw that she was breathing and then she groaned.

"You're alive! Thank God," Tom said, gently taking her hand in his. "I thought you were dead," he whispered, knowing that were it not for Persephone's courage it would be him lying there burnt to a crisp. "You saved my life."

Persephone lifted her head and smiled at him. "I'm glad about that," she said.

"Can you get up?" Tom asked.

"I… I think so." She glanced down at her charred school uniform and the blisters on her arms. "Ouch, that hurt. Interesting

273

job you have here… Did we win?"

Tom felt tears clogging up his throat and swallowed hard.

"Yes… yes we did. But the cost was high. I'm afraid the Professor…" Tom's voice wobbled and he couldn't say any more.

The others had come up behind him and now Edward crouched down at his side.

"He could see this day was coming," Edward said, placing a comforting hand on Tom's shoulder. "If you recall, he even warned us. He could see that it might cost a lot to defeat the Titans. He told me he knew a way to join with his other selves and become Titus again – the only one apart from you who was capable of banishing the Titans."

Wiping his eyes on his sleeve, Tom stared at Edward. "Why didn't he tell me his plan? Why make me believe that he was going to sacrifice me?"

"He needed you to be as far as possible along the path as a Potentate before he died. If he was going to leave the realities in your hands as Guardian, he needed to be sure not only that you were capable of doing anything to protect them, but also that you would do anything."

Tom shook his head. "Then I failed him. I thought he was going to sacrifice me and that is why I ran out of the Institute that time. I was afraid, Edward and I suppose I panicked."

"Yes, but despite being afraid you came back, Tom. You did not need to. More than that, you came here alone and tried to sacrifice yourself to save everyone else. After you left us frozen in his study… when we had recovered that is, the Professor told me he knew at that moment that he had been right about you. That was when he knew his plan was going to be alright."

Tom sighed and looked again at the spot where Titus had vanished.

"I will miss him."

"We all will, boyo," Septimus said. Having helped Persephone up from the floor, he now reached out one hand and pulled Tom to his feet. "We all will."

They strolled together back down the factory, towards the collapsed sandbags emplacement and the tank where Kronos had first appeared. Tom walked over to the dugout, surprised to see that the wounded machine-gunner was still alive. He was lying slumped against the sandbags, one hand holding a field dressing against his wound. Phil must have come out of his trance and helped him, but the big man was no longer there. Tom glanced all around but couldn't see him anywhere.

The gunner looked up at them as they approached then lifted a hand in surrender, fear standing in his eyes.

"Don't worry, mate we aren't going to hurt you," Tom said, as Edward stepped past him and knelt to have a closer look at the wound. "He's lucky; it could have been a lot worse," he said, before switching to German and reassuring the man that they did not intend to hurt him: "Unteroffizier, Ich werder sie nicht verletzen."

As he spoke, the wounded sergeant relaxed a little and murmured, "Danke mein Herr," then in broken English repeated, "Thank you sir."

"Er, where is Redfeld?" Mary asked.

Tom spun around to stare at the spot where Redfeld had fallen after Kronos had laid him out. With a sinking feeling he realised the captain was missing. He scanned the factory, suddenly anxious that they were standing targets and a bullet could appear from anywhere, but at that moment a familiar voice allayed his fears.

"Move along there, Captain. Don't try anything or the last

thing you'll feel is the sting of one of your own bullets!"

Coming out from the shadows behind one of the wrecked machines they saw Phil. He was pushing Redfeld in front of him and was armed with the captain's Luger pistol.

Phil winked at Tom and the others. "Hi guys. That was quite a battle. Sorry I missed taking part in most of it. Kronos had me under some sort of spell 'til a few minutes ago. When I came to I saw he had gone and then I noticed our friend here was not lying where I had last seen him. I went looking for him and found him sneaking out from the factory. I reckoned he was probably trying to get a safe distance away before Walking, so I jumped him and clapped these on him before he could scarper."

Tom could now see that Redfeld was wearing some of the Walker restraint handcuffs that the Institute had provided for the Resistance. With those round his wrists, Redfeld could not simply Walk away from the scene. And mightily angry about it he seemed, too.

Tugging at the handcuffs, he yelled over his shoulder, "You'll pay for this when I catch up with you and the rest of your Resistance criminals."

Phil gave Redfeld a nasty smile. "Oh, didn't you know. It's to the Resistance that you're going, my old son. My companions will be delighted to spend some quality time with you."

Grinning at the expression on the Nazi captain's face, Tom was just thinking that everyone now seemed to be accounted for, when he corrected himself. Not quite everyone.

"Where is Lapace?" he asked, scanning the factory once more. Then he spotted something moving among the sandbags deep inside the collapsed dugout.

"Come on out Rolf, we can see you!" Tom shouted.

Emerging from his hiding place, Lapace beamed at them.

276

"Well done team!" he said, clapping his hands. "I see that my plan worked perfectly. Everything was my idea, of course. It was me who suggested it all to the Prof and his brothers..." he hesitated and looked around the factory. "Er... where are they exactly?"

"You utter, misbegotten, traitorous sod!" Septimus said, stomping across the factory floor towards his former partner. "Betrayed us again, I see!"

"Well..." Lapace said quickly, backing away from Septimus, "er... I'll be on my way then!" But then a look of surprise crept onto his face.

Reaching him, Septimus seized him by the collar.

"I can't Walk!" Rolf whined. "Why is that? Why can't I Walk?"

"Because I have prevented it," Tom said. He spoke calmly, but had in fact surprised himself with what he had just succeeded in doing. As soon as he felt the disturbance to the Flow of Time that suggested Rolf was trying to Walk, Tom focused on it and simply stopped it so that Lapace could not leave. 'It seems the Professor was right about my Potentate powers, they are definitely maturing,' he thought. Thinking of Neoptolemas made Tom realise yet again just how much faith the old man had had in him. Resolving then and there not to let his old mentor down, it made Tom all the more determined to be a strong and just Guardian.

"You have a lot to answer for Rolf Lapace," he said, "and I'm sure that Edward will want to arrest you. You will come back with us to the Hourglass Institute. Then we will decide what to do with you."

Rolf Lapace looked every bit as outraged as Redfeld, who was still trying to get free from the Walker restraints.

"You!" Lapace spat. "You did this?" What gives you the right eh? For that matter, how did you do it? You're just a boy!"

"He is the Potentate, weren't you paying attention? Didn't you hear what Titus said before he vanished? Thomas Oakley is Tomorrow's Guardian," Edward said.

Tom smiled and gestured at his friends. "Titus did say that, but I think I prefer what the Professor himself said some moments before. He pointed out that it was time for him and his brothers to leave to others the task of protecting time. Others, he said, will be the Guardians of Tomorrow. He was speaking of all of us, not just me."

Lapace shook his head. "You are all self-sacrificing fools!" he said, his lip curling with contempt.

Edward shrugged. "Maybe - but it's our job, so get used to it. You are a thief and a traitor. In my day you would have been shot. It will be down to the Institute to decide what is to be done with you, but it is Tom here who will have the final say."

Rolf Lapace said no more, but his eyes widened and his face went suddenly very pale.

Edward turned to speak to Phil. "Are you sure we can be of no more help?" He waved his hand around the factory, the battleground on which they had fought the Titans. "I mean, I feel we should stay and try to help you change your world."

Smiling, Phil shook his head. "Oh, I think you have already changed it my friends. With Colonel Thielmann gone and with Redfeld captured and in our hands you have tipped the balance. Now I think my own group of Walkers can take the fight to the occupiers. With those two out of the way we can use our talents and see about bringing this Reich down. We can reach out and find others elsewhere around the Twisted Reality and form a new alliance. It will take a while but," he added with a wink, "I don't have anything else to do at present."

"Well, good luck then," Edward said, reaching out with one hand to shake Phil's own. "I am sure you can free yourselves, but we would like to help. Once we sort ourselves out I will be in touch and see what we can do. If nothing else, we can supply you with the equipment you will need."

"That will be welcome and I look forward to hearing from you. Thanks again to you all. Right then," Phil said. He turned back to the wounded gunner and said in German, "I'll send a medic back for you, mate. Hang on in there." Then he spoke to Redfeld, who had given up trying to get free and now seemed dazed and confused. "Time to go visit my friends, pal."

Captain Redfeld looked so alarmed at the prospect that Tom almost felt sorry for him. Almost, that is!

After Phil had Walked Redfeld away, Tom stared at the spot where they had been. "Well then," he said, "they are gone. Walking away to their war and their Britain. Time we went home to ours."

"I don't suppose you fancy leaving me here do you?" Lapace asked hopefully. He looked around at them all then his face fell. "No?"

"No!" they chorused.

"That is it then," Septimus grinned. "Crisis averted. Time to go home for tea and crumpets," he added joyfully, but the grin slipped from his face and he bit his lip. "It won't be the same, though... the Prof loved tea and crumpets."

Into the sad silence that followed, Mary asked in a small voice, "Do you think we can ever get him back?"

Tom and Septimus exchanged a doubtful glance and Mary's question went unanswered.

"Blimey!" Tom suddenly exclaimed. "I've just remembered that I left everyone at school thinking I had gone missing."

279

"And me," Persephone added.

Edward looked them up and down, taking in Persephone's burnt jumper and Tom's dirty and soot-covered face and blazer, and sniffed.

"Well, as I understand it, the teachers think there was a gas explosion. You certainly look like you've been in one. So you two had better go straight back and turn up at school – maybe you could stagger out of the rubble or something. With that appearance you won't have a problem convincing them," Edward said with a snort.

Tom glanced over at Persephone. "I guess we had best go back. No doubt your boyfriend will be worried about you."

She frowned, "My boyfriend?" she said vaguely.

"Andy, I mean," Tom said.

Persephone's singed eyebrows shot up and she shrugged her shoulders. "Well, Andy is nice and kind, but he is just a friend," she said.

"Oh?" Tom was suddenly aware that this mattered to him more than he might care to admit.

"I mean, he is fun and I quite like his company, but I can't tell him about us and even if I did, he wouldn't believe me." She waved her hand around the factory. "All of this... Walking, the Titans, Knossos and everything..." Her olive-green eyes widened and she looked straight at Tom. "And anyway, he would never understand like you do."

Returning her gaze, Tom felt suddenly hot and was aware that his face had gone bright red.

Edward coughed. "Er... Perhaps you two could discuss this later?"

"Yes boss!" Tom replied.

Edward gave him a sharp look. "What do you mean by that?"

"I mean you are the boss now. Neoptolemas made that clear by taking you into his confidence. You are the obvious choice. You are used to command and are clear-headed."

Edward looked doubtful. "What about you, Tom. You are the Potentate: Tomorrow's Guardian, as it were."

Tom shook his head.

"I am just a kid, Edward. One day maybe I can do more, but I think I will draw the line at studying French whilst saving the world before tea time! I need to be able to spend at least some time doing homework and seeing my family. Don't worry, though, I will be around whenever you need me."

"Me too," Persephone said then bit her lip, "That is if you will have me?"

Edward turned to her in surprise. "Of course. It goes without saying. You have proven your worth and I am sorry I ever doubted your loyalty. You are welcome as a member of the Institute." He looked across at Mary and Charlie, his eyes hopeful. "What about one of you taking command?"

Charlie laughed. "Me in charge? Are you insane?"

Mary also shook her head. "I will help you with all my strength, every day of my life, but I cannot lead," she said softly and from the slight blush to her cheeks, Tom felt there was more than one meaning in her words.

"I'll do it!" Lapace said brightly, "Of course, my first act will be to pardon myself."

Septimus reached over absently and slapped him over the back of the head. "Shut up you!" he mumbled.

"Septimus what about you?" Edward asked him. "You're the oldest, after all, and you've known the Professor and his ways longest."

Septimus shook his head. "Oh no boyo. I can't. Oh, I'll chip in

281

when I can, but I am going to be a bit busy the next little while."

"Busy doing what?" Tom asked.

The Welshman beamed at him. "Why, getting married to Julia of course. I proposed and she said yes. We set a date just before I left her in Vienna and she insisted that you are all invited." He glanced at Lapace, "Apart from you, needless to say!"

"A wedding!" Mary squealed. "I have nothing to wear. Oh, Edward, you need to buy me a dress at once! And I'll need a hat!"

"Yes, dear," Edward said, with a roll of his eyes at Tom.

Septimus laughed. "In that case you had better get a move on, Edward," he said. "Because the wedding is on June 15th … about five hundred years ago!"

The End

The Nine Worlds Series

Book One - Shield Maiden
ISBN: 9780956810373

This is the world as it might have been if the stories were true...

Shield Maiden is a Historical Fantasy Adventure For Children of Ages 9+

Anna is a 12 year old girl growing up in a Saxon village in 7th century Mercia. Her life changes when she finds a golden horn in the ruins of a Roman Villa. Soon an ugly dwarf, a beautiful sorceress and even her own people are after her.

What powers does the horn have and why does everyone want it?

And why is Anna the only one who can get a note out of it?

About Shield Maiden

Shield Maiden is the first book in The Nine Worlds series in which the historical world of Anglo-Saxon England meets the mysterious world of myths and legends, gods and monsters our ancestors believed in.

 This is the world as it might have been had those stories been true...

Won a Silver Children's Literary Classics Award in 2012.

Read Chapter One now ...

CHAPTER ONE
ANNA

"It's not fair!" the girl shouted as she stabbed her short sword down into the oak table, leaving it vibrating in the wood. Her deep green eyes fixed the man on the far side with a furious glare.

"Father, it's not fair! Why can Lar train as a warrior and not me?" she asked him, her arms folded in front of her chest and her foot tapping the reed-strewn floor in impatience.

The man she was talking to sighed, as if this was an almost daily argument, which it was, and as if he despaired of ever getting his way with this, his twelve-year-old daughter, which he did. He stepped forward, pulled the knife out of the table and held it out to the girl, handle first.

"Anna, we have been through all this before. Your brother, Lar will follow me as headman of the village one day and must be a warrior. You in turn will marry a warrior or a lord of another village and raise children."

"Lar is younger than me. I don't see why he should be the leader. Raedann tells me there have been warrior women before now - shield maidens - and even queens and ladies who have led their folk in battle. Why not me?"

Her father, Nerian, looked at her helplessly and, as was his habit when he was at a loss for words he scratched the bald patch in his brown hair.

"Your father has many cares, child.' These words were spoken by a man standing further down the hall, staring at the embers that burned in the fire pit running the length of the building. 'You should not distress him with these ideas. Nor should you take note of what that tinker, Raedann, says."

This was Iden, the priest of Woden, a fat man with grey hair, who enjoyed mead a little too much and as a result had a large belly and red cheeks. Anna, as well as the other children, thought him stuffy and when he preached found him boring and dull. Nothing like Radeann's fun tales of the gods, of great heroes, of the monsters that lived in the woods and hills and of the adventures he had supposedly had in the world outside their tiny village of Scenestane.

Iden was right in that Raedann was a tinker: he sold trinkets as he travelled around the villages of Mercia. But he sold stories too - anything for a bed for the night and maybe some food and mead. His stories were good ones and the children loved them.

"Are you saying that Raedann lies?"

"Child," Iden replied as he came to join them at the table, "he is a spinner of tales. He exaggerates. He makes stories seem more than they really are."

"But there have been shield maidens," Anna insisted, "women who fight alongside the men."

Iden nodded, but Anna could see he was reluctant to admit it. "Maybe,' he agreed, 'but not many and only when something unusual happens, when special times come along and they are forced to take up arms. It is best to forget such tales. You will soon be old enough to marry. You should be thinking about that and not this nonsense."

"I can be a warrior. I will prove it to you one day!"

285

"Please, Anna," her father pleaded with her. "Take back your seax and go help Udela prepare the evening meal."

Fists clenched, teeth gritted, Anna glowered at him for a while and then finally let her shoulders drop. Reaching out she removed the long knife which he offered her and slid it into the scabbard on her belt. With a nod she left the headman's hall and walked out into the village. Once there though, she did not go as ordered to the cookhouse to find the elderly cook, but looked around the village, past the wooded path that led up to the rocky outcrop upon which Iden's small temple was built, to the hut that lay beyond. This was home of the healing woman, Julia. Outside it Anna could see her friends loitering, playing a game of Tafel on the ground, with pebbles and a board they had created by cutting lines into the sun-baked mud. She joined them.

Her brother Lar looked up from the game as she approached. He gave her a kindly smile.

"So how did your talk with father go?" he asked, tilting his head towards the headman's hall.

She stuck out her lower lip and frowned at him, "What do you think? You are the boy so you will be leader and a warrior, whilst I have to have babies."

"Sorry, sister, but that is just the way it is," Lar said. "Shield maidens are all well and good in stories, but in the real world we all have to accept what fate has in store for us. If it helps I don't feel any better about it than you, but you can't fight fate."

Anna snorted. "Maybe I can. Maybe I can prove I am worthy to be a warrior and defend the village."

But Lar was not listening to her. He had turned back to the board, smiled and moved one piece.

"My game, pay up Wilburh!"

His opponent, ten-year-old Wilburh, gave Lar a dark look

from under a fringe of blond hair, his blue eyes darkened, suddenly seeming almost black.

Wilburh's twin sister, Hild, gurgled with laughter. "Come on, pay him," she said. Her own eyes, whilst also blue, seemed lighter somehow, just like Hild herself - bubbly and happy in a way that gave Anna headaches sometimes and contrasted with Wilburh's more gloomy nature.

Wilburh shrugged and reaching into a pouch at his belt brought out a tarnished old ring and handed it over. Lar held it up to the late afternoon sun and examined it.

"Should be able to sell that to Raedann for a new knife," he boasted.

"A knife? Why in Woden's name do you think that dirty old ring is worth the same as one of my knives," a man's voice cut in.

They turned around and saw the tinker looming over them. Tall, almost gangly, with curly brown hair and a hook nose, Raedann grinned at them. "I will give you this seashell bracelet for it," he said with wink, and Lar and Raedann were soon bargaining and trading.

Listening to her brother Anna shook her head in despair. Lar had no interest in swords and fighting. He had passed on to her all he had learnt after she badgered him into going off to the woods to teach her how to fight with a sword and how to fire a bow. No, Lar was a trader at heart and a good one at that, but he was no fighter. She sighed. If only her father could see that.

"Well, I must be off," Raedann said, after he and Lar had finally agreed a fair exchange for the ring and Lar had got his knife, although not as fine a one as he would have hoped. "I want to reach Wall before the sun sets and that's a couple of miles to go."

The tinker set off towards the Roman road that ran past the

west side of the village. Anna beckoned at the children and they all trailed along with Raedann, passing between the blacksmith's house and the one next to it, crossing a field and finally stepping onto the cobbled road beyond.

"We will go to just past the old Roman house with you, Raedann," Anna said. "Tell us about shield maidens again."

Lar groaned. "Not again, sister. Raedann, tell us something different. Tell us about giants."

"Giants? Ah, now there are many sorts of giants in this world. There are hill giants and cliff giants and fire giants and frost ones too. They come from other worlds you know, places like Jotunheim, Niflheim and the fire world, Muspelheim. They visit our world of Midgard from time to time."

He went on telling a tale about how he had once been chased by a fearsome fire giant and had escaped by swimming a river. By the time he had finished they had crossed the ford north of the town where a brook trickled over the old road, and soon they were passing the crumbling ruins of a Roman farm beyond.

"Did the giants build that?" Wilburh asked, gazing at the stone structure.

Raedann smiled at him. "You ask me that because it is made of stone, don't you? But no, the Romans were not giants, just men. They built many houses like that, walls and cities too, all over this land. Then they left because their empire was under attack. That was two hundred years ago. When our own people, the Saxons, came here across the Eastern Sea they gazed on such buildings, and because they could not build them they assumed the Romans must have been giants. That is why those ruins and many others like it make our people feel scared and why we keep away from them."

The children stared at the ruins and Raedann, chuckling at the expressions on their faces, said, "Well, I'll be on my way. I will be back in a couple of days. You'd best be getting home to the village, children. The sun is sinking. You don't want evil spirits to find you out in the dark do you?"

He pointed to where the old fort on the hills to the west was silhouetted against the setting sun. Then he was off, singing a song and strolling up the road.

"Come on, let's go home," Hild said, turning to head back down the road.

Anna moved to join her and then abruptly changed her mind. "No! Let's go and look in the ruins," she said.

"The Roman ruins? In the dark?" Lar asked, studying the decaying structure.

"Indeed, why not?"

The others stared at her. Lar opened his mouth to speak but did not get a word out. Around them the twilight was gathering, the evening air warm but quiet. Into that silence they heard a noise that made them all jump: the sound of running footsteps coming along the road from the direction of the village. They spun around to glance back towards the ford, but could see nothing apart from deep shadows at the bases of the trees.

No, there was something else there.

A shape was moving in the shadows....

The Northern Crown Series

Book One - The Amber Treasure
ISBN: 97809568103-1-1
"I will take care of the body of my lord and you can carry the sword, story teller. For all good stories are about a sword."

6th Century Northumbria: Cerdic, the nephew of the great warrior Cynric, grows up dreaming of glory in battle and writing his name in the sagas.

When war comes for real though, his sister is kidnapped, his family betrayed and his uncle's legendary sword stolen. It falls to Cerdic to avenge his families' loss, rescue his sister and return home with the sword.

Winner of a B.R.A.G. Medallion

Book Two - Child of Loki
ISBN: 97809568103-2-8
A divided land ... a divided family.

The Battle of Catraeth has been won and Cerdic's homeland is safe ... but for how long?

The Northern British were crushed but yet more enemies have risen to replace them.

Soon Cerdic and his friends must go to war again - against the Scots and Picts north of Hadrian's wall. He goes to help his country's allies - the Bernicians - under their great warlord, Aethelfrith.

But what is Aethelfrith's true design? How ambitious is he and how far will he go to fulfil his dreams? And what is Cerdic's treacherous half brother, Hussa up to in these fierce wild lands?

The Praesidium Series

Book One - The Last Seal
ISBN: 9780956810397
Gunpowder and sorcery in 1666…

17th century London - two rival secret societies are caught in a battle that threatens to destroy the city and beyond. When a truant schoolboy, Ben, finds a scroll revealing the location of magical seals that binds a powerful demon beneath the city, he is thrown into the centre of a dangerous plot that leads to the Great Fire of 1666.

"an awesome array of characters which definitely included the good, the bad and the ugly, and an amazing plot!"
" This young adult historical fantasy had me totally engrossed and I would recommend it to anyway who loves historical fantasy/fiction (especially British) whether you're a teen or an adult. "
FIVE STARS
The Slowest Bookworm

"Denning has a real thirst for historical knowledge and this certainly shines through in his books, with his descriptions of London in 1666 making you feel as if you were in the middle of the raging fire."
YA Yeah Yeah

Winner of a B.R.A.G. Medallion

www.ingramcontent.com/pod-product-compliance
Lightning Source LLC
Chambersburg PA
CBHW030030180626
46810CB00001B/295